DEDICATION

To the brave military men and wo
country. Thank you.

RESCUING HIS HEART

First edition. November 14, 2023.

ISBN: 979-8223805380

Written by Charlene Groome.

ACKNOWLEDGMENTS
I am grateful every day for the opportunity to share my stories. It's one thing to dream and
another to be doing it.
Sue Grimshaw, you're simply amazing. Thank you for your enthusiasm, support, and for making my characters shine. I'm lucky to be working with you.
To Dar, you are so talented! Thank you for designing my covers. You nailed it!
Writing this story took some research. One person I need to thank is Tom Huxley for helping me understand the mechanics of small airplanes. Thank you for your patience and knowledge.
Before I step onto a plane, I'll remember your words, 'it's safer to fly than to drive.'
Thank you to my family and friends for supporting me.
And to you, reader, for picking up my book and spending your time in Moonlight Valley. I hope you enjoy Sara and Colton's story.

1

Chapter One

S ara Quinn let the words from her inspirational desk calendar sink in.

Find love, find yourself, travel the world!

If the quote were right, Sara's vacation in less than two weeks would cure her adventurist mind, and she'd maybe find what was missing in her life. It was an opportunity she couldn't refuse having never traveled outside of the United States. It was something she wanted to

accomplish sooner rather than later.

Sara typed on her computer, not letting the *click-clacking* of Deloris' heels distract her from finishing writing her paragraph. She saved her story and emailed it to her editor before looking up at the receptionist.

"Special delivery!" Deloris sang, holding out a bouquet of mixed flowers. "For you, my dear." She set them down on Sara's desk and dusted off her hands. "My goodness. A flower delivery this week, a box of chocolates last week. Who is this charming fellow?"

"Oh, just somebody." Sara shrugged, feeling her cheeks warm. Keeping Johnathan Beck a secret created more questions and her answers were an extension of the truth, because how could she admit she was planning on meeting a guy she didn't know? She didn't realize how much people cared about her love life until the recent attention sparked curiosity after a dating dry spell. It had been five months since her last date, and it ended with a kiss she wanted to forget. She shuttered at the memory and dipped her head to smell the lily.

"This isn't from just somebody." Deloris touched the clear wrap surrounding the flowers. "They're beautiful. Are you sure you're not dating him?"

Sara shook her head. "Yup. I'm still single."

"Well, he has good taste." She gave a skeptical eye. "What's this gent's name?"

The idea of keeping her new friend a secret was harder than she thought. Maybe because she was twenty-seven, single, and up until now, she wasn't looking for a relationship. Until she met Johnathan online. Having similar interests kept her hanging on, even if she felt like the whole online dating thing was over-rated. What if he was nothing like she imagined? She didn't even know if she was attracted to him. Sure, they FaceTime, but it wasn't the same as being with someone in person. "Um. John." Her stomach clenched. "His name is John."

Deloris' eyebrows jumped. "So, where does John live?"

"Seattle."

Deloris clapped her hands. "Well then. When is he coming here?"

"I don't think he—"

"I can't wait to meet him!" Deloris' body shook with enthusiasm. "You'll bring him around, won't you?"

Sara's mind was spinning to say the next thing, but she drew a blank. They lived far apart. If she fell for this guy, would she consider moving out of Moonlight Valley?

She used her safe word. "We're just...friends."

Deloris laughed. "This is a guy trying to win you over. You're not interested?"

"I...don't want to date right now." Someone had to believe her.

"You should!" Her hands went to her ample hips. "You're young. This is the time."

"Yeah, but I want to travel and do things for me." The more Sara told the same story, the more she was believing it herself. "If I date now, I'll miss out on opportunities."

"What opportunities? You have everything here." She waved a hand. "What can't you do when you're with the right person? Wayne and I do lots of things together, and I've never missed out on anything." She brushed back her shoulder-length greying, brown hair. "When you're with the right person, it's a complement to your life. What happened to the last guy you were with, Derek? That was his name, right?" She side-stepped from the desk. "You dated him for a while."

"It didn't work out," Sara said casually. She failed to mention bad-kisser guy, but he didn't count.

"When you meet someone you can't live without, you'll know."

If Sara wanted to date, she had to look outside of Moonlight Valley, where everyone didn't know everyone's business. It was the only way she could build a relationship without anyone's interference, so she joined a dating website for singles, and Johnathan seemed to be the best match, at least one with potential.

"You're young," Deloris sang. "You'll meet someone. Just don't wait too long. It gets harder the older you get." She tapped her beaded necklace. "We get set in our ways."

It was unfortunate but true. Deloris wore the same hairstyle for years, and her makeup was always the same: Blue or cream eyeshadow, dusty rose color lipstick, and blush on her plump cheeks.

"I'm not worried." Sara placed her hand on the Fall Festival flyer sitting at the edge of her desk. She slid it towards her, glancing at the bold print.

"Maybe the man of your dreams will be playing bingo and taking part in the pie-eating contest." Deloris chuckled.

The idea made Sara's spine straighten. "I sure hope not."

"Don't forget the pig races." Deloris pointed a finger and turned on her foot. "I've got my bet on Bronco to win."

Sara closed her eyes briefly before sinking into her chair. Is this what her life had become? A revolving door? Same stories. Same people. A change was what she needed, and maybe she'd appreciate the local banter and silly games while she was away. Satisfied with her decision to spend the first two days in Seattle to meet Johnathan, then fly solo to Australia would do her some good.

The timing couldn't be so perfect.

Her heart fluttered, thinking about the Seattle newspaper reporter. He had a pinched smile, a little mischievous, a bit intriguing and...average? How could one judge by a photo or live screen, anyway? Would it be enough to fall in love? They had a lot in common, having the same job, wanting to travel, and being family-oriented. He said all the things she wanted to hear and gave her high hopes for a promising companion. He even called her sweet and sweetest when addressing her name, like her dad used to do. If it worked out, could she move out of town?

Sara logged off her computer and grabbed her phone from her duffle bag. She checked her messages before packing up.

"Sara!" Jerry rounded his neck at his office doorway, like he was afraid to step out into the light. "I need to speak to you for a minute."

"Okay. I'll be right there," Sara called back. Maybe Jerry changed his mind and agreed she could write an opinion piece or write about trends. Something to boost its lifestyle section. It needed a new look to attract a younger crowd.

Sara stood up, picked up her phone to message Johnathan.

Hey Johnathan! Thanks for the flowers. They're beautiful. It was very thoughtful.

Hey Sweet Sara, You're welcome. I've told my family all about you, and they can't wait to meet you. I hope it's okay. My mom wants us for dinner on one of the nights you're here. Let me know.

TAPPING HER HEEL, SHE stared at her phone. Was it too soon to meet Johnathan's family? She hadn't even met him! It wasn't like they were dating. She winced. Maybe Johnathan wanted his mom's opinion. Her skin prickled.

> **Sure. Meeting your family would be great. I'm there for only two days. If it doesn't work out, maybe next time?**

What if there was no next time? No chemistry? It was impossible to know someone in forty-eight hours. Was it enough time to see if she liked him enough to see him again?

Sara shoved her phone into her bag and stepped into her editor's office to remind him she was leaving in twelve days. The smell of stale air lingered in the windowless room. Sara wrinkled her nose. Jerry was hunched over his desk, surrounded by loose papers and old newspapers. He looked up in a daze.

"Why did you change the font of your headline?" he asked, running his hand over the newspaper.

"I thought it added to the page. It made it stand out."

"We don't need it to look like a tabloid. It's a community newspaper." His voice rose. "Save the fancy stuff. We just need the story to be legible. It's what people want."

Sara slid her teeth together.

"You added a border around the second news story," he said. "We've talked about this before. We don't need to change it. No borders."

Sara sighed. "I thought it added to the piece. Making it stand out. Without a photo, my eyes go directly to the story."

"Nothing wrong with white space, either." Jerry's eyes shot up over his glasses. "Why do you want to change it?"

"I...I'd like to freshen it up a bit. Make it, I don't know, modern?"

"People are reading for information, not for art. Although the photos are good, it's not a magazine." He creased the corner of the page.

"Okay." It didn't matter how hard she tried to make the paper look better. Jerry wasn't into it. He didn't care, so why did she? Maybe her trip would give her a long break she needed to forget about work and everything else in her life she didn't have control over.

"Did you give any more thought to the lifestyle section?" She gripped the armchair and swung her feet from under her.

"We need to stick to local stuff. It's a small-town paper." He adjusted his glasses. "What's going on? You've been working here for five years. Nothing's changed."

That was the problem.

"I thought we could add some soft news, you know, touch on what's happening outside of town. Freshen it up." She gave a playful smile to hide her disappointment. "Make it...interesting."

"We cover what happens here, not what happens in Hollywood. If people want garbage, they can search the Internet."

Sara's mouth swished to the side. She wasn't winning the battle, so why was she trying?

Jerry placed his hands on his desk. "The reason I called you in is to tell you my mother is ill." He jabbed his fingers under his glasses to massage his lids. "She's dying..."

"I'm...sorry." Sara crossed her arms. Her stomach muscles tensed. "I didn't know she was sick."

"She's been battling cancer, and there's nothing they can do for her." He took off his glasses and pinched the bridge of his nose. "I'm going to see her before she...she dies."

"Of course."

"I need you to cover for me."

"Oh, but I—"

"Her dying wish is for me to sing Come Fly With Me...Frank Sinatra." His voice

monotoned. "I need to be there."

"You sing?"

Jerry put his glasses back on his face. "I used to." He opened his eyes and blinked double time. "You'll have to postpone your trip if I don't make it back. I don't know what else to do. I have nobody to cover for me."

Sara shook her head and swallowed.

"When I get back, you can go."

She stared at him, hopelessly. "I bought my ticket." Her voice hitched. It was an expensive ticket. If she didn't act on impulse, she would miss the opportunity to meet Johnathan. What if he was...*the one?* She needed to give it a chance. And what about Australia?

"I know. I know." Jerry slumped in his chair. The lines in his face grew deeper. It was like the years of stress were catching up with him. "I don't know what to say."

Her heart picked up. "I'll find someone to cover for me. I'll edit while I'm away."

"You can't do that."

"No?"

"No." His voice sharp and irritated.

She huffed. "I never take vacation. This is all I'm asking for." Her heart started to race. She never asked for anything. Maybe she should start.

"This isn't my ideal situation," he shot back.

"I can edit on my flight," she said. "It will be for a couple of work days."

"No. It won't work. I need you here."

"I have no one to cover for us. I don't know how long I'll be gone." Jerry's brown eyes were wide behind the lens. "Sorry, but what can I do?" He shrugged.

"What's wrong with Liam? He can write copy and—" She stopped herself from telling him he should split the assignments with the sports reporter, but she didn't know how much Liam could handle. If she didn't meet Johnathan now, she'd lose her chance and it was too soon to

invite Johnathan to Moonlight Valley. She couldn't offer him a place to stay when she didn't know him. "I'm sure if I—"

"My mother is dying."

"Yes. Do you think it would be a good idea to hire someone, a temp, for situations like this?" She leaned back in her chair. "It would be good to have a casual person."

"Not right now." His sparse eyebrows came together. "We're managing fine."

"Are we?" she challenged because it would be helpful to have someone to count on.

"Liam could write a news story, but I can't make him cover for you or—" He shook his head. "Edit the newspaper." He flattened out his hands on his desk. "I'm counting on you to do my job."

Sara pinched her lips together, refusing to believe she couldn't go on her trip. She'd been waiting so long to date a respectable guy. Someone who she could be proud of showing her mom and her friends. A guy who she could relate to and build dreams together. She let out a breath. "When are you leaving?" Sara gripped the armchair. There had to be another way around this.

"Tonight." His hands braced the edge of his desk." I've got a ride to Omak. Taking a

private plane to Idaho and I fly out from there. My mom lives in Wyoming. You have

cancelation insurance, right?"

She closed and unclosed her hands. "I don't." Her stomach sank. "I didn't think I'd need it." Her shoulders ached—all the money she saved. "You told me it was fine for me to take holidays."

He cupped his hands on his head like he had a headache. "They're giving my mom days."

She felt a pang in her chest. "I'm sorry." Life was more important than a job or meeting her potential boyfriend, but she never asked for time off. There wasn't anywhere to go until now. He brought up his head. "It must be hard for you."

"It is." His face faltered. "When I get back, we can find someone to cover for you. Maybe you can extend your vacation. We'll figure something out when I get back. I appreciate your understanding. It's unforeseeable circumstances, as you know."

She didn't have a choice, did she?

"You're the reporter people know and trust," Jerry said. "They depend on you. Without you, I can't run this paper alone."

"We should hire a casual reporter," she said again. "Someone who can fill in when one of us is away, sick. It doesn't help when we both are gone."

"I'd consider it. I'll run it by Georgia. I'm supposed to have a meeting with her soon." He patted his thinning hair. "Someone who can step into our shoes and work without fail. No handholding."

As flattering as it was, it didn't help right now. Sara wanted to meet Johnathan. She wanted to hang out with her cousin, tour beaches, see koala bears and kangaroos. Begin an adventure. She would experience more in her two-week vacation than she had her whole life living in a small town. She was tired of the same people and the same routine. It was her chance to explore and add some excitement to her life. She was ready to fall in love, even if it was with someone outside of Moonlight Valley.

Jerry folded his hands and leaned back in his chair. "Well, maybe I can look at hiring someone." His eyes scanned his desk as though looking for something.

Deloris popped her head inside.

"Do you know anyone who would be interested in a causal position?" Jerry's eyebrows knitted together.

"I don't," Deloris answered. "But Sara might."

"I do?" She looked over her shoulder at Deloris' wide eyes.

"You do?" Jerry asked.

"Your friend, John," Deloris said.

"He. Has. A job." Sara's eyebrows narrowed. If they only knew Johnathan worked at a

major newspaper, they wouldn't ask. "He's too far away."

"Jerry, line one. Do you want me to send him to voicemail?"

"I can take it. We're done." Jerry darted his eyes at Sara.

"We're done?"

"Unless you need to add something." Jerry bumped up his glasses. "I hate to be a disappointment, Sara, but there's nothing I can do." He tapped his hands on his chair and leaned into his desk. "I might be back by the time you need to leave. I don't know how long my mother is hanging on. Plus, I'll have to make funeral arrangements while I'm there."

Sara spun out of the door and went to her desk to collect her belongings and stomped out of the office. She would make a surprise visit to Dan Briggs hoping to get a story about why he was selling his apple orchid. Maybe the town got to him, and he was ready for something more, just like her.

Letting the questions build in her head, Sara drove out of the parking lot in her Honda and headed onto the main road toward Highway 97. With two hands on the wheel, her radio turned down; she passed TJ's Tavern and Cottage Hills winery. The road curved a little and then straightened again, passing Homeward Bound Animal Shelter. There was an empty cornfield in the distance, and Dan's farmhouse would come into view. Rethinking Jerry's conversation, she was entitled to a vacation. It was Jerry's fault for not hiring a part-time reporter for times like these. She didn't want to blow her chance at meeting Johnathan and the opportunity to see a country she'd always wanted to visit. Men don't wait around to find out if the woman they met online was the one, did they? She didn't want to believe she had to cancel her trip. Jerry could be back the day she was leaving, and it would work out.

She looked to the hazy sky and caught a light shining through the low grey clouds. A plane looked like it was falling. *Planes don't fall, they fly*. Sara squinted. And planes didn't turn the way it did. She stared harder while keeping an eye on the road. Moonlight didn't have an airport. Judging by the plane descending fast as though out of control, Sara realized it was heading toward the empty cornfield.

Sara's chest heaved. Her pulse quickened and she pushed her foot on the gas pedal, getting as close as possible. Did the pilot have a heart attack? Did the pilot think the cornfield was a runway? A pilot would know that.

She talked herself through the possibilities. Unless he was making an emergency

landing? Watching the plane going down in a nosedive, she jerked her wheel and stomped on the brake, parking on the side of the road. In disbelief, she watched the airplane hit the ground, nose-first. A smack to the earth, it tumbled once and flipped, the sound of a medal door coming off its hinge.

Sara got out of her car, adrenaline shooting through her. Hands shaking, she slipped off her heels and stuck her feet in her rain boots. Grabbing her camera and notebook, she took out her phone from her cloth purse and dialed 9-1-1 as she raced toward the wreckage. The closer she came, she knew it was a life-or-death situation.

Chapter Two

M ajor Colton Brooks had experienced pain throughout his life, both emotional and physical, but he had never experienced throbbing in his head like pressure of a balloon about to burst. Hell, it even hurt to breathe.

Struggling to keep his lids open, the sun was so bright, all Colton wanted to do was close his eyes to ease the tension and rest, but he was upside down and needed all the strength he had to get out of the plane.

He lifted his lids enough to see he was at eye level with troweled dirt and bits of cornstalk left from the combine. "This isn't...the way...I wanted to die." Colton spoke with a challenging breath. The pain in his ribs silenced him.

Six months ago, and maybe even yesterday, he wouldn't have cared about living, but today, this morning, he promised himself on his twenty-eight birthday, he had a mission to accomplish. He had been anticipating the date for weeks. Psyching himself up to find peace within himself, or a new calling, an outlet, whatever the hell it was that would get him out of bed in the morning.

Colton coughed. An ache radiated his lungs, and he breathed incautiously, avoiding a jab to his chest. The only thing satisfying would be to sleep but the sickening feeling bubbling in his gut, and the fact of being restricted, hanging upside down had its limitations.

Colton closed and opened his eyes to the late afternoon sun, reflecting off the broken windshield. His head feeling lighter by the second, the rush of blood pooling in his temples.

He had chosen the best landing strip in the middle of nowhere.

A quick breath stabbed him, and he grunted at the discomfort and remembered to take shallow breaths. He stayed calm, so he could escape before he passed out from being light-headed.

Colton patted his chest and lowered his hand to his achy side until he reached the door

handle. With legs spread to brace himself, he pulled off his headset and tossed it to the side. His legs cramped against the controls; he had to get out of his seatbelt without injuring his head.

Colton put one hand on the buckle, the other behind him as though going to do a handstand, he steadied his breath and clicked the belt. "Ah." A thump, his body tumbled, smacking his head again and straining his neck. He pushed on the ceiling to hold up his body, taking pressure off his head. He used both hands to steady himself and rolled over, bumping his left foot and gritted his teeth through the discomfort.

The weight of tiredness overtook him, and he closed his eyes in response. How could an accident he survived make him so tired? Struggling to lift his lids, he extended his hand to reach the door handle. He felt so weak. When did his arm weigh so much? He tried again,

using as much strength he had to open the door. With clutched teeth, he forced the door open. Pain shot up his arm, and he dropped his hand for relief. Too much grit but determined to get out of the confined space. A blast of fresh air came through the cab, and he pushed himself out and fell to the plowed dirt with a thud.

The honking of geese flew over him. Slow and steady, he crawled across the dirt. His chest heated, he collapsed to take a breath. Cheek to ground, he pushed himself up and rolled onto his back, laying on the rocky overturned soil. He wiped his forehead with his hand, squinting at the bright, grey clouds, blanketing his tired eyes. He snapped his lids shut, and seconds later, he forced them open again, struggling to see if the plane was leaking fluid.

Colton tapped the side of his cargo pants and slipped his hand inside one pocket, feeling for his wallet and phone. He brought his hand to the inside pocket of his coat, where he caught the corner of the envelope. He sighed and closed his eyes with relief. Colton had everything he needed. With a slow breath, he opened his eyes to the dust bunny of cloud above him. It was still too bright to see, so he closed his lids halfway, easing the pressure behind his eyes.

Through shallow breaths, the sound of swishing and cracking formed a beat in the distance. Colton blinked and turned his head until it was uncomfortable. He spotted flapping hands in the distance; someone was running toward him, a woman, trying to sweep her hair off her face. She held one hand against her bag, which bounced against her small frame.

Colton closed his eyes again because the energy to keep them open took effort, but he

managed to lift them to her radiant, brown eyes and pink, O-formed lips. She fell to her knees.

"You're alive," she gasped, touching the base of her neck. "Thank God." She exhaled. "You got out." Her head whipped over her shoulder to view the plane, then leaned into him. Her golden strands hung past her angelic face, and she let out a sigh as though draining her body from fear. "Is there anyone else on the plane?"

Colton shook his head slightly and turned up a half-smile, comforted by her pretty face. He didn't have the energy to speak.

She got to her knees and placed her hands on her thighs, assessing the situation. "Are you okay?" She squinted at him as though tasting something bitter.

"I'm—" Colton closed his eyes and exhaled. "Yeah," he muttered.

"Um, okay. Good. You're talking. That's great." Her lips came together, stretching her pink smile. "Help is on the way." She hunched over and then rocked back on her boots. "I—I don't have a first aid kit. I should have. I mean, in case something like this.

In...case of...a...plane crash." She laughed to herself. "You don't see this every day. What's your name?"

Colton didn't feel like talking. He just wanted to sleep.

"I need you to open your eyes," she said her face circling above him like an owl. "You can do it."

He knew he could, but he didn't want to.

"Where are you from?" she asked.

Colton moved his head back and forth. His neck muscles tight, head pounding, he let out a groan. Too many questions. Too much talking. He watched her through a crack of his lids.

"You're doing great." She laid her hand on his arm again.

"Where were you headed?"

Colton see-sawed his upper body to rid the rock pressing on his back.

"Maybe don't move around." She threw her hand on his chest. "We'll wait for the paramedics to get here." Her narrow shoulders concave, creating a lovely valley between her breasts, but it wasn't enough to keep his eyes open. Her sweet perfume tangled his senses, relaxing him. If he could close his eyes for a moment or two and she could stop talking so he could sleep.

Her hand tapped his shoulder. "What's your name?" Her voice interfered with his mellowed brain. "I'm Sara." She took a deep breath. "My name is Sara Quinn. And I'm a—" She narrowed her gaze at his forehead. "Never mind. I need to know what your name is." Her head moved with his. "What's your name?" She tore through her bag and pulled out a package and stuck a wad of tissue on his head.

Colton flinched.

"Sorry," she said. "You have a cut." Her teeth came together. "You're bleeding."

Colton grunted and touched his stomach. "Major." His title rolled off his tongue without thinking. There was no reason to correct himself. He had been proud of what he worked for. "Brooks."

Sara brought her head close to his ear, and he breathed her in.

"Major Brooks," she said with authority, determination. "Nice to meet you."

He shuttered at her warm breath against his skin.

"Hang in there. Help is on the way." She patted his arm. "They should be here." She looked over her shoulder and strained her eyes on the highway. "I can't see them, but they'll come. We have paid and volunteer firefighters." She stroked his arm while the other hand applied pressure to his forehead. "You flew by yourself?" She ducked to see the inside of the plane.

He nodded slightly, blinking because every breath was a challenge to say.

"Flying by yourself. That's brave." She rubbed her hand down his arm, and she clapped her smooth hand in his, giving him reassurance. He managed to open his eyes a little more, focusing on her tense expression. He got another whiff of her sweet-smelling hair or body or both. It didn't matter; she settled his mind. Having her beside him was better than being alone.

"Let me see if I have any more tissues. This one needs changing." She took back her hand and dug through her large bag and found a wrinkled napkin. "It's clean. It was an extra I took with my oatmeal muffin I bought this morning at Betty's." She opened it up and reversed the fold, gently placing it on the side of his forehead.

"Ah!" His body seized.

"Sorry." She clutched her jaw and gently dabbed the spot. "Let me hold it here."

"It's...bad?" he muttered.

Her lips and nose bunched. "A little."

"A lot," he said, touching his palm to the side of his face. He smudged the warm, wet liquid from his cheek and wiped his hand on a broken corn husk.

Her eyebrows narrowed, and she leaned in and focused on the top of his head. "You'll be okay," she soothed. "I think I hear them." She tilted her head, ear to the sky. "Help is coming. They're coming."

Colton couldn't hear the sirens, but he loved listening to her voice. Her grin was a mix of worry and fright, but her smile gave him hope.

"How bad do I look?" He moved his jaw to exercise his muscle, freeing the tension.

"You need a little fixing." Her voice faltered. Her lips loosened into a frown. "You'll be okay."

He survived the crash and would heal. He wasn't giving himself a choice this time. Being unemployed and single was enough. He didn't want any more time to think about his past. He didn't want any more time to think about what he did wrong. "You're not...con...vincing."

She gave a nervous laugh, brushing her hair away from her face. "I'm not a doctor." She cringed. "I don't know."

"I'm bleeding?" His face muscles tightened, ignoring the pain in his side and the swishing of liquid in his stomach. "I have a headache."

"I know you must." She smiled at him, switching hands to apply pressure. "Amazing you're doing okay. All things considered." She glanced at the wreckage and brought her eyes back to his. Her lips parted, warming his insides.

He tilted his head to the faint sound of sirens.

"Hear them?" She patted her hand on his arm.

"Hmm."

"Where are you from, Major? Where's home?"

He had considered his life in Texas, but Jenny didn't exist in his life anymore.

"Belling...ham." Colton closed his eyes.

"Talk to me, Brooks. I want to see your eyes open."

"Tired." He exhausted a breath.

"I know." She rubbed his arm and then cupped her hand over his. "I know it's hard, but hang in there. You're doing great. You're going to be okay."

Her hands soothed him. It felt good to be touched, to be cared for, even if it wasn't going to last. But Colton knew affection led to heartbreak. It didn't matter what kind of relationship it was, he wouldn't leave his heart open for invitation again.

"Major? Look at me." Her eyes searched for his. There was a faint smell of coffee on her breath. "Do you know where you are?"

His eyelids flickered. His head dizzy. It felt like an intruder had taken over his brain.

"Moonlight Valley," she said before he could attempt to answer. "Do you know where it is?" Her voice was gentle, but the words were crashing into each other, feeling like a storm in his head. "North-east Washington," she informed.

The sirens came closer, louder. Firetrucks and an ambulance? With his eyes closed, he slipped his hand into his coat pocket and pulled out an envelope and dragged it across his chest and into her hand because it was too heavy to lift.

Sara relieved it from his hand. "What-what's this?" She eyed the envelope carefully and looked at him with a grim expression.

"Keep it...safe." Colton's stomach clenched. His head felt woozy as though he drank too many whiskey sours. "I can't lose this."

"How will I get it back to you?" She swiped a strand away from her drawn face and blinked rapidly.

He squeezed his eyes shut — the pain...the fatigue. "You know...where... I'll be." He exhaled.

Focusing on Sara's eyes, the trust he saw there eased his mind before interrupted by paramedics, and the loud voices filling their space.

GOING TO THE HOSPITAL was a blur. Colton woke up in a seafoam green room. Across from him, an older man was snoring. How could he sleep in a place where machines were beeping, and doctors were talking, and the paging system was going off every few minutes?

Colton wrapped his leg around the thin, white sheet. He lifted his bandaged hand with the IV and brought it down, remembering he couldn't do much with it. He used his other hand to scratch the growth on his chin. His eyes moved to the footsteps at the door.

"You're awake." A doctor in a lab coat carried a clipboard walked toward him and stationed himself at his bedside. "How do you feel? Any pain?"

Colton winced at the doctor's louder than expected voice. "I was hardly sleeping," he grunted. Although his eyes were heavy and his body ached, he wanted his own bed to sleep in. "Yeah, I have pain. Everywhere." He tried lifting his foot and then brought it down to stop the ache.

"I can give you something." He made a note on his sheet of paper.

"What's my prognosis, doc? When can I go home?" The word home had never felt so Foreign, but it was better than staying here and in an unfamiliar town.

"Not so fast." The doctor's black eyebrows lowered. "You just got here. You had head trauma. We're going to monitor you overnight." He pointed in the air with his pen. "See how you are in the morning."

Colton lifted his free hand to touch his injured face, and on second thought, he lowered it. He had a clean image and was proud of it — no scars or tattoos. In high school, they called him a pretty boy, and Colton fought it for years until he married Jenny. She liked his image, and now he wondered if he'd have any visible scars this time.

"You have some bruising on your ribs," the doctor continued. "I'm sure you feel it."

"My whole body feels it." Colton put his hand to his head. The ache wasn't as intense, but if he could get over his tiredness, he'd feel better.

"Concussions can make you feel irritable, tired, ill."

"It would explain the headache." Colton squinted. "When do you think you'll be discharging me?"

"We have another test to run." The doctor looked at his watch.

"What test?"

"An MRI. Just a precaution to make sure you don't have blood on your brain."

The man across from him choked and caught his breath, alerting him awake. Colton looked past the doctor.

"I don't remember my head hitting anything." The accident was a blur. He fought to remember the details but his mind was like a blank canvas. Getting out of the plane...did he die and come back to life? There was a woman with pale skin and shimmering hair. Her voice was soft. Although he couldn't remember what she said or why she was there with him, he had an angel with him, protecting him and keeping him safe until paramedics arrived.

The doctor wrote something down. "The nurse will be in to check on you."

Colton closed his eyes, trying to rethink the event and what happened when he was out of the plane. What did he do with the envelope? Unless he left it on the plane. He fought his memory. He must have left it on the plane. He needed to get out of the hospital stat before someone tampered with it.

Chapter Three

Sara didn't leave the accident site until she found out the pilot's name. Every emergency vehicle they had in Moonlight Valley was there. Poor Dan Briggs got home to the crisis and offered to help any way he could. She went back to the office to start her story with the little information she had. According to one, first responder, the plane was going to Omak Airport.

The more Sara thought about writing about the plane crash, the more she started thinking about the envelope. Why did he want her to hold onto it? And why didn't he just mail it? She didn't know who Colton was, and she was determined to find out so she could write about a proud American working for her country. It was the best way she could show her support and gratitude in her dad's honor.

Sara tapped on her computer, searching for anything she could find on Major Colton Brooks. Her heart sunk a little, thinking about comforting Colton while they waited for help. The way his eyes struggled to look at her when she spoke and how his lips came together in the effort to smile. He was counting on her to get help and she felt the need to do what she could by not leaving his side. Even after the first responders came to his aid, she wanted to find out who he was and if there was something she could do to ease the military hero's mind.

"Did you video it?" Liam asked, sauntering past her desk.

"I didn't think about it. Honestly, I didn't know what was happening." She turned her attention back to her computer, skimming names. There were lots of Brooks, and one, in particular, was a Roger Brooks, an attorney in Bellingham. "I'm trying to find out who he is," Sara said without looking at him. "There's nothing here with his name."

"Why not ask him?"

She spun her chair around. "I would, but I want some background info first."

Liam bobbed his head. "He has his own plane?"

"Apparently so."

"You can find out who it's registered to."

"Good idea." Sara turned around and searched for the photos she took of the plane. Opening up each picture, she found the one with the most evident serial number and transcribed the upside-down digits. She made a phone call and then another until she found out the information.

Roger Brooks, from Bellingham, Washington, was apparently the owner. She picked up the phone and dialed the number.

"Brooks Attorney, how may I help you?" the female voice answered.

"Hi. I'm looking to speak to Roger Brooks."

"He's in a meeting right now. Would you care to leave a message on his voicemail?"

"I would. Yes. Thank you."

"Just one moment and I'll put you through."

There was a pause, followed by a ring, and a male voice recording came on. When she heard the beep, Sara cleared her throat. "Hi, Roger, this is Sara Quinn with The Observer

newspaper in Moonlight Valley, Washington. I'm looking to speak with a relative of Major

Colton Brooks. If this is you, please call me back, and if it's not you, but you know who I can reach, I'd appreciate a call. Thank you." Sara ended with her phone number and hung up. "What are the chances he'll call me back?"

"Fifty-fifty."

"Right." Sara looked up from the click-clack of Deloris' pumps. She stopped at the filing cabinet and shoved a piece of paper into a folder.

"Any more news about the plane crash?" Deloris asked.

"I'm working on it." Sara clicked on her mouse, dragging a photo of the upside-down plane to fit the page.

Deloris slammed the drawer and leaned over Sara's shoulder. "Good picture." She adjusted her glasses and stood up. "Amazing, he survived. The plane is nothing more than a tin can."

"It is," Sara agreed. There was no way she'd fly in one.

"It's home time for me," Deloris said. "Have a good night."

"Good night." Sara scrolled the Internet to see what she could find on Colton. Wasn't there a website to find military personnel? There had to be some information on the young pilot. She scrolled the screen, clicking on links which took her to articles she ended up reading. She rubbed her eye and clicked on the next story.

CAR CHASE ENDS DEADLY

She bit her lip and skimmed the article, anticipating the tragedy.

A joyride ended in tragedy Saturday night when an erratic driver barreled through the streets of Dallas, Texas, killing a pedestrian and injuring another.

Police say the senseless crime started when two thieves stole a Chevy Camero and lost control, crashing into a building. The identity of the deceased is Major Owen Combs of Omak, Washington. Investigators say Combs was walking out of the Soups & Subs restaurant on Main and Evergreen, when the vehicle exhilarated and drove into Combs. Major Colton Brooks, 27, was with Combs and said, "We were grabbing lunch when, out of nowhere, the vehicle came at us. I didn't know what was going on," says Brooks, a six-year navigator with the Air Force. He told news sources that the pair wasn't aware of the

commotion when they exited the building. Brooks explained that when he saw the car racing toward them, he didn't think it would 'mow them down,' but when it got closer, Combs pushed Brooks aside to get out of the way. "For a second, I thought we were safe," Brooks said. "And the next thing I knew, Owen was flying through the air." Distraught, Brooks covered his face with a hand, pausing to collect his thoughts. "I knew it was fatal. If only I had seen it coming, I would have saved Owen. He was my best friend."

SARA PUT HER HAND OVER her mouth. The men were at the wrong place at the wrong time. There was no telling how long Colton would be in the hospital for, and she didn't know how to reach him if he left, so she needed to go there. Then what would she do with the envelope? If Colton was on his way to Omak, perhaps Denise lived in Omak. Her brain unraveled like a ball of yarn.

Jerry shuffled out of his office. "I'm heading out." He slung his briefcase over his shoulder.

Sara looked up at him, blinking.

"If you need me, my cell phone will be on," he said. "I can't promise I'll answer it, but text or leave a message if you need to reach me." He gripped his fingers to his forehead. "Layouts are done, just insert the front page. It's all we're waiting on."

"I found out some information about the pilot." She sat up straighter. "He was flying to deliver something."

"Just cover the plane crash." He shuffled his feet. "We need hard news."

Sara's insides sank. Why was Colton headed to Omak?

"Email me. I'll edit what I can." He hung his head. "Smaller stuff send to Liam and Deloris. If a bomb goes off, I want to hear about it." He looked up, his thick eyebrows creased.

"You'll be back." Her voice hitched. "Soon," she added. Hoping he'd be back before she left on her trip. She couldn't bear to cancel. She had been looking forward to it the whole year and then meeting Johnathan...it seemed like the perfect time to go.

Jerry sighed. "I'm sorry you have to postpone your trip. I'm sure your cousin will understand." He patted the side of his head, his fingers caught in a ruffle of greying hair.

What about her entitlement to vacation? Johnathan took two workdays off to be with her and her cousin, although she hadn't spoken to him recently and was pretty chill about when she would arrive, said he'd be waiting at the airport for her. Everything was planned. She wasn't supposed to worry about a thing.

"When I get back, you can take some extra days off." His mouth came together abruptly.

"What if I found someone to cover for me?" It wasn't a bad idea. There had to be a part-time reporter somewhere who would be willing to work a couple of days.

"I can't have that," he snapped, and she lost all hope. "If you're gone, who's going to do your job? Liam can't handle this place himself," he said gruffly. "What would it do to the quality of our paper? I can't afford to hire anyone on short notice. We don't have a spare reporter floating around from paper to paper, although—" He shrugged. "It's not a bad idea." His shoulders rose, squaring his upper body.

Sara felt a squeeze of her stomach. Her chest hurt as she took a breath.

"I'm not in the position to hire a temp," he said. "I need you to take my job, so there's no mess up while I'm gone."

"What if I wrote and filed stories ahead of time?" She cleared her throat. "Community stories, light stuff." Stuff their newspaper was known for printing. "Then maybe I could go."

"And what if something big happens? We've already had a plane crash."

She frowned.

"We're a twice-weekly newspaper," he said. "We need news stories. We need consistency."

"I get it." But what was wrong with a little change? Her eyebrows came together and she released her hand on her strap. "I'll figure out something." She had no idea what. If she didn't meet Johnathan, she might as well forget about being adventurist. The whole idea of meeting someone online was because she gave up on finding a relationship in town. She was also bored with the same-o, same-o. The only way things would change for her was if she took matters into her own hands and took a leap of faith.

"Don't be here late," he warned, walking away. "I'll lock the door behind me. You're the last person here."

It was at five o'clock. It wasn't like someone was waiting for her at home to have dinner. For five years, she had been fair with Jerry. She had done everything he asked for her, and he won't help her find someone to take a couple of days off?

She turned her attention to the computer.

AIRMAN QUESTIONED IN FRIEND'S DEATH

Major Colton Brooks, 27, is in questioning tonight after witnesses say he pushed Major Owen Combs towards an oncoming car.

One witness, who doesn't want to be identified says, 'the pair appeared to be good friends, but Brooks was jealous of his misfortune.Th e witness added, 'while it seemed to be a targeted accident, Brooks used the opportunity to get back at Combs. When Brooks was asked about the situation, he called it 'BS,' and added, 'I'd never dream of hurting people I love. He was my best friend. People say things out of anger, and I'm angry too. Owen didn't deserve to die.'

Sara stared at the words. The unsettled assumption rocked her gut. If he was guilty, wouldn't he'd be in jail? She searched online for a marriage record for Owen Combs. She blinked, finding out he was married to Denise Wall on October twelfth. She stared at her screen, rubbing her cold hands to warm them. Colton was delivering the envelope to Denise, but why? When would Colton be out of the hospital? He survived an accident on base and now a plane crash.

There were two sides to the story, but what if the report was right? What if Colton wasn't one of the good guys? Her phone rang just as she pulled into the parking lot. She scooped up the receiver. "Sara speaking."

"Hi, Sara. This is Roger Brooks. I'm Colton's father, returning your call."

"Hi," Sara said and paused. "Yes. Thank you." She scrambled for her notebook and pen at the edge of her desk. "He had a plane crash here in Moonlight Valley. Did you know?"

"Yes. I was told it was minor, and he's okay. He's okay, right?"

"I don't know."

"I'm told Colton should be home in a day or two."

Sara felt a bit of relief. "Well, I think he's lucky to be alive. I mean, the plane, in my opinion is a write-off. It's laying upside down in a cornfield."

"The plane is light. It's small. It doesn't take much for it to flip."

"Then, you know the details." She was saved by telling him what his son suffered. Why wasn't Roger on his way here to see Colton?

Sara cleared her throat. "The reason I called was to find out about Colton. I understand he's an Air Force pilot."

Roger coughed. "Miss Quinn, I can't elaborate on my son's personal life."

"Do you know why he was flying to Omak?" Sara twirled her pen. It would help if he could help her out with the facts.

"I don't know," Roger huffed. "No idea. He said he was visiting a friend. It's his birthday. He did what he wanted to do. I give him space."

Sara swallowed. "Does the name Denise ring a bell?"

"I don't know a Denise," he shot back. "He doesn't tell me much anymore."

"Wasn't he living with you?"

"He was, but I hardly saw him. I work a lot." He paused. "Colton doesn't like talking, and as I said, I've been giving him space."

"It was your plane he crashed."

"That's right."

"How are you going to arrange for it to—" Sara couldn't think of the right word. "Come home?"

"Colton will figure it out. He won't want my help. Never does. He's smart. Worked on planes his whole life. He graduated with honors."

"Um, okay," Sara said.

"Anything else? I have a meeting." He huffed.

"Was Colton jealous of his friend, Owen?" Sara's heart raced like it always did when she was onto a story and breaking news.

"Colton is not the jealous type," he said.

"Is Colton guilty or innocent?"

"He'd be in jail if he were guilty," Roger said with a horse laugh. "Look, Sara—"

"Does Colton have friends?" she asked, not wanting to miss a beat.

"Of course." Roger breathed into the phone.

"Can you give me a name? It's to round out the story." She was on borrowed time with Roger. She was amazed she had him on the phone for as long as she had.

"His childhood friend. Steve. Steve Bailey."

Sara scribbled down this new information in her notebook. "Does Colton stay in touch with Steve?"

"I don't know. I haven't heard his name in a while."

"Steve lives where?"

"Bellingham. Look, Sara, I didn't call to be interviewed."

"I appreciate it," she carried on. "You taught your son to fly. At what age did he learn?"

"How do you know?"

"I, um, read about it." She clenched her teeth. "It's your plane."

"Colton taught me. He was in high school when he took lessons."

"Sounds like he loved planes from an early age."

"He did. Miss Quinn, I have to go. Is there anything else?"

"No. Thank you for your time, Roger." Sara hung up. What kind of relationship did the father-son have? Sara didn't know what to make of the conversation, but she did have a story to write, and adding a few facts, according to Roger, would give her story balance. Hard news facts mixed with human interest about Colton.

Sara would be doing Colton an honor by publicizing his dedication to work. Her dad would have been proud of her for doing so. The question Sara had for Colton was the importance of the letter addressed to Denise. Why did he need to hand-deliver it? And was Colton a jealous person? Could he have used the opportunity to kill his best friend?

Sara's stomach sank. The situation was unsettling. She needed to learn more and get answers to a story she was desperate to write. It had been years since she felt the journalism flame light inside her to follow a story.

She looked at her phone. It was close to seven, so she packed up and headed home to answer Johnathan's call.

Chapter Four

The sound of screeching brakes and shredding metal rattled Colton's head. He tried to lift his eyes from the horrid memory, but he couldn't let go of seeing Owen's body jolt, and his wide-open stare flashed with terror. Heart racing, Colton's eyes sprung open from a reoccurring nightmare.

He breathed out, taking a moment to erase his mind for what would happen next. Owen was mauled over by a speeding car, tossed in the air like a test dummy. Colton ran a trembling hand above his forehead, wiping the sweat away. His heart racing, he took a sharp breath and separated his feet from the tightly wrapped sheet, scissoring his best foot to cool his body temperature down. When were these nightmares going to stop?

He wished he could erase the image of terror on Owen's face, but the moment when he pushed Colton away from the oncoming car was stuck in his mind. His friend thought he was saving him, but what he would never know, was a part of Colton would die too. He'd live with the guilt because Owen should have been the one to live. He had everything to live for.

Colton's insides turned as always when thinking about what he could have done differently. Had he not stopped to tie his boot, taking away from what was happening around them, would it have saved Owen? Had he looked up seconds when his gut told him to?

Colton's heart ached. Owen had a son he would never see grow up and a wife who supported his career, loved his silly jokes, and framed his poems. Colton grinned like he had a frozen mouth. Guilt filled him, and he refused to be grateful to have survived.

"Major Brooks." A voice cut through his dream, and his eyes sprung open to the door.

A petite woman with shoulder-length golden strands walked toward his bedside.

"Hi," he said, his eyes coasting over her delicate features.

"Hi. I'm. Sara." She brought her hand to her chest, eyelashes fluttering. Her shoulders sank and she widened her smile as though receiving good news. "I stayed with you after you crashed your plane. You probably don't remember."

The angel.

It was Sara who was there after the crash. She stayed with him. Okay, so he wasn't hallucinating.

She came a little closer, stopping at the foot of his bed. "You're doing better?"

"Yeah." He brushed his fingers under his chin.

"That's good. Really good," she exhaled. "Glad to see you're awake and alert. You seemed like you were out of it. I mean, it took a lot for you to answer a question." She met his gaze. "Obviously," she laughed.

"Did I answer them for you?"

"You did the best you could." She nodded, pursing her rosebud lips, bringing warmth to his chest. "I was happy when help arrived. I felt helpless." She played with her hands. "I didn't have a first aid kit in my car or a blanket. Something I should. Never know when you'll need it."

He smiled at her quirkiness. "Yeah, appreciated your help. It seemed like the middle of nowhere."

"It's just on the outskirts of Moonlight Valley," she said as she unbuttoned her long, black coat, revealing a cream sweater and black pants.

"How did you know my plane went down?" He moved his head around on the pillow.

"I was driving when I saw you...your plane. It was all over the place. I couldn't figure it out, and then you took a nosedive right into the cornfield. I've never seen that before."

"You were in the right place at the right time," he said.

"Maybe, but I'm not the best person to offer help. I didn't know what to do." She rubbed her coat sleeves. "I still don't know if I did the right thing."

"You stayed with me and called for help. Right?"

"Yes." She lowered her chin, eyeing his forehead. "Looks like they stitched you up."

"Only three stitches," he said.

She scrunched her face. "I used whatever tissues I had to cover up the cut. Do you have any broken bones?"

"Na. My left foot is sprained. I have bruised ribs." Colton squirmed his head to find a soft spot on his pillow. "I'll heal."

Sara jumped. "Here, let me help you." She stepped toward him and pushed his pillow in. "Better?"

"Yeah. Thanks." He breathed in a mix of flowers and vanilla. "Hospital beds. Never hotel quality."

She laughed, showing off her pretty mouth. Damn, Colton wondered if her lips tasted as good as they looked.

"It's for a reason," she said. "They don't want you to stay long. That's why they don't have chefs in the kitchen."

"They should. Maybe people would get better faster."

"Great concept. Why hadn't anyone thought of that?" She smiled and threw her hands into her coat pockets. "Have you eaten? You're probably starving."

"I'm not." He lay his hand across his stomach. He was too sore to think about food.

"I can run over to the bakery across the street and get you something. Betty's makes delicious cinnamon buns and muffins, and they make espresso too if you drink coffee."

"I drink coffee, yeah." He nodded. "I don't need one."

"Are you sure?" Her shoulders rose. "It's no problem."

"I'll be fine." He didn't want her to go out of her way. She had already done enough for him. She had stayed with him until help arrived and was kind enough to come and check on him. It was more than enough. "What time is it?" He scratched the side of his head.

"Nine A.M."

She craned her neck, glancing around. "I probably wouldn't have an appetite either if I were here." She returned her gaze to his. "I'm glad you're recovering and doing okay. When I saw your plane go down, I didn't know what to expect. It must have been scary."

"I didn't either." He pulled on his sheet to cover his leg without irritating his sprained foot. "It kinda happened fast."

"It looked bad. I mean, it was bad." Her eyes lit up. "Glad you're okay."

Colton struggled with the sheet.

"Here." She jumped to the foot of his bed. "Tightly wrapped or loose?"

He felt the heat of her hand through the sheet, sending a shock to his nervous system. Her fingers curved over his right leg and wrapped it over his foot. He flinched.

"Sorry." Her eyebrows narrowed. "Painful?"

"No." He gave a slow grin.

"Ticklish?" Her shoulders dropped. "Sorry."

"A little. That's good." Laughter bubbled in his throat. He didn't know why it brought a flutter to his gut.

"So, you have your own plane?" Her eyebrows furrowed and then released.

"My dad's. He used to fly."

"He doesn't anymore?"

"No. He has nowhere to fly to."

She nodded. "I guess now he doesn't."

Colton's upper lip pulled to the side.

"Sorry," she said. "Bad tease."

"All good."

"You're alive. That's the most important thing." She gave him a grave expression, feeding his insides with uneasiness. "So, what happened? Why did you crash?"

"Engine failed."

"Really?" Her beautiful brown eyes danced with green flecks — a sparkle of brightness to his dull day. "How does that happen?"

"It just does." He shook his head. "The magneto stopped working. I was flying with one engine and accidentally shut off the good engine." He felt his cheeks warm. Had he been calmer and didn't let his anxiety get to him, he wouldn't have dropped the key. He definitely wasn't the man he used to be. How did he become so anxious? He had always been a confident flyer.

Colton had tried turning the key of the magneto switch to the left so both engines would run at the same time, but his trembling fingers turned another notch to the off position. When he turned it back to the left, his shaky hand pulled the key out and it slipped through his fingers, falling to the floor. The engine did what he imagined it would do seconds before he turned the magneto to off. His aircraft was spinning slowly.

"And you had no indication beforehand? Before you took off?" Her eyebrows narrowed.

"Not at all."

"So it just...stops working?" Her mouth fell open. "Oh, my goodness." She touched her chest. "That's scary."

Colton had never explained it before. Being around airplanes since he was young, he knew how they worked, and the mechanics came second nature, but to solve engine problems? He couldn't find the words. Not simple enough to wash the panic off her face.

"Gosh. I don't think I could ever go on a small airplane. I mean, what are the chances it will go down?" She sucked in a breath and at the same time clutched her fist to her chest. "It doesn't sound safe."

"Safer than driving." He didn't want to scare her, so he chose his words carefully. "It rarely happens," he added to calm her apparent fear. "Driving a car is dangerous."

"Yeah, but falling from the air is just as scary. I'll stick to the jumbo jets. At least they feel safer."

They go down too, but he kept the thought to himself. The light in Sara's eyes disappeared, and her bottom lip dipped like she was about to be kissed. He rubbed his forehead. He needed to stop thinking about her before he slipped up and said the wrong thing. He didn't deserve to start a friendship with someone when he wasn't good at keeping them.

Her body shifted. "I can't think of about it."

His stomach stirred. Maybe Sara had a fear of heights or airplanes or both. He couldn't imagine not flying even if there was a risk. If he was her pilot, he'd make sure she had nothing to fear. He'd keep her safe. "There's a risk in everything we do. You can't live out of fear, or you can't live." Why was he giving her advice? He was the last one who should be offering.

"I guess. Any advice for putting a passenger at ease?"

"Ah. So, you've got a flight booked?"

Her eyes glanced up at the clock on the wall. "I do. I leave in eleven days." She sucked in her lips.

"Where to?"

"Australia." She shuffled her feet. "Give me some advice. I don't travel often."

"No? You should." He paused before answering, finding humor in her tone. "Listen to music. Bring earbuds." He pushed himself up with his free hand. He wanted to get out of the bed, touch her, hold her, thank her for not leaving and for keeping him company.

She made him feel better and he felt stronger than yesterday, but just as lonely. The good thing was his mind was clear. "It helps me with anything."

"Music?" she asked. "I've got earbuds. Thanks." Her body straightened. He wiggled for comfort. "Need help?"

"I'm fine. Ugh." He grunted as he rolled his shoulders back. His neck muscles tightened, and when he took a breath, a stabbing sensation made him freeze, and he automatically touched his side. Exhaling, he stayed in a position to gain the courage to move again. He hated sitting still unless it was work-related, and it had his full attention.

"Are you sure?" she asked, her voice a mere whisper.

"Yeah." His teeth came together. "I supposedly have bruises. I feel like I cracked a rib."

"It's a sign to take it easy."

"Probably."

"Your advice is listening to music." She nodded. Her body swayed. "I'll do that."

"Inhale lavender too," he added. "It's calming." *Like your voice, your presence.*

"I never thought of that, but okay. Is that what you do?"

"I don't. I like the adrenaline flying gives me." He met her eyes. "My mom uses it for her patients, though."

"Oh, is she a doctor?" Sara took a step forward.

"Not a doctor. A doula," he said slowly. "An aid for expecting mothers." It's the way his mom describes her job to someone who asks.

"I know what a doula is." She giggled. "That's amazing. I bet it's exciting too."

"She thinks it is." He stared a little too long and looked away, but he came back to her. "I think it is too. From what I hear, she's good at it. I haven't witnessed her work, but she gets little gifts and cards, so she must be doing a good job."

Sara giggled, and Colton knew he was rambling and sounding like he couldn't find his words, but Sara was making him forget why he was there and the life he used to have.

"So, music and inhale lavender. Got it."

"Taking a couple of Dramamine doesn't hurt either."

"Thanks, doctor." She laughed. "I should be fine then." Her smile lifted his chest. She was the best thing he had seen in days, months. A breath of fresh air. Her company took his mind off of the sorrow and grief he had fought days before. It didn't vanish from his life. Not completely. Every day was healing and trying to get stronger, mentally. He was ready to start again and close the door of his past. It was time to bury his losses and force on getting out of the hospital so he could find the envelope and deliver it to Owen's wife. It would give him closure. He held onto it for too long, but couldn't bring himself to the realization that was haunting his dreams.

She looked up at the clock. "I have to go, but I can come by later to see how you're doing and if you need anything." She spun around and left before he could say goodbye.

Chapter Five

Waking up from a nap, Colton used what strength he could muster to push himself up and readjusted the pillow. It would be nice if he could get out of bed and see how well he could manage walking. The sooner he showed independence, the sooner he could leave.

The same doctor who came in earlier, popped in, tapping his clipboard with his pen.

"Hey, doc, are my results in?" Colton asked. "I'm feeling good to go." He'd heal better on his own and would get a night of better sleep without the sound of peeping machines and getting poked in the middle of the night by the nurse. The days would go by faster too if he slept. He did it before, and it worked when he wanted to forget about his ex-wife, his dog he left behind, and the friend who died for nothing.

He pressed his tongue against his cheek, tasting the bitterness of his past he wished would disappear. His counselor said it would take time to find a focus, a new love, and strength to free himself from his demons, but to Colton it was more about forgetting his past and working through what he lost.

"Yes. Nothing turned up on your MRI." The doctor shifted his jaw. "Do you have someone to take you home?"

"I don't need anyone." Colton winced. "I can find my way."

The doctor clutched his clipboard with both hands in front of him. "You'll need someone to pick you up."

He didn't need a chaperone. "My parents should be coming." He knew they wouldn't be. He hadn't asked them, but if he needed his dad, he could ask. He just didn't want to, and his mom wouldn't come without his dad, so he had nobody.

"You need to get up and walk," the doctor said. "Get some strength before you're discharged."

His stomach tightened. He hated that word.

"We'll keep you one more night to see how you are tomorrow." The doctor's lips sealed; he glanced at his paper, wrote something down, and looked up. "I don't want to be the one to release you when you've suffered a concussion and have no one to take you home."

Colton sighed. "It's just a headache now." He regarded his left hand hooked up to the IV and his sore foot. He hadn't even tried walking on it yet. Maybe he could ask Sara to drive him somewhere. Although he wasn't sure where, he needed to figure it out. He might never see her again. Why did she care about his wellbeing? She was a passerby and he was a stranger.

Colton balled the sheet with his right hand. All this thinking made his headache worse. He should have said something meaningful to Sara, heartfelt like he appreciated what she'd done for him. He had to work on expressing himself, something his counselor encouraged. How did Owen do it so naturally? His friend's memory was what kept him going when he didn't want to, but damn, it was hard.

His past was all Colton knew, and learning to live again, finding his way, imposed a

challenge because moving forward took effort. He wasn't ready to let go until he could deliver the envelope and somehow express his sympathy to a woman with the most significant loss. If he wanted to deliver the envelope on time, he needed to get out.

Colton closed his eyes to ease his headache and because it was the best way to past the time, but when he heard footsteps against the vinyl floor, he opened his eyes and knew he had fallen asleep again. Rolling his head toward the door, he twitched at the room's brightness and the silhouette approaching him.

"Sara," he tried to say and swallowing to moisten his dry throat dry. When that didn't help, he coughed and covered his arm over his stomach to calm his achy muscles. "What day is it?" He scratched his head. Had he slept a full day?

"Hi," she greeted and giggled, stepping cautiously toward him, holding a tray with two medium-size paper cups on either side. Her eyes following the bandage on his forehead to his toe, sticking out from the bedsheet. "It's afternoon. I came back because I thought you might feel like a cup of coffee and a muffin." She stood at the foot of his bed then slowly made her way around to the wheelie table and set down the tray.

He put a hand to his facial hair on his chin. He probably looked as rough as he felt. "I do, thanks. I could use one." Her eyes lit up causing a pang to his chest. "They tried giving me a cup this morning, but I swear it was made from a used filter."

Sara wiggled the paper cup out from the tray. "What do you take in it?"

"Cream or milk. Whatever you have."

"I have some here." She shook a capsule of cream and poured it in. "How many?"

"Two would be great. Thanks." He lowered his gaze to his hand. She didn't need to look after him. He was more than capable of looking after himself, but he didn't mind her company and her soft touch on his skin.

Sara stirred the cup with a wooden stir stick. "Do you want to take it?" She lifted the cup up. "Or would you like me to leave it here?" She lowered her arm to the table.

"I can take it." He held out his hand, and her fingers slid under him in a warm embrace. His heart quickened.

"I brought you a muffin." She slipped her hand away and opened the brown paper bag. "You must be hungry."

"I'm not." He eyed the bag. "But thanks."

"They're delicious." Her bottom lip curved.

"I'm not...really hungry."

"I can leave it here for later." She dropped the bag on the table. "You might change your mind. How do you feel? You look better than this morning."

"You're nice." He kept his eye on her.

"I try to be." She tempted to take a sip of coffee. "So, when are they sending you home?" Her mouth hid behind the paper cup. "Must be soon."

"I don't know." He stretched his neck side to side. "Tomorrow. Maybe."

"Do you have family living close? Is someone coming to get you?"

Colton pushed his shoulders back into the pillow. "Yeah, someone will."

"Your family knows you're here, right?"

"They do. Just have to let my parents know when I can leave." Colton pushed himself up, squirming to get comfortable.

"Are you okay?" She put down her cup and jumped to his side. "Can I do something?" She grabbed onto his pillow and pushed it under his head. "Is that better? Or a little more?" Her hand cushioned the back of his neck, and as she pushed the pillow further down, her hand slipped through a sliver of his opened gown, touching his skin. His shoulders tingled. The combination of her sweet perfume and a soft hand seized his mind.

"Thanks," he said, meeting her eyes as she stepped back. "Do you want to sit down? You can pull up a chair."

She looked around the room. "I'm okay. I can't sit. I just wanted to bring you a coffee and muffin and see how you were doing."

"Thank you."

"So what do they do with your plane, have they said?"

"No. Probably have to wait for a flatbed and tow it to Omak. I don't know what the extent of damage is."

"Not like it can fly again, right?" Her lips pursed. "It's been in an accident now."

"Oh, yeah, it could fly again." He nodded, "As long as everything gets replaced and tested. Why not?"

"The nose of the plane is broken." Her eyes widened, lips pulled apart. "What if it wasn't fixed properly?" She blinked rapidly. "I don't know. It seems pretty risky to me."

Colton smiled from the side of his mouth. She was so damn cute; he couldn't help himself. "Life is a risk. I made it this far."

"You would fly again? The crash didn't scare you?"

"Scare me?" He wanted to laugh.

Her eyes widened. "You could have died. Next time you may not be so lucky."

He reached for his cup. "I've flown a Boeing C-40 Clipper and a Lockheed C-5 Galaxy. I can't afford to be scared, and I can't think about luck. Timing is everything."

"I don't know what those are, but they sound big and scary."

Colton's hardened smile gave way. "I don't think about the danger. If I did, it could get the best of me. I can't let it."

"Still." She raised her cup. "You could have died."

"I didn't."

"You were lucky."

"I guess if that's what you want to call it."

"You don't believe in it?"

"Luck?" He shrugged. "I don't know what to believe anymore." He pulled the sheet over his chest. If someone asked him a year ago he'd be divorced, lose his dog and accused of killing his best friend, he wouldn't have believed it. "You could die a lucky man. It depends on what it means to you, I guess."

"So, what's next for you? Leave here, then what?" She changed her tone. Why was she so interested?

He pressed his shoulders into the mattress. "Hopefully, get back to work."

"Okay." She took her coffee in her hand. "Where are you stationed?"

"Texas. Have you ever been?"

"No."

"Beautiful state. I guess you won't be back to the base for a while."

"No." There was no use telling her he took an honorably discharged. It would only open up questions for her to ask and he wouldn't be here long enough for her to care.

"Can I bring you a book? A magazine? A deck of cards?"

"Na. I'm good. Thanks. So, what do you do?"

"For work?" She rocked on her feet and took a small sip of her coffee.

"Teacher? Caregiver?" She had to have a career helping people. "Nurse?"

"No." She grinned to the side. "I'm... a reporter." There was a sparkle in her eye. "The Observer...for Moonlight Valley."

He bit his tongue — a good thing he didn't say any more than he did.

Her fingers slid around the paper cup. "Did you always want to work for the military?"

"Not really." He ran his tongue over his lip. He didn't want to follow in his dad's footsteps like his brother. "But when I was a kid, I used to build burrows in the backyard," Colton said, looking past her. "I would use my toys and blankets. My mom hated it." He grinned at the memory. "She would curse and tell me I wrecked her good sheets.

But I wanted to be a pilot." His lips parted. "The military came later. When I was a teenager."

"You followed your calling."

"I guess." He brought his focus back to Sara. "It's what I know. It's part of me." He didn't know what else he could do with his life and wondered again what he would do now if he could relive his decision.

"We have to dream, or we're going nowhere." She clutched her cup to her mouth.

Colton nodded. "What's your dream, or have you lived it?"

She laughed. "I think you might have changed my mind." Her face grew serious. "I wanted to travel." Her eyes widened. "It's always been my dream, but I think you might have wrecked that for me."

"Sorry." He exhaled. "Traveling's a good one." His voice throaty. "There's a risk in everything. It depends on what you want badly." He reached for his coffee cup and took a sip.

"I guess you're right." Sara looked up at the clock. "I should go. I've got a meeting to get to."

"Thanks for stopping by." He raised his cup to her, feeling a tightness in his chest. "Just curious. Are you always this kind to strangers?"

"It's what people of Moonlight Valley do. We help when we can." She bowed out and headed for the door, passing the doctor coming in. "Get better soon."

The doctor walked toward Colton. "There's a good chance you'll be going home tomorrow," he announced. "Let's see how you do tonight." The doctor shoved his hand into his coat pocket. "You may still feel off balance, dizzy, but we'll see how you do in the morning. You'll need a ride. Do you have someone now to get you?" He looked at Sara. "Would you be the person?"

"Me?" She touched her chest. "Okay. Sure."

"No," Colton interjected. "I'll call my parents."

If Colton called now, it would give his dad time; he could leave in the morning and get here by afternoon as long as he wasn't in court or in a meeting with a client. Colton would be bothering him, but he didn't have an option.

"I can pick you up." She shrugged. "It's probably easier for you."

Colton's eyebrows lifted.

"I'll be here." Sara beamed. "But I'll come by tomorrow in case something has changed." She winked at him, turning on her foot.

His body sunk into the bed, and he felt a lightness in his chest. He didn't want Sara's help, or anyone else's, because if he gave in, he'd start to care, and having friends was the last thing he wanted.

Chapter Six

Sara walked out of Moonlight Valley General Hospital. The one-level building had been added on to accommodate the need for more rooms and departments. She headed toward the main doors and shoved her hand into her purse to retrieve her dinging phone.

What was she supposed to do with Colton tomorrow when she picked him up? He didn't have a place to go. She should have asked him to call a family member. Roger didn't say anything about coming here, and by the sound of his abrupt and unsympathetic demeanor, she doubted he was hopping on a flight to be by his son's side.

Hey Sweet Sara,

Sorry, I missed you last night, and I got caught up this morning in a meeting and interviews. You know how it is. I was looking forward to our chat, but I was covering a protest, and it went past midnight. A dozen people got arrested. You probably saw it on the news. Anyway, by the time I got home, it was too late to call you. I hope you weren't waiting up for me. Can we chat tonight? Same time?

Sara dropped her shoulders and sent a quick reply. Her stomach twisted as though she was out of sorts.

Hi! It was probably for the best. I was working late. There was a small plane crash here. Big news!:)We can chat tonight.

Sara put her phone back into her purse and strut across the parking lot. In just over a week, she'd leave it all behind and focus on gaining life experience and meet new people because if she wanted to live and find love, she'd have to do it outside of Moonlight Valley. Meeting Johnathan in person was a good start. Was he as nervous as her? He mentioned he lived in a condo, so she assumed he lived downtown, not that it mattered, she booked a hotel room for her comfort level.

What if Johnathan was nothing she imagined? She didn't want to be a victim of her own misjudgment, so she was going to play this one smart and stay only two days in Seattle before heading to Australia. It seemed the perfect opportunity to ease into the dating scene again without being committed to just Johnathan. Maybe her cousin would introduce her to one of his friends. Sara was open-minded, even if dating wasn't her top priority, she wanted to at least experience life outside of Moonlight Valley and the only way she knew how was to take a vacation for a change of scenery. Her phone dinged again. She scooped it out to read her message. **Plane crash. Wow. I bet it'll hit the front page. Lol**

She smiled and clutched her phone when it rang.

"Sara? It's Steve Bailey. You called me?"

"Hi, Steve. Yes. Thanks for getting back to me." Sara walked as fast as she could to her car so she could sit and take notes. "I'm told you're a friend of Colton Brooks?"

"Yeah. I mean, we grew up together."

"Do you talk to him often?" She moved faster through the parking lot, fingering through her purse for her keys.

"Not as much as I used to. I guess when he's home we might see each other. Is he okay?" His breath shortened. "He's alive, isn't he?"

"He is. He's in the hospital recovering from a plane crash. He'll be okay," Sara said confidently. "He's in good spirits and doing fine.

I have a couple of questions about your relationship with Colton. How is he as a friend?"

"We don't talk anymore. He was a good friend. Yeah."

"Was he a jealous person?"

"I don't know about jealous. Colton's a humble guy."

Sara unlocked her car door and slipped inside, throwing her bag on the passenger seat.

"Has he done anything out of character?" The idea of Colton wanting his friend dead didn't sit right with her. He had been under investigation; surely, he didn't commit a crime.

The pit of her stomach knotted. She wanted to hear first-hand.

"Can't think of anything. You can't count the time Colton stole my girlfriend in high school. They got married, so I guess it was legit. They're divorced now."

"Divorced?"

"Yeah."

"Do you know why?" Sara suspended her pen from her notebook, listening carefully.

"I don't think Jenny could handle him being away. Honestly. It's hard on the marriage. Any marriage, right? Being away for months at a time." Sara's own mom and dad somehow kept it together.

"Jenny didn't know how hard it would be, and they grew apart. It's not a secret. I'm telling you stuff everyone knows."

"Okay." Sara took a steady breath.

"They were separated, and Colton had some stress at work."

"What kind of stress?"

"Work in general. It wasn't easy dealing with harsh situations. Do you know his buddy died at work? It was an accident. I think everything snowballed for Colton, and life got worst for him. He had to get help. That's what I heard. By that point, he was on leave. It was for the best. A guy with so much mental strain...you can't have him working in life and death situations. Right? It's a tough call. I don't know what he's doing now."

"So, Colton is divorced?" She felt a flutter in her belly.

"Yes. If Colton were a jealous guy, he'd hate me."

"Why is that?"

"Because I'm with Jenny," he said matter-of-factly.

Sara sat in her car, deliberating what she should do about Colton. The tiniest idea of him being a murderer played in her mind. She didn't feel threatened by him, although lying in the hospital, there's not much he could do. A part of her felt sorry for him, losing everything. He must be suffering emotionally, or he didn't care and was relieved.

Sara ended the conversation and called her friend Kelly. She checked the time on her phone before putting it to her ear. "Hey, Kel. Got a sec?" Sara asked when Kelly answered.

"I've got a few minutes. You caught me. I was just in the staffroom, grabbing water. What's up?"

"I'll give you the short story and fill you in with details later. The pilot who crashed his plane, you heard, right?"

"I did. Crazy."

"Yeah, well, I found out some stuff about him. He's in the hospital still, and I went to visit him. The doctor asked if I could pick him up tomorrow, drive him somewhere. I don't even know where." She sighed, rolling her eyes. "The doctor doesn't want him leaving by himself. He has a sprained foot and a concussion so he can't drive. I offered. I don't know what I was thinking, but now I'm having second thoughts. I don't know this guy. Do you think Brad would pick Colton up for me?"

"You can ask him."

"Brad has good judgment on people, and I need to ask this pilot more questions, but I don't want to be alone with him."

"Ask Brad. He'd do it."

"Have you talked to Brad recently?"

"No."

"Oh."

"It doesn't matter. You're friends with him too."

"I don't want it to be awkward."

"It's not. I don't know what to say to him, and even if I did, what would it matter? He doesn't want me. He's moved on," Kelly said.

Sara's body slacked, and she felt an ache in her chest for her friend. It must be hard not to have someone you love.

"I'm sorry," Sara said.

"You don't have to be. It's over. I just can't think about him. I have to move on."

"You're strong."

"I don't have an option." She paused. "This doesn't have anything to do with him and I. If you want Brad to help you, he will. You know he will and you don't need my permission."

Sara put her head back against the seat. She felt sorry for her friend. Kelly and Brad were the perfect pair, and yet they couldn't make their relationship work.

"Maybe we can meet up at TJ's soon," Kelly said. "I'm busy this weekend. I'm working Saturday and doing something with my sister. I'll ask Emily if she's free Monday night. Are you up for it?"

"Sure."

"We can see you before you leave on your trip. We're going to miss you."

"It's a short trip." She wished it was longer. Sara said goodbye and called Brad.

"Hey. What's up?" Brad answered.

"I have a favor to ask you."

"Shoot."

"You know the pilot who crashed?"

"Yeah."

"He gets out of the hospital in a day or two and he doesn't have anyone here to help him. Any chance you can pick him up?"

"And take him where?"

"That's the thing. I don't know. Hotel? I'm not sure where he will go."

"Why is this your problem?"

"Trying to help," she said. "I'm sure his parents are coming to get him. He did mention it. I assume they would." Sara clutched her teeth. Most parents would find their child and bring them home, wouldn't they? "I offered but having second thoughts."

"So you want me to pick him up and take him somewhere?"

"Could you?"

"Yeah, sure as long as I stay in town. I'm working."

"Thank you." She breathed a heavy sigh. "Okay. That's great. Can you also let me know what you think of him in terms of a murderer, a bad guy?"

"Whoa, what?"

"I don't know him," she protested. "I need to interview him, but if he's a bad guy, then I don't want to be by myself."

"You think I'll be able to tell?"

"You have a good sense of judgment on people. Remember when that guy was selling us on that nutrient supplement, and you told him it was a scam before he had a chance to tell us about it?" Sara lifted her shoulders; she stretched her neck. "This guy, Colton could be crazy, but you, you're good at judging people and if you can let me know—"

"You're helping him so you can use him for a story," Brad said. "That's fine. I can do it."

When Colton got out of the hospital she could exchange his envelope for a story.

The sound of rushing water came through the phone, guessing Brad was at work, so she ended their conversation and tossed her phone into her purse. At least Brad would tell her if the pilot was dangerous and if she should be worried.

Sara took out the sealed, white envelope and read the name. Denise was written on the top right corner. Its thickness was more than a one-page letter. Perhaps legal papers?

Chapter Seven

Sara drove to her mom's house for her mid-week visit. The three-bedroom bungalow was the same house she lived in as a child. Her mom updated it over the years, changing the laminate kitchen countertop to quartz, and the tile floor was now wooden planks. Sara feared her mom was going to put it up for sale and down-size as she and her brother moved out, but their mom convinced them living there gave her peace and tranquility, easing the pain of her late husband.

She opened the front door and stepped inside. "Hi, mom."

"Hi!" Her mom called back, scurrying through the living room, wiping her hands on a dishtowel. "Do you smell it?" She waved the dishtowel in the air. "I burnt the zucchini loaf. How are you?" She pecked a kiss on Sara's cheek and raced into the kitchen. Sara took off her shoes and followed her mom.

"I don't smell anything."

"This new oven is sensitive. Higher heat." Her mom tossed the towel on the counter and used a glove to move the loaf pan over an unlit burner. "It's not like my old one. That one took twice as long. Do you feel like a cup of coffee?"

"Sure," Sara said. "You got your hair done."

"I went lighter." She tossed her hair and took out two mugs from the cupboard. "I turned the machine on a few minutes ago. I knew you would be here. Right on time." Her face eased into a smile. "I can't guarantee the loaf tastes any good." She dropped her head and poked it with a knife. "It's a little dark along the edges."

"I'm sure it's good, Mom. You're baking always turns out. You did something with your...eyes." Sara tilted her head, taking in her mom's new look. "And you're wearing makeup."

"A little eyeliner. That's all." She waved her hand. Her cheeks pinched with pink. She poured the coffee and handed one to Sara, leaving her cup. "It's still warm." She took out a cooling rack and carefully flipped the pan over. The loaf popped out.

"Your baking never goes to waste." Sara leaned against the counter, hands cupping her coffee while watching her mom move from the stove to the sink.

"Were you on assignment?" Her mom put the pan in the sink and ran the water to soak it. "I didn't see your car parked at work when I drove by."

"I was at the hospital, visiting the pilot who crashed." Her insides lifted, thinking about Colton. "I want to interview him."

Her mom snapped her head over her shoulder. "How's he doing?" She shut off the tap and dried her hands. "Pretty banged up?"

"He's actually good. Better than I thought." Sara brought her mug to her lips. "He didn't seem like he was in too much pain, considering."

"Phew. That's a relief." Her mom took a sip and placed her cup down on the counter. "Small planes scare me. There's nothing to them."

"Have you been in one?"

"Yeah," she faltered. "A couple of times."

"Why?"

"Oh, I don't know." She shrugged. "For fun."

"Why don't I know this?"

Her mom waived her hand. "You must have been working."

Sara nodded. "Well, Colton's an experienced pilot."

"With his training, he's probably not thinking about being hurt, he's thinking about how well he is to go home or back to work."

"Was that dad's thing? Home briefly and then back to work?"

"He was committed." Her mom put down her mug and wiped down the counter with a wet cloth. "He liked keeping himself busy. I don't think he knew how to relax."

"I remember him taking us for ice cream," Sara said, batting her eyes. She missed her dad's booming voice and playfulness. Ready to shoot hoops with Evan or playing board games with Sara. He was up for anything when he was home. He loved his family.

"Oh, yes. At the food stand at the lake," she said dreamily, shifting her gaze to the window. "We'd sit on a log and eat ice cream." The late afternoon sun was dulling. "It was the only time he was himself."

"What do you mean? Dad was always laidback. The most easy-going man I've known."

"With work on his mind twenty-four-seven, he tried his best to separate his home life around you kids. It was tough for him sometimes. Thinking about what was happening in the world, how his friends were coping, and when he was due back, or if he'd get a call. It was hard." Her mouth came together. "On me, on your father." Her shoulders sank. She sighed, squeezing the wet cloth in her hand.

"I never noticed." Sara strained her eyes on her mom whose face was washed with sorrow. "Is that why Al Anderson stopped by so often to check on us?"

"He, he didn't come over all the time." Her body jerked and she wiped off the counter. "He came over when we needed something."

"I didn't mean all the time." Sara took a sip and put down her mug. "Sometimes, he stayed late."

"He's a caring man." Her mom washed the cloth under the tap and rang it out. She wiped the other side of the sink where it was clean.

"Do you ever see him?"

"Who?"

"Al."

"No. Oh, well, yes, sometimes," she faltered. "At the store. Stuff like that." She shook her head. "So, is this pilot you're talking about young or old?"

"He's my age, I think." Sara blew the steam off her coffee before attempting to take a sip.

"Really?" Her mom threw the cloth into the sink and dried her hands and cut a piece of the loaf. "It's cooled off." She put a piece on the plate and slid it in front of Sara. "Where was the pilot headed? Do you know?"

"Now, I know where I get my reporter instincts from." Sara laughed, breaking off a chunk of the loaf and shoved it into her mouth. "Omak." She chewed and washed the crumbs down with coffee. "It's not burnt, mom. It tastes delicious." She licked her thumb.

"I added more cinnamon this time." She glanced at her watch. "Is it too much?"

"No, it's perfect. Aren't you having any?"

"I had a bite. I'm not hungry. I had a big breakfast."

"It's afternoon. You should have lunch."

"I had a bowl of soup. You don't have to worry about me. I'm fine." She dusted her hands and put them on her narrow hips.

"Are you going somewhere? Out for dinner?" Sara asked, noting her hair and makeup. "You're dressed up."

Her mom looked down at herself. "I don't think so."

"I have some running around to do." She dried another bowl and placed it in a cupboard.

Sara swallowed and drank. "Is everything okay?"

Her mom grabbed a spatula from the drying rack. "Oh, yeah. Great. Don't worry." She glanced her way. "I'm pretty good. Have you talked to your brother lately?"

"No, why?" Sara raised her chin, soaking up her mom's flawless expression.

"He broke up with Jessica."

"Really?" Sara put down her mug, her eyes bugging. "What happened?" Sara touched her chin. "They were so compatible."

"I don't know." Her mom shook her head. "He said it wasn't working out."

"That's bad news. I thought for sure they'd get married." Sara ate another piece of loaf and pushed away her empty plate.

Her mom scrunched up the towel and left it on the counter beside the others. "Do you want another piece?"

"No, thanks." Sara looked at her half cup of coffee. "I have to get back to work. I'm covering for Jerry while he's away."

"Where is he?"

"He left to see his dying mother. I don't know how long he's gone. He better come back by next week, or I won't be going away."

"And cancel your trip?"

"I don't have a choice."

"Well, you can't put a time on death," her mom said lightly. "People will hold on until their loved ones are there before they die."

"I know." Sara scratched her neck. "It's just this was a great opportunity for me. I don't know when I'll get another chance."

"You will. I never liked the idea of you traveling alone."

"I was going to stay with Scott."

"I know. I'd rather you travel with someone. Getting to the airport, flying by yourself, getting your luggage. It's stressful trying to navigate your way." Her mom leaned against the counter and folded her arms across her chest. "Are you sure you're going to be okay?"

"Yeah, mom. Fine." Sara took a sip. "Are you still going to the gym?"

"Three times a week."

"And your friend's lunch, Sunday afternoons?"
"I haven't missed one."
"Work is good?"
"Couldn't be better." Her mom tilted her head. "You don't have to worry about me. I'm doing well." Her mom's lips curled into a gentle smile. "Better now."

"Just making sure. I can take you shopping sometime if you want."

"That's nice, sweetheart. I'm okay." She unfolded her hands and held onto the counter behind her. "Are you seeing anyone?"

"You know I'd tell you if I was. I'm taking a break," Sara reminded her. Her stomach clutched. She hated to keep Johnathan a secret, but there was no way it would be an easy conversation if she told her about meeting a guy she met online. "I have to run. I have a story to write." She jumped up and cleared her dishes, putting them in the sink. "Thanks for the snack." She hugged her mom and inhaled. "You're wearing perfume."

Her mom smiled at her acknowledge. "Be safe."

Sara rushed out the door and got into her car. As she drove away, Sara glanced at the rearview mirror. A new blue pickup truck slowed down and stopped in front of her mom's house.

It was good to see her mom had friends and was looking after herself. Maybe her mom didn't need Sara to worry about her well-being, after all.

Chapter Eight

Colton woke up from a dreamy state when he heard footsteps stop at the door and into his room. His first indication was Sara, but his heart shrunk when he realized it was his nurse, padding the empty IV pouch. "The doctor said you have no infection. All looks good, so I can take out your IV."

It had been three and a half days in the hospital. Too long, according to Colton. He couldn't leave fast enough, except he'd miss Sara. Her daily visits had sparked hope and comfort to an already over-active mind. Yesterday, they talked about the weather, the town, the fall fair—not much of anything really, but he liked having her around. The familiar scent of her perfume, her laugh after she told a story and an attentive gaze that distracted him from where he was. She was becoming a friend and saying goodbye was the part he hated.

The nurse placed a fresh gauze and Band-Aid on the bed and began to tear off the tape. "Take a breath in." She pulled the IV needle out, placed it into the disposable needle bin hanging on the wall and applied a cotton ball for pressure. "Put a finger here," she instructed and ripped open a Band-Aid, placing it on his hand. She glanced at the foot of his bed. "You should try and walk around. I'll get you crutches to borrow."

Colton moved his foot around. His left foot still ached under the tenser bandage, but he knew he'd be fine once he started moving. "I'll be okay. I don't know how long I'll be here, in Moonlight for." He didn't want to borrow anything when he was planning on leaving right away.

She patted her coat pockets. "You'll have to elevate your foot as much as possible. At least for the next few days to bring the swelling down. I'll be right back." She walked out of the room.

Colton whipped off the sheet, pressed his hands into the mattress, and swung his legs off of the bed, gently lowering his left foot to the floor. He brought a hand to the ache on his side. His head felt a little woozy, and he stumbled, trying to get his balance.

"Easy," the nurse said, coming into the room with crutches. She quickened her step and extended her hand to his arm.

Shifting his weight to his right to feel for balance and to relieve his left side. "I'm good." He didn't need her help. He could manage on his own. "I'd like to try walking without crutches."

The nurse lifted a brow. "Okay." Her voice came with a warning.

Colton shuffled his feet and after a few steps, the nurse let go of his arm.

"Don't make it hard on yourself," she said.

He took another step.

"Just take it easy. Looks like you're ready to go home," the nurse said.

Home. Wherever it was. His parent's house was supposed to be short-term, and it turned out to be six months. He needed to find a place to live, but Bellingham didn't interest him anymore. He wanted to be away from his family be around people who didn't know him.

Somewhere to heal on his own and find a new job. Get a new life.

"Here, let me fix you." The nurse tied the string of his gown. "Walk around the ward and see how you feel."

Colton headed for the open door.

"I'll leave the crutches if you need them." She placed them against the wall.

"Nurse," the old man hollered from across the room.

"I'll be right there," she said, darting an eye. "You're doing very well," she told Colton. "Keep going."

"Nurse? Wanna give Major my cane to use?" He lifted a bent finger and pointed to the side table.

She looked over at Colton. "Do you want to try using a cane?"

Colton braced his step. The pain jarred his ability to move. Without answering, the nurse brought him the cane. It was easier than using crutches. Colton looked over. "Thanks."

The older man saluted.

With one foot at a time, Colton made his way around the ward one step at a time. By the time he got to the nurse's station, his joints felt looser, his steps slow and unbalanced but he could manage. That alone freed some anxiety of how he'd cope on his own.

He strode around the desk where nurses were hanging about, talking about patients, and reading from clipboards.

"Major Brooks?" He heard his name and looked over his shoulder. "Yeah, he's right there." It was his nurse, pointing someone in his direction. Someone Colton didn't know. He brought up his chest and threw back his shoulders, eyeing the casually dressed twenty-something guy.

The man approached with an extended hand. "Major Brooks. I'm Brad Stevens. I was one of the first responders when your plane went down."

Colton relaxed his shoulders. He couldn't remember faces. There were too many that day, but the only one he couldn't forget was Sara. "Thank you," Colton said, clutching his jaw.

"You're moving around." Brad shoved his hands into his jeans. His blond hair was swooped at the front and shaved on the sides, similar to Colton's hairstyle when he cared about his appearance. "It's good to see you're recovering, walking around. I wasn't expecting you to be mobile."

Neither did Colton, but he was determined and believed a healthy mind overcame the weak. "I am." Colton relaxed a bit. "I should know today. I'm getting ready to leave. I'm waiting for the doctor to release me."

"I can take you somewhere."

"I'll be okay, thanks. My parents will be flying out to get me as soon as I tell them when." It was a good lie, so he wouldn't be annoyed by people wanting to help. He could find his way out of town.

Brad looked at his Ironman watch. "Okay. Well, I have to get back to work. I can be back later in the afternoon. I'll give you my number in case I'm not here by what, two?" He turned around and made eyes at the nurse. "May I borrow a pen and paper?" He took the pad of paper and draught down his information. "Here," Brad said and handed the paper to Colton. "Call me when you get out. I'll take you where you need to go. Do you know where you're going?"

"I—" Colton shrugged. "Don't. Not yet. Maybe stay at a hotel. Get cleaned up and head to the airport. I can catch a cab." When he was ready, he had to figure out what to do with the plane. Staying a night or two at a hotel didn't seem like a bad idea.

Brad laughed. "We don't have cabs. Don't worry, man. Whatever you need. I'm happy to help. It's with great respect for you and for what you do for our country. It's my honor." Brad touched a hand over his heart.

"Thanks." Colton's stomach pushed up to his chest. A job he was proud of and memories he wanted to erase. "By any chance, did you see a white envelope?"

"Envelope?" Brad narrowed his eyebrows. "No."

"I had it with me, but I don't remember where I put it or if someone took it."

"I didn't see one. I can ask my buddies. If they did, I'd let you know." He raised a hand.

"Okay. That would be great." He breathed through his teeth. Maybe he should recheck his pockets.

"Do you have money for food?" Brad asked.

"Yeah." Colton nodded. "I do, thanks."

"Just let me know if you need anything. I can bring you something to eat. Clean clothes."

Colton was the one who should be helping people. "I'll be fine."

"Just want to make sure you're okay." Brad squared his jaw. "I gotta get back to work." He pointed his thumb behind him. "Glad you're well."

"Thanks."

Colton waited until Brad disappeared through the open double doors and walked to a lounge area at the end of the hallway to make a call to his parents.

Colton plunked himself down on the thin padded chair, clutched his phone, and dialed his mom's cell number because he didn't know if she was at home or with a patient. Anticipating her voice, he heard a quick hello answered instead.

"Colton. I'm glad you called," his dad's voice boomed. "We've been worried about you. Are you coming home? Do you have a ride to the airport? We'll pick you up when you land."

He didn't have a plane ticket, hadn't even stepped out of the hospital. "I'll come home when I can. I have to figure out some things." He had to find the envelope and deliver it.

"Just let us know how we can help you. We want you home safe. What are you doing with the plane? Did you get it towed?"

"I'm working on it. Is Mom around?"

"She's here. I'll get her. Hold on."

A muffle through the receiver followed by a burst of energy. "Colton! Honey. How are you? How are you feeling? Are you alright? Are you coming home?"

"Hi, mom." Colton's chest warmed. "I'm good. I'm still at the hospital. Getting ready to leave."

"That's great. I'll make your favorite."

"Don't bother, Mom. I'll call you when I've left, and I'm on my way."

"I was so worried about you." Her voice pitched. "Your dad was worried too. I couldn't sleep. I was going to fly out to see you but your dad thought it would be a bad idea for me to go by myself. We don't even know where Moonlight Valley is! We do now, of course." She sighed. "The whole time, we were thinking about how to get you home."

"No need to stress, Mom. I'll find away. You know I'm fine, so you don't need to come here. I'm figuring something out. I've already got a ride."

"I want to be there. What did the doctor say? Are you out of the bed? In a wheelchair?"

"I have a sprained foot. I'm walking around. Using a cane."

"I called yesterday to ask a nurse how you were. Of course, she wouldn't tell me much, just that you were okay and waiting on the doctor's report. Made me sick, not knowing. She could have at least told me you were walking around."

"I just started to. Five minutes ago."

"Making progress great. I spoke to Jenny."

Colton's stomach dropped. "Why? What for?" Heat traveled up his body.

"I wanted to see how she was doing. The divorce is hard on both of you, I know, but I wanted to say hi. I told her what happened. She hopes you feel better. Wishes you well."

Colton rubbed his forehead. "You don't have to tell me when you speak to her. I'd rather not know at this point."

"Okay, well I'd thought you'd want to know."

"Mom, I don't care. It's over, okay?" He tried not to care, but he'd always care about his first love. The woman he married. He couldn't love her the way she needed to be loved, and he realized he needed the same treatment — something she couldn't give either.

"Did she remind you that you don't have to be friends with her anymore?" he asked, wondering if she felt the same way he did.

"Colton, she's kind and caring and doesn't have a bad bone in her body. I don't either. That's why I wanted to talk to her, so she knows we're not against her."

"Okay," Colton mumbled. "Fine, but so you know I don't want to hear about Jenny anymore." It was over and he hated living in his past. It only brought him down.

"Well, it would be good of you to at least be civil."

"I was. I don't have to be now since we're divorced. I'll never see Jenny again."

"It's too bad."

"What? That we're divorced or not see her again."

"Both."

"Visit her if you want. I don't care, Mom." Colton's voice rose. "I don't need to hear about

it. Okay?"

His mom fell silent.

"I'll call when I get out," he said and ended the conversation. He took a breath and stood up, putting little pressure on his left foot. He glanced down at the newspaper on a small table. The picture of his dad's plane, on the front cover, caught his eye. It was lying upside down with a broken wing and crushed nose. Colton read the caption. **PILOT SURVIVES PLANE CRASH.**

His heart raced. Colton picked up the newspaper, his eyes soaking up each word. The reporter claimed he suffered non-life-threatening injuries; however, it would be a road to recovery, and there wasn't any telling how long it would take to get back on his feet.

It was news to him. He wasn't going to let some small plane crash cripple his abilities to get back on his feet. The reporter didn't know him. Toward the end, the story explained where he was headed to and why. Colton rubbed the throbbing ache his head. How did the reporter know he was delivering a letter to someone in Omak?

He rubbed above his eyebrows. *Sara.*

His stomach clenched. How did Sara know about the envelope? He read the article further. There was mention of Owen's death and how much Colton had gone through in the past year. She had to have done some research or found someone to talk to who knew him.

He closed his eyes briefly, reflecting on the sequence of events that had happened after the crash. The juices in his stomach crashed like waves. His throat constricted. He couldn't get away from the tragedy. He was dealing with one event, putting it behind him, but the envelope? Where was it?

A flame lit his chest on fire. He put his palm to it while his eyes scanned the byline. He needed to stay away from Sara Quinn before she found out more about him. A past he wanted to forget. He needed to leave before she came for him. How could they write a story about him without being interviewed?

Colton went back to his room and opened the plastic bag the nurse had used to keep his clothes. He took each piece out, laying them on the bed and checking every pocket for the envelope just in case it was stuck between the fabric. Nothing. His arms ached and his body stiffened. Colton rubbed his tense jaw. Drawing the curtain close, he undressed. There was a bruise on his left side, and his legs were achy like he just finished a set of burpees. Stretching his shirt over his head, he raked his hand through his oily hair, feeling desperate for a shower. His fingers touched the bump on his forehead, and he jolted with a shock of a sharp prick. Maybe he was more hurt than he realized.

Putting on his jeans, he then slipped on one of his sneakers, and then loosened the other so he could slide his sore foot in. He tossed the hospital gown on top of the ruffled sheets and moved slowly, bringing his hand to the back of his neck. Once he moved around, he'd feel better, Colton thought. He didn't want to rely on using a cane. How else would he get back to 'normal?' Shuffling over to the old man, snoring, Colton placed the cane where he could reach it and hobbled to the door. He hadn't called Brad yet to let him know what time he needed to be picked up, but it didn't matter, he wasn't in a hurry anyway. He could manage on his own.

Colton rubbed his neck and looked around at the nurses working at their station.

"Are you all set to leave?" a nurse asked.

"I'm ready to leave," he said, shrugging on his coat.

"Is your ride coming?" the older of the two nurses asked.

"Yeah. I expect him here any minute. I'm going to wait outside for him. Fresh air would do me some good."

"There's a nip in the air," the nurse behind the desk said. "Felt it this morning when I was coming into work. There was frost on my car, too." She smiled as she wrote something down. "Take it easy."

Colton staggered to keep his balance and headed for the exit, welcoming the slight chill in the air; it was what he needed after restricted to a hospital bed.

A small group of people huddled in a corner away from the double doors lighting up a cigarette. Staff in scrubs came and went. Colton sat on a nearby bench keeping an eye out for his ride. Did he remember what Brad looked like? Tall with a similar hairstyle, but was it dark brown, light brown, blond?

Colton stood up and wandered the sidewalk. His head held high; he took in his surroundings and watched for a man who'd match Brad's description. For a little town, it didn't seem so small. Across the street, he noticed the sign for Betty's Bakery. A cup of coffee and something to eat sounded like the best solution as he figured out a plan. Colton took his time, walking to the intersection. He crossed the street with a slow shuffle, breathing in the fresh air and realizing he needed to take smaller steps to ease the pain. The windows of the bakery were foggy, and from the outside looking in, tables were full.

He pulled the door open to a blast of heat. He lifted his chin to the buttery, cinnamon aroma, which activated his hunger. Cinnamon buns and coffee sounded like the best reward — a treat he hadn't had in a long time.

"Hi, there," the woman behind the counter greeted. She closed the cooler door and side-stepped to meet him. "What can I get you?"

"A coffee." Colton blurted out. "Please. With milk." He lowered his head. "And...a cinnamon bun."

"Sorry, we ran out." Her mouth tightened.

His body slacked, he looked to the cooler. "Okay. I'll take—" He spotted an oversized cranberry-orange muffin and pointed to it. "I'll take one of those."

The woman grabbed a plate from the stack and used a pair of tongs to grab the muffin. "Heated?"

"Sure. Thank you."

He put down his money and took his coffee and muffin. Eyeing a place to sit, he decided on the empty table close to the window beside two men, drinking hot beverages and laughing with each other. It seemed like a friendly place to sit for a few minutes and to rest his leg.

Colton concentrated on getting to the table without spilling or dropping the plate. It was a steady walk, but he managed. He put down his cup and plate and sat down. The men beside him made eye contact, and Colton lowered his head to his muffin.

"You that pilot who crashed?" one of the men asked.

Colton turned his head. "Yes, sir." He tore a piece of muffin.

"Well, I'll be darn."

Colton nodded. Maybe he looked worse than he felt. It took a lot of energy to speak to someone, and the more he talked, the more people would learn about him.

"Welcome to Moonlight Valley, son."

Colton forced a grin and picked up his coffee, inhaling the rich, spice beans.

"Thank you for your service. You're a good man." He tipped his hat. "Sorry for your loss of your friend. Can't imagine."

The damn article. Colton's stomach clenched. He forced a grin.

"I hope Moonlight gives you good hospitality while you're here," the other man said. "It's a good place to come to...relax, take a load off...no matter how bad life treats ya, someone will listen."

Or write a story about you. Colton looked over with a slight grin.

"If you need a place to stay, the Snuggle Inn up the road-—" He pointed. "Serves continental breakfast."

"Thank you." Colton took a sip of his coffee and stared straight ahead at the front windows of the bakery.

"How long you here for?"

"Not long." Colton picked up his coffee and plate and took it over to the counter. "Can I get this to go?" He raised his cup.

"Sure thing." She took a paper cup and emptied his coffee into it.

Colton snagged a napkin from the dispenser and wrapped his muffin.

He turned on his foot and headed for the front door. He should go back to the hospital in case Brad was looking for him.

He shuffled to the front door, trying to walk without getting attention. Once outside, he dropped his shoulders and inhaled, looking at what was around him. There had to be a motel nearby. How far would it be?

"Colton."

His pulse raced. He brought his chin up and caught his breath. Her light brown hair, the color of cashew, was at her shoulders, and her dark eyelashes fanned her brown eyes. "H—hi." His mouth fell.

"You're out. That's great. Awesome, really, hey?"

"Yeah."

Her eyes scanned his body and landed at his bandaged, left foot. Her eyebrows knit together. "You're walking?"

"Fresh air."

"Good to see you," she hummed.

Colton put one foot in front of the other.

"I can drive you somewhere." Her lips were taut. There was concern in her eyes, but he

wasn't buying it.

"I'm good." He took another step.

"Are you okay?" Her glorious smile vanished.

"Fine. I gotta go."

"Where?" She laughed. "Where are you staying?"

Colton lifted his coffee and used his index finger to scratch his temple. "Somewhere."

"Somewhere?" She leaned forward, squinting. "As in a motel?"

"One of the first responders offered to pick me up. Brad."

"I know Brad." She narrowed her eyes, silencing the conversation. "Is he for sure picking you up?"

"He is. Is he good on his word?" Colton asked.

"Usually."

"Good." Colton began to walk away, and Sara skipped ahead and walked with him.

"Is everything okay?"

"Everything's great." He couldn't hide the sharpness in his voice. Colton pushed the crosswalk button and looked at Sara.

"It's not. Did I do something?" She lowered her gaze to his.

The crosswalk beeped, and they stepped off the curb.

"So what, you're not going to answer me now?" She walked in pace with him.

"If I talk to you, it might end up in the newspaper."

She hung her head, her bottom lip curled over her top lip.

"It was a survivor story," she finally said when they reached the sidewalk leading to the hospital. "Human interest story."

"For you, maybe."

"What's that supposed to mean?"

"You should have asked me before you go and print something you don't have all the answers for." He squinted, looking her in the eyes.

"I covered the accident. The plane crash was news."

They slowed down their pace, and when they reached the empty bench close to the front doors, Colton sat down to relieve his throbbing foot. He slouched and took a drink of his coffee. Easing up his fist from the wrapper, he opened it up to see crumbs. Suddenly it wasn't appealing, so he rolled it back up. His eyes drifted across the parking lot, as far as he could see. No sign of Brad.

"Do you want me to call him?" she asked.

She wasn't smiling anymore, and it bothered him that she looked sad, but Colton reminded himself he wasn't there to attract women or make friends. He wasn't good at it, and God knew he wasn't good at keeping them.

"I'm not going anywhere." Colton leaned forward a little more. "I can wait."

The afternoon autumn sun caught her golden strands. She was beautiful, and although he didn't want to think anything more of Sara, he was intrigued by her willingness to help a stranger.

"Slow news day?" Colton crumbled the bag and took another sip.

"You could say that." She crossed her legs and kicked one out, rocking her boot.

"I'm not giving you anything to write about." Colton took a sip of his coffee. If he made it clear, she might leave him alone.

"Why not? You're an interesting person. This town would love to hear about one of our country's heroes."

"I'm not a hero," he shot back. He was doing a job he was meant to do. He lost his best friend because he wasn't quick enough to save him. Colton cupped his coffee with both hands and hung his head. "Did it occur to you that maybe you should have asked me about my personal life rather than print what you found out?"

"My sources were—"

"I don't care who you spoke to," he snapped. "You didn't ask me." He narrowed his gaze to ease the wave of pain running through his head. "It wasn't your right to dig up personal information about me so you could entertain your town."

"It wasn't for that kind of entertainment." Her eyes widened and she craned her neck. "I was reporting a fact, an incident. It was a news story."

"My personal life isn't for public entertainment," he snapped, then looked away so he wouldn't be stuck on her beautiful, brown-eyed stare. He was frustrated and mad and the last thing he needed was to be convincing at what she did was ethical.

"I'm sorry," she said, tilting her head to meet his eyes. "I wrote what was already public knowledge."

"Well, there isn't any more that I'm going to tell you about and you better not go digging around." Colton shook his head. The less he said, the better.

They sat in silence for a few more minutes. The cool breeze reminded Colton he was alive. Sara shivered and crossed her arms. He tried to get her innocent face out of his mind. Didn't journalists write whatever the heck they wanted about everybody and nobody can complain?

"You don't have to stay here," Colton reminded her.

"What time is Brad supposed to be here at?"

"Anytime I'm guessing."

"So, you're going to wait here until he shows up?"

"I'll leave soon."

"Where are you going to go?"

"Find a hotel. Get myself organized. Anyway, no need for you to worry. So, you know Brad?"

"Brad Stevens. Yes."

"Clean-cut guy."

Sara laughed. "He's sort of dating my friend." She pursed her lips. "On again, off again for years. Late should be his last name unless it's a fire or someone needs medical attention. He's usually never on time."

"How late should I expect him to be?"

"How long have you been waiting?"

Colton shrugged. "An hour or so." Time meant nothing, not when stuck inside a hospital.

"He probably didn't get the message or was on a call." Sara dropped her foot to the ground and smacked her thighs. "I can drive you. Stay here, and I'll get my car."

"I can walk."

"Your foot is swollen. Walking is the last thing you should be doing. You need to take the pressure off it."

Probably, but he didn't want to listen to her. "It's the tensor bandage you see." He lifted his

pant leg.

"Looks like you should be elevating it." She tilted her head. Her lips anchored to the sides and he blinked away the thought of what his lips would feel like on hers.

"That's what the nurse said." Colton's heart pulsed. If Sara didn't write the article and he hadn't sworn off relationships, then maybe he'd consider getting to know her. He took one last gulp of his coffee. What was he thinking? A relationship with Sara? He wasn't thinking straight. He needed a walk as soon as he was able. It was what he did when he needed to clear his mind. "Do you happen to have an envelope with the name Denise written on it?"

Chapter Nine

The cold air brushed against the back of her neck making her shiver as she took out her keys. "I was keeping it safe." She stopped beside her Honda.

"You didn't tell me you had it." Colton put a hand on his hip. He felt a bit of relief and frustration at the same time.

"You gave it to me. Told me to hold on to it." She flipped her palm open. "You don't remember?" She opened the passenger door and scooped up a traveler's guide, *Destination Australia,* and tossed it behind her seat. "Don't mind the mess. I wasn't expecting company."

"Don't mind at all." He cautiously got inside, paying careful attention to where he placed his left foot.

"My car is my second office," she explained and pulled out her phone to send a quick text to Brad to let him know she was with Colton. "You told me you trusted me and to keep it safe." She looked up from her screen. "Quote unquote." She threw her phone into her bag and started the ignition.

"I don't remember." He unzipped his jacket and she got a whiff of his sour clothes. He needed them washed, and he probably wanted a shower. He had bedhead, and the scruff on his chin and cheeks made him look rough.

"Must have been a bad concussion." Someone needed to look after him. Although he seemed functional, she was concerned his equilibrium was off and didn't want to see him fall.

"I'm doing better. Much better." He buckled his seatbelt. "Do you still have the envelope?"

"Of course. It's at home." She didn't want him to worry. She couldn't imagine what was going through his head, trying to get his bearings in an unfamiliar town.

"I need it."

"Yeah, sure," she said. "We can go there right now and get it."

"Perfect." He nodded, holding her gaze. "It's important."

"I figured." Sara swallowed and put the car into reverse and backed out of the parking lot.

"You can drop me off at the Snuggle Inn. I heard it's close. I can get my envelope later today if that helps."

She laughed and shook her head, keeping her eyes on the road. "You don't want to stay there."

"Okay, well, another hotel, motel, inn, whatever. It doesn't matter." His lips formed a line, and he looked around.

"There's the Traveler's Motel." Her lips pursed. "Up the street here."

"Sure."

"We can stop at my house first, and I'll grab the envelope. I'm sure you'll want it back before you leave."

She drove further down the main drag. "You gave it to me for safekeeping," she reminded him. "I've been waiting for you to get out of the hospital so you could have it back."

Colton scratched his head. "I appreciate it."

"You seriously don't remember?" She glanced his way and smiled, anticipating his mouth to curve into a grin like he had before.

"No. What else did I say or do?"

"Nothing. You spoke very little." At the crash, he had touched her hand, and she felt his loneliness and distress.

Sara drove passed the shopping center. "We're almost there." It was the benefit of living in a town. She didn't have to go far, and there wasn't traffic to beat.

"I assume the envelope had important documents inside." She glanced his way. "That's why you asked me to hold onto it."

"I can't tell you what's inside because I don't know." He threw his head back on the headrest, staring ahead.

"Are you curious what's inside?" Sara gripped the wheel. She wanted to know more. There could be another story hidden somewhere and she might learn more about Colton.

"Not at all."

Sara swallowed, wanting him to explain, but he didn't. Was Colton always this way, or had he changed from being in the Air Force? The military did change people, and she understood how much the job transformed a life. When her father came back from Afghanistan, he refused to talk about it. It was like he'd crawled up in a shell and needed time to adjust to family life, and he did, but being a father and husband, then leaving and focusing on his job strained him. Every time he left, Sara told him she loved him and to be safe. He would reply with an 'I love you and a yes, my sweet Sara. Always.' until one day, he didn't come home.

Sara's eyes jogged back and forth from Colton to the window. They passed the collection of stores and drove past residential streets. "Why didn't you mail the envelope?"

He paused before he answered, "'Cause it didn't feel right." He held his finger to his face, grazing the scenery. "This place is bigger than it seems."

"It's spread out," she said quickly, easing up on the conversation he was obviously trying to change. "It feels bigger than most small towns. I think." She turned the wheel. "We're lucky we have the lake and mountains." Then why was she so stuck on leaving? It was the best place to live and had everything she needed. Her friends, her job. What else did she need?

"I saw them when I was flying over. The lake too."

Sara drove past downtown and made a couple of turns until she got to her street where the houses were all small and boxy and in need of new paint and landscape. She had paid the neighbor kid to cut her grass, and the planter out front still had marigolds and cosmos in them.

Her car bumped along the gravel driveway and parked her car in the usual spot. "We're here," she announced and grabbed her purse from behind her seat.

Colton tucked his head under the visor and opened his door to get out. Slowly he got to his feet.

Sara walked around the front of her car. "Are you okay? Need help?"

"I'm fine." He shut the door and limped behind her to the front door.

Sara slowed down, pacing her steps with his. She rattled her key in the lock and swung the door open, tossing her keys on the entranceway table. "Would you like something hot to drink? Coffee?" She shrugged off her coat and hung it on the rack. "I've got tea, juice..."

"Water would be good. Thank you."

"I'll message Brad again—" she said, walking away. "To tell him I can drive you to wherever you want to go." She grabbed a glass from the cupboard and took the water pitcher out of the fridge.

Colton took his time taking off his sneakers and slowly made his way into the kitchen. "I'm sure I can walk from here."

"You could, but it would take you a long time, and you've probably put enough pressure on your foot for a day."

"I'll be fine."

She poured, shifting her weight on her hip, and handed him the glass. "Thanks." His hand brushed against hers, taking the glass.

She flinched, let go and met his lofty grin. She slipped a strand away from her face when she heard her phone beep. Leaping to the counter, she snatched her phone. "It's Brad," she announced and read the message.

> **Sorry! I missed this. I was at work. I had practice. The pilot got out earlier than expected, huh? Let me know if I can do anything.**

> **Do you have a T-shirt he can borrow? He needs clothes.**

She looked up from the screen and swallowed. Colton was staring at her. Then her phone
beeped, and her eyes dropped to read the screen.

> *Yeah, sure. I'll come by in a bit. Are you home?*

Sara replied and put down her phone. "Brad says he was at work and will come by later." She filled the electric kettle with water, feeling the need to do something. Was she supposed to entertain him while he was here?

"It's fine." Colton put a hand on the counter. "He doesn't know me. Well, you don't know me either." A quick grin touched his lips and vanished. "I don't expect anyone to help."

"When someone says they'll do something for you, they should." Sara dug through the
small box of instant coffee and pulled out a sleeve. "Brad's the type of guy who would give his shirt off his back to a stranger." She poured the coffee grounds into her mug. "He's got a big heart."

"I don't want to put anyone out." He shifted his weight, resting his left foot on his heel.

"I'll get the envelope and get going."

"Where do you want to go?"

"A hotel, motel, wherever." He lifted his hand. "What's around here?"

"I can drive you around to find someplace, but there's not much to choose from." The kettle clicked off and she poured the hot water into her mug. "I have some work to finish."

"Yeah, I'm holding you up. I can walk somewhere, at least try."

"I'll drive you. I don't mind. Honestly." She met him eye for eye. "Why don't you take a shower first?" He had to know he needed one. Besides, it was the least she could do for him. Her dad would be happy she did. She put the kettle down and her eyes moved up his chest. His shirt snug, outlining his solid frame. Sara bit her bottom lip. "I can wash your clothes." She pulled at her strands, imagining his wash board abs underneath. She was sure he was super fit by the way he carried himself, but he was unshaven and smelled like dirty socks. What had gotten into her? She hadn't dated in a long time and now she was attracted to Colton?

"Are you sure?" he asked and drank his water down, his Adam's apple bobbing with each swallow.

"I don't mind." It would benefit the two of them. She was sure he'd feel better about himself, maybe it would help to relax him.

She opened the drawer to find a spoon. "If you don't want me to touch your clothes, I can show you how to work the washing machine." She put the spoon in the sink and held up her mug. "Whatever you're comfortable with."

"I smell that bad?" He grinned, showing off a sliver of white teeth. He took a few steps toward her.

Her stomach flip-flopped. "I think you would feel better." She'd feel better too. Sara put down her mug because it was too hot to drink. "I'll show you where the bathroom is." Her arm brushed by him. He held out his hand and touched her sleeved arm, stopping her in her tracks. She froze and looked at him, staring at his aqua blue eyes, reminding her of the sandy beaches she'd be visiting soon.

"Thanks. I appreciate it." He dropped his hand. "But I can get cleaned up at a hotel. I don't need to bother you."

"You're not. I don't mind. Come on." She side-stepped and walked around the corner. "The bathroom is down here." She held out her hand." Laundry is right beside the bathroom. Just a closet, and at the end is the spare room." She didn't know why she was telling him. It wasn't like he was spending the night. She didn't have a bed or blowup mattress anyway. They circled around. "And the living room."

"Perfect for one," Colton said, standing, leaning to one side.

Or a small family, as her mother reminds her from time to time.

"Yeah, it works." She turned on her foot, heading back to the laundry. He stepped back and followed her. "I'll grab you a towel." She opened a linen closet on the other side of the bathroom. "Help yourself to shampoo and conditioner." She dropped the clean towel on the counter and eyed her bra. She snatched it up and tucked it into her side, feeling a flash of heat to her face. "I wasn't expecting company."

Colton chuckled.

She took out a new bar and placed it on the tub. "I have razors too. A new one. Right here." She opened a drawer. "Help yourself."

He flexed an eyebrow. "Okay. Thanks."

"Great. So, make yourself comfortable." She waved her bra around. "'Ill be in the kitchen." She snapped her hand back, realizing she was shaking her bra in the air, so she hid it behind her back and jumped out of the bathroom. When she got beside the washing machine, she tossed her bra into the laundry basket.

Sara closed the closet and went into the kitchen, her face flaming. She'd leave Colton to do what he needed to do, and she would try and erase her crazy thoughts brewing in her mind. Correction. Dirty thoughts. Colton was in her bathroom. Naked under hot water, soaping his hard abs.

She sipped her coffee. What had gotten into her? He was a stranger, recovering from a plane crash and a divorce. He was off limits. Looking out her kitchen window, she sipped her coffee. Her trip was coming fast. She'd first stop in Seattle to meet Johnathan. Would she find him attractive? Would she be happy to leave him and then travel to Australia for her vacation? She wasn't sure what her mom and friends would think about when they found out, but for now, it was better to keep it a secret.

"Sara? Do you want to—"

She jolted almost spilling her coffee. Sucking in a breath, her heart quickened and she pulled on a strand to face him. "Sorry. I—" She butted her lips together. "Yes?"

"Didn't mean to scare you." Colton walked in, only wearing a towel tied around his waist.

She closed her mouth, staring at his hard pecs and broad shoulders. Her cheeks felt like they were going up in flames. Her stomach fluttered. He had the perfect indent of muscle between his hip bones, leading up to his lean-cut abs. He was a work of art, just as she suspected.

"Do you mind showing me how the washer works?"

She blinked at his transformation. He shaved. His hair parted, so it swooped to the side, it was short in the back and his cheeks red from the heat of the shower.

"I'm sure I can figure it out," he said, stepping back.

She cleared her throat. "I can help!" Sara snapped out of her trance, putting down her mug. Not looking to where she placed it, the cup was over the edge of the counter. Colton sprung toward it with his hand extended, pushing it back so it wouldn't fall.

She froze by Colton's swift motion behind her.

"Saved it," he said.

She dropped her shoulders. "Thanks. It's my favorite mug, too." She took a breath. A bubbling sensation rose through her chest, and she shook the thought of him out of her mind. She was being silly. It was Johnathan she was interested in. He was waiting to meet her. They've spent two weeks getting to know one other through text and email messages, and yet, she was attracted to Colton, a guy she hardly knew.

Sara opened the washing machine door and took out the bottle of liquid soap from the cupboard above. Colton went into the bathroom and came out with his clothes rolled up in a ball.

"You can throw them in," she said. Colton tossed them in, and she closed the lid.

Her eyes slowly reached his sincere gaze, and she felt a pang of guilt. Colton was a genuine guy. He just needed help to get back on his feet and she had the ability to help him.

"Thanks," he said.

"You're welcome." She turned on her toe, trying hard not to look at his half-naked body or it would send her mind spinning with ridiculous thoughts. Her stomach bounced, so she went into the kitchen to get her half mug of coffee. She really should be drinking a decaf to bring her down a notch, but coffee was what kept her going. She had a story to write and Liam's stories to edit.

There was a knock at the door. Sara slammed her mug down on the counter. "You have to go to the bathroom," she hushed, shooing him. "Now."

"Why?"

"Because." She looked at his half-naked body. "Because. I don't know who's at the door and if they see you." She felt her eyes stretch wide. What would people say if they saw him here looking like that? Even if she was truthful, it looked like a sin.

"Okay. Okay." He held up his hands in defense. "I'm going."

Sara walked in the opposite direction to the front door and pulled it open. "Oh. Hey, Brad."

He extended his hand to her with a folded-up hoodie and T-shirt. These are new from the hall. I don't have pants, sorry. It's all I got." Brad combed his fingers through his hair. "I can get him pants. Need to know his size though."

"I think he's okay, but I'll let you know."

"Are you okay? You look a little...flustered." He bent his head inside and a blond strand fell on his forehead. He scooped it back with his hand.

"Do I? Oh, I'm good. I just guzzled hot coffee." She fanned her face with a free hand and laughed. "Didn't realize how hot it was," she laughed.

"Where's the pilot?"

"In the shower."

He eyed her carefully. "I'd get him to stay with me, but I have plans tonight. One of the guy's I work with, it's his birthday. I can pick him after if that helps."

"How much later?" Colton needed to stay anywhere else but with her. He was too distracting. How was she going to get any work done? She didn't know him either, and it would conflict with her job. It would interfere with a future story about him. After he left of course because God knows she didn't want to live through his wrath again. Besides, she had Johnathan to think about.

"I don't know." He shrugged. His round shoulders fitted against his jacket. "Could be later."

"I have to get up for work tomorrow. I'm in bed by ten."

"I'll drive him to a motel. He mentioned it."

Brad put one boot on the step and turned around. "Have you spoken to Kelly lately?"

"Of course." Sara's eyebrows narrowed. She spoke to her friend often. Brad knew she did.

"How's she been?"

"Good. Great, actually," Sara said. "What's going on?"

"Nothing's going on. I just want to know if Kelly's okay."

"You could call her." Sara lowered her chin, darting her eyes up to reach his. "She'd love

to hear from you."

"She screens my calls."

"Maybe you catch her at a bad time. Do you leave messages?"

"No."

"You should. She's busy with work and her new business startup." He nodded and folded his lips in.

Sara's heart doubled in size. They needed to come to some agreement, but then they were both stubborn, so it's no wonder they haven't put their past behind them and started again.

"She does?"

"Oh, yeah." Sara bit her bottom lip.

"When you talk to her, can you tell her I say hi and hope she's doing okay?" He circled his head.

"Sure."

"Okay. Thanks."

Sara closed the door and spun around when she heard the bathroom door squeak.

Colton stepped out, his fingers tucked into his towel. "All clear?"

"Oh, yeah. That was Brad. He just left. Um. He brought you a shirt and hoodie from the firehall." She raised the folded clothes. "They're new. Tags are on them. I'll wash them when the load is finished."

"It's okay. I can wear the T-shirt now."

And cover your pecs? She placed the hoodie on the armchair and handed him the shirt.

Colton pulled it over his head. It fit him just right. "Nice outfit," she teased, unable to help

herself.

His lips widened. He looked down at himself. "I'm not impressing anybody."

"I guess not." She raised an eyebrow. Her cheeks felt warm again.

"Unless you care." He grinned from the side of his mouth. It wasn't a full, happy reaction, but it was smooth and cute like he amused himself with his attire.

She smirked. "Your clothes will be a few more minutes," she said calmly. "And I'll pop them into the dryer."

"I appreciate this."

"No problem."

Colton put a hand on his hip. "You know, I'll finish up here, get my clothes and head to a hotel. I'm putting you out, I know. I appreciate everything, but I'm interfering with your life."

"What? You're not interfering. Not at all. I'm happy to help. I have work to do is all." She cringed. "You're welcome to stay here. I'm sure you're tired..." She paused. What was she saying? "You can take the couch." She folded her lips in. Having a stranger stay at her place was not the best idea. He seemed harmless, but weren't all serial killers?

"I'll wait for my clothes to dry and then head out." He ignored her offer.

"Where are you going?"

"A hotel." His lips came together. "I shouldn't stay here. You don't know me." He turned his head. "Is that the washer dinging?"

Sara jumped up. "Yes." She took out his clothes and put them into the dryer. She turned the knob to quick-dry and closed the door. "It should take twenty min—" Standing in front of her, gazing, Colton put a hand to his hip. His chest right there bold under the fitted T-shirt.

"If I could offer you a pair of pants, I would." Her eyes traveling down, getting a glance at his bare feet. His left foot was swollen and bluish-purple; he was clean and had trimmed toenails. "You should probably sit and elevate your foot. Looks sore."

"I'm okay."

She got a whiff of cleanliness: soap and her apple-scented shampoo.

"And I'm fine in a towel. Unless it bothers you."

"Bother me? No. No. As long as you're...comfortable." She swallowed. She turned left to right, unsure what to do.

He lifted a hand. "I'm fine."

"Okay, well, do you want to sit? Watch a show? I can throw something together for dinner. You're probably hungry." Why did it feel like she had a lump in her throat?

"I can grab something. What's here that's around?" he asked.

"Depends on what you feel like eating. Do you like perogies?"

"I love perogies." He straightened his back.

"You do?" She smiled. She wouldn't have to eat alone.

"Yeah."

"Well, if you don't mind—" She used her thumb to point behind her. "I have to finish writing a story." She stepped backward.

"Sure. Take your time." Colton plunked himself on the couch.

"Okay. The TV remote is right there." She pointed and grabbed a toss cushion from the couch and placed it beside his sore foot. "This is more comfortable." She went into the kitchen and took out a bag of peas, wrapped it in a dishtowel, and placed it gently on his foot.

He jerked his leg.

"Sorry. This should help." She made sure he was settled before taking a seat at her desk— an old table in the living room and fired up her computer. The flipping of channels clogged her creative mind as she logged onto her story.

Typing the last sentence, the room fell silent.

"Is there something I can help you with? I can clean your gutters, haul furniture if you need something moved."

Sara leaned against her chair. "Thanks, but you can't do anything with a sprained foot."

"I can. I don't need to be sitting around if there's something that needs fixing. You're washing my clothes and giving me dinner. I need to do something."

"That's kind of you, but I don't need anything. You just need to get better so you can go home."

Colton stood up, his towel slipping, he grabbed the edge and tucked it back into place. "Are you helping me because I'm a good story for your newspaper?"

"No." She sucked in a breath. "I'm helping you because you don't have anyone here. You're in a town with nothing. The least I can do is help." She strained her eyes, and a flash of her dad came to mind.

"I don't need help." He glanced past her at her computer screen. "Is there a rental car company here?"

"No. The closest one is in Omak."

"Well, that's where I'm headed." He tilted his head.

"I can drive you," Sara offered.

"I don't want you to. Isn't it far?"

"About an hour away. Why don't you want me to drive you?"

"Because you've done enough. The sooner I leave, the better it is."

"Where are you in a rush to get to?"

"The envelope. I'm returning it."

"It's not from you?"

"No." He shook his head slowly.

"You're not going to tell me."

"You might write a story about it, and it's not my place."

"I won't write about it. Is that what you think I'll do? Write a story on anything I come across?"

"You wrote about me and why I was here."

"I did. Yes." She pursed her lips together. "There was a reason to."

"You wrote a story about me." He pushed back his head. "I don't want people to know about me."

"Why not? People care."

"They're nosey."

"Maybe, but they care."

Colton stood up, catching his balance. "I'm a private person. I don't like the attention, and I don't want to be known as the pilot who crashed a plane in town and is too hurt to leave. People already know why I'm here." He shook his head. "And they know about me." The words came out in a harsh tone. "And there's nothing you can do about it."

"I'm sorry." She took a step toward him. "Tell me how to help you."

"You've already done enough."

"I don't think I have." Would her father agree? He was a man who took charge and made things right. The time Sara was a little girl and he promised her he'd take her horseback riding, but then he got called to work. He felt bad and when he came home, not only he took her horseback riding, he signed her up for lessons.

His voice echoed in her head. *Help a soldier, and you're helping our country.* "I can write later. I'll make us something to eat." She dusted off her hands. "I'll boil the water."

Colton followed her into the kitchen.

"Why are you being so nice?"

She squeezed her lips together. "I like to help."

"Why?"

"Because I do." She took out a pot and filled it with hot water, then carried it to the stove.

"What can I do?" He extended his hand. "Give me something."

"Nothing. I've got this." She pulled on the freezer door and took out a bag of store-bought perogies.

"Well, you should let me do something." He tilted his head, his eyes followed her. "Are you like this with other people you just met?"

"You're not so much a stranger anymore. I mean, you are, but you're not." She took out a frying pan from under the stove and faced him. "Does that make sense?"

"Because you saved my ass?"

She put the pan on the stove. "I didn't save you. I called for help. Turns out they were in the process of tracking you. They knew you went down."

He cleared his throat. "I called for help when I knew I had to land."

She gave him a look. "Crash," she corrected. "I knew you'd survive. You've trained to survive." She glanced at him and then brought her attention to the stove. She turned it on. "I mean, you're fit. Obviously." She rolled her eyes. "You can afford to eat without gaining anything. Muscle burns more than fat. Ha. Okay." She clapped her hands together. She had to stop before she made a bigger fool of herself.

Colton smirked. A surge of self-consciousness came over her. She rubbed her hands on her jeans and returned to the stove to open the bag of perogies sitting on the counter.

The dryer buzzed.

She dropped the scissors she was using and emptied the bag into the boiling water. "Your clothes are ready."

"I can get them," Colton said, walking out of the room.

Scooping the perogies out of the water and into the hot pan, she put together a plate of vegetables and dip as a side.

Colton returned into the kitchen, wearing clean clothes and smelling of soap and freshness.

"Put me to work." He clapped his hands.

"I, I got this. Really."

He got up close to her. "You don't like help in the kitchen?"

She froze in mid-step. "I...do, but I'm on a roll and—" she looked over her shoulder at the perogies frying on low.

"Have you been single for a while?" he asked.

She walked past him to place the veggies in the middle of the four-seater, round table. When was the last time she sat here?

"Yes. Why?"

"Just wondered," he smirked, eyeing the pan. "Do the perogies need flipping?"

"Shoot!" She turned on her toe, dropped the plate on the table and rushed to the stove. "I think I burnt them." She used the spatula to chisel them from the pan and when they came free, she flipped them. "A little crispy. I don't burn things." *Only when a hot guy is watching me.*

"Here, let me do this. I need to do something." He stepped over and took the utensil from her hand. For a moment, he held her hand, and an electric surge came through her body, weakening her arms. She released her fingers from the flipper and took a step back.

"I didn't mean to interfere. I just need to do something." He turned his focus to the pan and tossed the bacon bits. "These are done. Do you have a plate?"

"Plate. Right." Sara spun and leaped to the cupboard to take out her plates. She handed him one.

"There's a lot of food here."

She looked at the table to the pile of veggies and the pot of water with perogies floating on top.

"I thought you'd be hungry."

"I guess I am. Hospital food suppresses an appetite." He filled the plate and handed it to Sara. Colton scooped out the reminder of perogies and placed them in the frying pan.

"Do you cook at home?" Sara wanted to know. He looked serious and she wondered if he was pondering to tell her something personal.

"Sometimes. I don't do much of it. When I was away, all I craved is home-cooked meals."

"What's your favorite?"

Colton tossed the perogies around and glanced at her with an uneven smile. "I'm not picky, but I enjoy anything baked. Do you cook for yourself?"

"Not really." Sara stood in the middle of the kitchen, playing with her hands.

"Sorry. You want to take over? I interfered with you cooking."

"Oh, no. It's fine." She laughed. She never thought he'd relax a little, and here he was standing in front of her, a little stiff and guarded, but able to carry on a conversation a bit easier.

"I'm not used to having someone cook for me," she admitted.

"That's a shame."

"Is it?" She caught his eye.

He chuckled, and for the first time since their first encounter, Colton relaxed.

"You eat better when you're not alone."

"Is it true?" She dipped her shoulder and puffed her lips.

"It's true." Colton stuck the flipped in the pan. "These are ready."

Sara brought back the serving plate, and Colton added more to it.

"Do you want anything to drink?" She opened her hands. "I'm sorry I can't offer you a beer or soda..."

"Water is good. I don't drink alcohol anyway, and I stay away from soda. Too much sugar."

"So, you're a healthy guy."

"I try to watch what I put into my body." He shrugged.

"But you'll eat bacon?"

"Once in a while."

Sara opened her fridge and took out a lemon from the bottom drawer.

"I'll get the cups. Where would they be?"

"That cupboard." She pointed with the knife. "I have filtered water in the fridge." She sliced the lemon. Colton filled their cups and set them on the counter. She dropped the wedges into each cup, splashing water. Maybe it was a good thing she didn't have soda or dessert; she didn't need the sugar either when Colton was eye candy.

Chapter Ten

Colton lifted his water glass up to his mouth, reflecting on the beautiful woman trying so hard to help him, and he had nothing to give in return. He wasn't staying in Moonlight Valley for long, and she'd forget him as soon as he left. The sooner he was gone, the better. For everyone.

Colton sipped and put down his glass. "So, what do you do in your spare time?"

Sara picked up a carrot stick from her plate. "I should be the one asking you the questions," she laughed, waving her carrot in the air. "I enjoy taking photos."

"Of what?" He cut into his food and took a bite.

Her lips flared out. Like they were teasing him for a kiss. "Nature, but I mostly do studio shots."

"You have a studio?"

She swallowed and turned her head to the back door. "Yeah. It's my shed, actually. It's nothing fancy."

"That's cool." He nodded. "It's your space, helps when you can separate from your home." Colton forked a bite. "I've taken some photos over the years, not professional. I did it for fun." He shrugged. "I haven't in a while now." It was during his happier days. When he was married to Jenny, he'd snap a few of her or when his dog did something cute like drank from the sprinkler. "I guess I ran out of things to take pictures of."

"You can't go wrong with scenery shots. Especially in the fall and springtime when the colors change. It's pretty. I bet you could take some nice ones from the sky." Her lips parted into a shy smile. "Maybe you have."

A buzz of a cell phone came from the kitchen counter. Sara jumped up and went over to check. Colton watched her grip the phone, and in seconds she put it down again without replying.

The kitchen window was dark, and he wondered if he could manage to find a motel on foot. Even with Google maps, he wasn't familiar where he was, but he couldn't stay here. Colton didn't want to put Sara out.

"Sorry about that," she said, returning to her seat. "Are you finished? There's more in the pan."

"I'm done." He pushed his plate a smidge. "It was good. Thanks."

"Look, if you want, you can sleep on my couch. I have to get up for work in the morning."

"No thanks. You've done enough already." He stood up and pulled the dishes from the table, carrying them to the sink, aware of his limp. "I don't want to intrude."

She swept a gaze to his foot and then held his stare. "You're not. When do you have to go back to work?"

Colton's body tensed. "I'm on leave," he said quietly. Shame had a way of working its way into emotions. "I'll go back after I deliver the letter."

She put her plate in the sink. "Honestly, if you need to stay one night here, it's fine. It's the least I can do. My dad would have scorned me for not offering."

Colton chuckled. "For not offering a stranger to sleep on your couch?"

Her lips came together and gave a quivery smile. She closed the fridge door and took the half-eaten veggies off of the table and placed them into a container.

"He was a man with heart," she said. "It's what people told me." Her eyebrows lifted.

"My dad would be running a criminal check and asking a hundred questions." Colton snickered. "You said your dad was in the military?"

"Yes. My dad died when he was on a mission overseas."

"I'm sorry." Colton's insides dropped, not understanding why he got a second chance at living. "He died in an attack. My dad was doing a counter-terrorism mission when his vehicle was hit by a roadside bomb." She shook her head. "I don't like to think he suffered death."

"I'm sorry." His shoulders sank, feeling her pain. "I am." He touched her arm. Her gaze cut across to him with sincerity. "It's tough. The job is hard enough without having a family on top of it all."

She nodded with a grin and ran a sink full of soapy water. "I remember saying goodbye to my dad, just like we always did when he was deployed. He'd give us hugs, tell us to look after our mom, and promised to have ice cream with us when he returned." She smiled. "As if it was a guarantee he'd be back." She paused and blinked. "There's an ice cream stand at the lake. It's where we would go," she whispered.

Colton's stomach knotted. He never made promises to anyone anymore. It was giving someone false hope for something he had no control over. It wasn't because he couldn't commit to the person he promised. He had pledged to Owen he'd give the envelope to his wife if he never came home. He wasn't sure what exactly was inside, but he knew his friend loved poetry and had probably written poems for Denise and their son. It was a priceless gift that Owen had given Colton for safekeeping and now he had to find a way to give it to Denise before, what would have been, her and Owen's fifth wedding anniversary.

"Why did you join?" Sara rinsed a plate and placed it in the drying rack. "Do you have a relative serving?"

He took a drying cloth from the counter. He wanted to make his family proud. "I wasn't going to be a lawyer like my dad and brother, so I had to do something."

The light in her eyes brightened her smile. "So, your option was to become a lawyer or join the Air Force?"

"It sounds like a good option though, doesn't it?" He met her eyes. His gut fluttered with unknown emotion, but he liked the feeling. "I've always loved planes. I like flying them, and I wanted a job that I could learn more about them."

"Why not be a commercial airline pilot?"

Colton dried the plate and put it back in the cupboard. "I wanted to give back." He rubbed his tongue against his bottom lip. He wanted to make his family proud. The military gave him stability.

"Do you know where you'll be stationed when you go back to work?"

He didn't want to be dishonest with her, but he couldn't tell her about his unemployment for fear of knowing his truth. He felt like a failure and didn't want to be reminded. It was hard enough living with guilt. "I have a few weeks off. I'll go back to Texas."

"Do you know if you'll be deployed?"

"Probably not." He shrugged. "I've been domestic only." On base, he was needed for mechanical issues and he didn't mind. He liked it. It was what he was good at. Plus, he didn't have to think about where he would be the next day. He was safer on base, or that's what he thought.

She scrubbed a plate with a cloth. The suds crept up her arm. "Thank you for doing what you're doing," she said. "For our country. I don't think I ever told my dad."

"I'm sure he knew."

"I didn't know how important it was. I mean, I did, but I didn't, you know?" She glanced at him. "On the one hand, I was disappointed my friends had their dad attend school concerts and birthday parties, and I missed out."

"I'm sure it wasn't fun for him, either." He took the clean fork from her hand, skimming his fingers across hers. "It sucks. I've been there." Owen wasn't there for his son's birth, and it bothered him. "My dad, he was always working and doing his thing. I had to beg him to come to a Christmas concert."

She pursed her lips. Colton caught looking at her strained, honey-brown eyes.

"He said they were boring," Colton continued, hesitating to laugh.

"He didn't." Her eyebrows came together. "Serious?"

"He did. Yeah." Colton didn't know why he was smiling. It bothered him every year when he was a child. "My mom would make him go, which I thought was worse than not going."

Colton dried the last plate, threw the towel over his shoulder, and put the plate in the cupboard.

"I haven't spoken about my dad for a long time." Her face softened, and her naturally pink, kissable lips came together. "I don't want him to be forgotten."

"He won't. Not if you keep him close. Pictures, memories. It's good to talk about him, too." Colton closed his eyes for a moment. He was trying to let things go but didn't know how. His counselor was the only person he unloaded on, and yet, talking to Sara was comfortable and fulfilling. She got him. Sort of.

Sara dried her hands, and went into the living room, picked up a picture frame. "This is my dad and me." She wiggled in her stance, holding up the picture proudly.

It was a man holding his daughter on his leg with an arm wrapped around her waist.

"Where was this taken?" Colton asked.

"At the lake here. I have a lot of memories there. My dad loved to sit and watch my brother and I play and going with us for bike rides." She took back the frame and put it on the shelf. "I don't know why I showed you." She gave a perplexed expression.

"Thanks for sharing. It's therapy, right?" Colton played with the dishtowel in his hand and tossed it over his shoulder. He knew all about it.

"I guess it is. Do you want to sit down? Watch TV? Maybe something better will be on."

"I thought you were writing, and I was leaving."

"I'm done writing my story." She glanced at his shoulder and then at him. "I can take the towel." She extended her hand and Colton plucked it off himself and handed it to her. "I'd love to see your studio."

"It's not much, but okay." She came toward him. "Back door." She pointed. Colton

followed, eyeing her figure. Her long-sleeve shirt came to her waist, and the jeans she was wearing drew his eyes to her behind. She glanced over her shoulder to hold the door for him, and Colton shot his stare upward, hoping she didn't catch him looking.

"Right through here." She swung her arm. A short path to the shed and they were inside. "It's a little cool in here." She hugged herself, rubbing her hands on her arms.

"You have a heater?"

"I had someone put it in. I can't leave my camera in here when it's cold and I need it to be comfortable."

Colton looked around the room. "It's a real studio." He was in awe the small, but organized space. "You wouldn't expect anything like this in a shed."

"It works for me."

One wall had a horizontal pole with sheets of thick paper rolled on it for background color. There was a camera on a tripod, huge lights, and a side table under the one window with a drawn curtain.

Colton went over to the tripod and put his hands in his pockets. "Nikon. I have one. It's old, though." He stepped back. "What's the name of your business?"

"It's not a business." She twisted her body, looking around at the space. "I just take photos when people need them. They pay for what they want."

"I guess it's hard if you work full-time."

"I don't advertise. Don't need to, really. I do what I can and when I want. I was busier last year, but then I had more time."

"What's changed?"

Her teeth came together, and her eyebrows lifted. "Life, I guess." Her smile turned his gut. "Isn't that the way?"

"I can relate."

There was a brief silence. "Can I ask you who Denise is?"

It was probably the question that had been on her mind. "A friend's wife."

Her face fell, eyes drooping. "Another civilian?"

Colton nodded. He kept his eyes on her light brown hues. "I have to see her in person." Colton's mouth dried. "I need to talk to her. I can't do it over the phone."

Sara folded in her lips. "Good idea." The sparkle in her eyes told him it was okay. He didn't need to explain. Not right now.

Colton stepped toward the door. "If I come across short, I don't mean to be."

"I understand." She nodded, eyebrows flexed.

He was sure she did, but he wasn't ready to open up to an outsider. He didn't know if he wanted to have a conversation without fearing judgment or being criticized for making decisions he did. He didn't know how much she knew about Owen's death, and he didn't want to ask. He wasn't expecting anyone to understand or to give him sympathy.

"Is it you being you or you adjusting to being off of work?"

"A little of both." He shrugged. "I don't know," he admitted. He always thought of himself as easy-going.

"If you talked about what's bothering you, you might feel better and get better faster. And you wouldn't be carrying around a grudge."

"I'm not bitter." He dropped his hand from the door. Okay, most days, he forced himself to get outside and to talk. "You think I hold a grudge?"

"I don't know." She shrugged. "I think you have a lot on your mind. I'm just saying. If you keep things inside, it's hard to move on."

Colton walked out and back into the house. Sara shut the door behind her. "I'm just honest," she said when she got into the kitchen. "I saw what happened to my dad. He was a constant bundle of fear and mixed emotions. Anytime someone offered to help my mom or us kids, and my dad was around, he took it as an insult."

"I'm not like your dad."

"Maybe not, but I see similarities. Your memories of work are with you forever. It's getting past it and focusing on your future. If there's something wrong—"

"There's nothing wrong." He felt his voice rise to the point he wanted to shout.

"Then why haven't your parents come here?"

Colton froze. The back of his neck tensed.

"I'm sorry," she said, waving a hand. "You're right. I'm a stranger. It's not my place."

He hung his head. He put his hand on his hip and brought his chin up to a somber face.

"I just want to help you," she said.

"Why? I have nothing to give." It would be better if he left, but where would he go?

"I couldn't help my dad because I didn't know the signs."

"Signs for what?" He twitched.

"Never mind. I'm referring to my dad, not you." Her forehead creased.

"What did he have?"

"Depression."

It was anxiety Colton fought with, but he blamed it on everything thrown at him at once. Who could manage to see and hear a best friend die? A wife who fell out of love and took their dog when he had nothing left. He was out of work and didn't know what to do with his life.

"I think you put on a brave face for people."

He hated it when people made him out to be a victim. "Thanks for dinner. Thanks for letting me stay, but I'm going to go." He hobbled past her, out the kitchen and into the living room, trying not to put pressure on his left foot. It was starting to ache more.

"Where are you going?" she asked.

"To find somewhere to stay." He searched around for his jacket, the only possession he had besides his wallet he had with him.

"It's getting late. You can stay here," Sara said softly. "I don't mind."

His eyes swept the room. "I think it's for the best." He found his jacket and picked it up from the couch.

"Wait. I'll get you the envelope." Sara jumped and turned on her foot, hand to her forehead. She returned wearing a coat and took her keys from the dish on the table at the front door.

He didn't want to leave, but he knew he had to.

Her lips pursed, and he thought about kissing her, and when he thought about kissing, he thought about sex. It had been too long to go without feeling a woman's body in his arms. He promised himself he wouldn't fall in love, so it was just sex, but Sara deserved more than what he could offer.

He headed for the door.

Sara put on her shoes and followed him out.

"I can walk," Colton told her.

"Hardly and it's dark," she called. "I'll drive you."

Chapter Eleven

The no-vacancy sign flashed red at the Sleepy Inn. "You don't want to stay here anyway." She turned her car around in the parking lot and headed back on the main street. "I haven't heard good things about this place."

"What about the motel? I saw one somewhere."

"There's the Traveler's Motel. We can try." She looked up at the dark sky. It was only seven o'clock, but it seemed later.

"Sorry. I'm inconveniencing you." He cupped his hands in his lap.

"You're not. I'd be at home working anyway." Guilt seeped into her mind. She was driving around to find a place for Colton to stay when she had a couch he could sleep on for the night. Letting him leave wasn't the Moonlight Valley thing to do.

She drove up to the Traveler's Motel and saw the vacancy sign lit. It was white stucco with a blue trim. Beat up trucks and a minivan parked in front of the rooms. A man staggered down the sidewalk to his place, and a kid escaped from another, followed by a woman screaming after him.

Colton rubbed his hands on his knees.

"By the looks of it, sleeping is optional," Sara said.

"Are there any others?"

"A bed and breakfast. You'd have to reserve those in advance."

Colton nodded.

Sara kept the car running. The same guy who staggered into his room came out and lit a cigarette.

"Are you sure you want to stay here? You don't have to."

"I should. I can't stay at your place. You don't know me."

"I don't. No. I wouldn't offer if I didn't trust you. It's not like me to invite strangers to my place, but if you need somewhere to sleep and eat, I don't mind, honestly." Her dad's quality of goodwill had stuck to her. She wanted to do the right thing. "We can drive to the Bed and Breakfast place and see if they have a room." It gave Colton options. Sara drove to the next site, stopped at the entrance, and it was under construction. "I didn't know." She turned up her lip. "News to me. Well, what do you want to do?" She folded her hands on her lap, looking at him for the next instruction.

Colton stared out the window. "Are there any other options?"

"I'm afraid not."

Colton turned his body toward her. "If I stay with you for one night, I owe you." His eyes were steady on hers.

One night. It was the least she could do to help a veteran. "You don't owe me anything."

"I can't stay for free." He ran his hand through his hair. "It doesn't feel right."

"It's not a big deal." With Colton's inability to accept help when he needed it, Sara had to play it down to ease his mind. "But if I think of something I'll let you know."

"Okay. Is that a grocery store up ahead?" Colton pointed at the town center.

"It is."

"Mind stopping? I should grab a few things."

"What do you need?" she asked.

"Stuff. I don't have an overnight bag."

Respecting his request, she pulled into the parking lot of the outdoor shopping mall, in front of Lee's Grocery and turned off the ignition.

"I'll be a few minutes." He jumped out, finding his balance and shut the door.

Noticing his limp, Sara could only imagine his discomfort or pain.

Her phone rang and she unzipped her purse, to pull out her phone. Sara forgot to message Johnathan back when he texted at dinner. She hadn't even thought much of him. How would this potential relationship work? A week ago, it seemed like a great idea, except now, with helping Colton, her mom acting funny and not knowing when Jerry would be back, she had less time to think about anything else.

If she didn't leave on her trip, would Johnathan wait for her until she could meet him? It didn't seem realistic. He'd find someone new if he hadn't already. The distance between them didn't offer bonding time, and she hadn't even felt his affection physically. What if she wasn't attracted to him? There were too many things to think about. Maybe she should have waited to take a trip when her friends were able to. She had her ticket; she might as well enjoy it and get to know a cousin she hadn't seen in years.

"Hi sweet Sara," Johnathan said.

She giggled. "Hey, Johnathan. How's it going?" she asked, keeping her eyes on the grocery store exit doors.

"I read your plane crash story online. It's quite a story about the pilot being in the Air Force."

"It is, right? Nothing like it has happened here before."

"We've had some fluke accidents and tragedies this week, too," Johnathan breathed into the phone. "It's been a hard news week."

She sank into her seat, running her hand along with the wheel.

"What are you doing right now?"

"Um, I am at the store," she said.

"Small town is quieter than I expected."

She threw her head back. "Yeah, not much going on," she mocked.

"I want you to meet my best buddies. Thought we could stop at the club or bar, wherever they'll be."

She saw Colton head out of Lee's Grocery. "Sure." Her stomach sank. Sara hadn't even thought of Johnathan introducing her to his friends. It was bad enough he wanted to introduce her to his parents. It wasn't a *relationship. Maybe? Sort of? Was it?* She didn't consider

Johnathan her boyfriend. She was still single until they made it official. Why hadn't he made it official? The back of her neck prickled. Was Colton a friend? Maybe. Or was this moving too fast when they hadn't even started? "I better bring some club clothes," she laughed, scanning the parking lot for Colton but couldn't see him.

"I thought you'd want a heads-up. You probably don't have to dress up for work. Not like here where you're prepared for meetings and interviews daily."

Did he think she was working in a barn?

"I dress up! I go out." She had to remind herself not to be offended. Johnathan didn't know her. They hadn't seen each other yet. Maybe he was worried she wouldn't fit in.

"Perfect. You're going to have a great time."

"Listen," Sara cut him off. "I have my hands full of groceries and I'm at the register, so maybe we can chat tomorrow?"

"I'm out tomorrow night after work. It's the midweek bash."

Sara wrinkled her nose. "And what is that?"

"Co-workers get together and bash out the week. Talk about our highs and lows. It's a way to meet without bringing partners."

"Do you have a lot to bash about?" Was Johnathan a complainer?

"Sometimes I do. I never have it as bad as some of the guys."

"Why is that?"

"Well, they have families, so the stress is higher."

Sara looked down and examined her fingernails. She wasn't one to paint them or wear rings; she didn't have a reason to. It had nothing to do with living in a small town. She needed to educate Johnathan. "I should go," she said.

"Send me a text," he told her, and they disconnected.

Sara looked up and saw Colton at the passenger door. She startled and fumbled her phone, then caught it before dropping it in her lap and into her purse.

He opened the door and got in. "I didn't keep you waiting too long, did I?" Colton asked as he sat down, placing the grocery bag between his feet.

"No. You were quick." She swept a strand behind her ear and started her car.

"Are you okay?" Colton asked as they drove away.

"Yeah, I'm good." She smiled to reassure him. Meeting Johnathan would be a test. "Did you get what you needed?" She looked down at his feet but couldn't see how many bags he had with him, but it appeared he had one from Well Clothed, a unisex clothing company tailored to more trends than comfort.

Take that, Johnathan.

"I picked up some essentials at the clothing store next door."

"It didn't take you long."

"I got to the door before the woman locked it." His lips arched to the side. "I hate shopping. I told the woman what I needed and she picked it out for me. And a woman at the grocery store let me go in front of her in line." He dug in his bag. "I got you this."

"A first aid kit," she said, feeling warmth in her chest. "Thank you," she cooed. "That's thoughtful."

He reached around and dropped it behind the seat. "Now you're prepared."

"I will be. I just need to renew my first aid certificate and I'm all set." She put her car into reverse and drove out of the parking lot. "When are you going to Omak?"

"I have to figure it out."

"Your foot's bothering you."

"You can tell?"

"It's hard not to notice you favoring your right foot. Why didn't you get crutches?"

"I don't need them."

"I'm sure I have Advil if you need something for the pain," she suggested.

"I don't need anything."

"It would help with the swelling."

He looked out his window. "I'll see how I feel."

Sara pulled into her gravel driveway and turned off the ignition. She rubbed her hands together for warmth. "We had such a warm September. October has been warm too, but at night it's getting cooler." She unlocked her door and stepped inside. "I should turn the heat on. Do you find it cold in here?"

"It's perfect. I don't like it when it's stuffy."

"Okay. If you get cold, you can turn on the thermostat."

Colton took off his shoes and coat. He left one bag by the door and carried the other two into the kitchen. The fridge opened and closed. A jar hit the counter when Sara walked in.

"What's this?"

"I did a little grocery shopping."

"I see that. One thing about me, I'm a good sharer."

"I figured so." He looked over the fridge door. " It's the least I can do." Colton closed the fridge and scrunched up the bags. "Where do you want these?"

"I have a spot under the sink." She held out her hand to take them and placed the bags in a plastic cylinder. When she stood up, Colton was standing in front of her. She flinched and rubbed her hands together.

"Still cold?"

"I'm okay." She didn't know what to do with them. A flutter in her chest interfered with her thoughts. How could a man like Colton, attractive, career-minded, and sincere, be chatty one minute and closed up the next? "Feel free to help yourself to anything you need." She wiggled her body as though she needed to shake the nerves away. Good nerves. Like, feelings she shouldn't be feeling for a guy she barely knew. As she turned away, her eyes caught his. She licked her lips with apprehension. The muscles in his T-shirt formed a groove in the fabric. His broad shoulders, toned biceps, and strong hands gave him a stable posture. He looked at her thoughtfully and gently touched her arm.

She swallowed in response. Filing her lungs with air, she felt short of breath.

"I want to give you space, Sara. I'm not looking for special treatment. It's not my intention to be anything more than a stranger living in your house for a day or two."

Her pulse raced, hanging onto his words. She was guessing what he was trying to say and the meaning behind it. His callused hand was on her arm. Her skin prickled. All she could do was nod to agree. They shouldn't start something that wasn't concrete and viable to a relationship, especially when she had a trip planned.

"You don't feel like a stranger," she whispered. Or a friend, but she would do anything for him. In her heart, she knew her dad was happy she was helping a fellow civilian and doing her best to help him with whatever he needed. When would he tell her he was honorably discharged?

Colton dropped his hand. His body squared with hers. Sara waited for him to say something because from what she knew of Colton, he took his time to talk, to eat, to show what was on his mind. He probably received his time to make love to a woman he wanted to keep. Her insides squeezed. She bent her weakened knees slightly, draining her eyes from his cautious blue stare.

"What?" she finally asked. "What is it?"

Colton blinked. "You're going to make it hard for me to leave." The corner of his mouth gathered. "Your hospitality...treating me like a friend."

"Everyone's a friend here." Her skin flushed. "We can stay in touch." It seemed it was the only way relationships were going for her these days. She couldn't keep a long-term commitment if she tried, and friendships were all she could offer. "You can write to me, email me, call, whatever you like." Maybe he still needed the connection. She heard about the opportunity to be pen pals with servicemen and women. A way to connect and send thank you notes and words of

encouragement because handwritten notes were concrete and still far better to receive. "Would you write me back?"

"I would." His voice was solid. "Could you do me a favor?" He took a step closer.

"Sure." Her mind raced at what it could be. Driving him to Omak would be expected.

Hanging out with him under the tent at the market would be okay, too, but anything more could lead to trouble. She wouldn't be able to write a story about him if she was with him day and night. It would be an unbalanced story.

Sara's arms hung to her sides unsure what to do with them. Colton placed his hand on her arm, squaring her with him. She listened carefully, taking in a shallow breath.

"I need to clear my head," he said. His hand fell to cover hers.

"What do you need me to do?" She blinked, not letting his touch, his masculinity interfere with what was brewing within her.

What was it again? "A favor?"

"No, not a favor. Besides, you've done enough for me already."

"What is it?" she pressed. Whatever it was, why couldn't Colton say it? She wanted to snap at him and squeeze his hand, maybe even hug him to tell him to relax.

"Would you come for a walk with me?"

"When?"

"Now."

She squinted in disbelief. She hardly ever went for a walk around her neighborhood. It was mostly at the lake or parks when it was light out. It seemed pointless to go when she was alone.

"Where to?"

He pulled her toward him, stopping her body before she landed right into his arms. He took a step back, distancing himself as though teasing her with his desires.

"Around here." He looked over his shoulder toward the living room. "Around the block."

"It's dark."

"I'm not afraid of the dark."

"I don't mean afraid," she said, laughing. "I mean, it's hard to see anything. There isn't a

view and cold. How about your foot?"

"What about it?"

"It has to be sore."

"I'm not thinking about it." He dropped his hands. "Got a flashlight?"

"Somewhere. I'll go find one," she said and stepped back. She went into the kitchen opening cupboards and drawers. When she couldn't find one, she stood on her tiptoes and reached to the top shelf where a small basket was stored and brought it down to check. "Got one." She clicked it on and off. "It works."

"Great. I'll get my shoes on." He was at the door, waiting for her by the time she put on her coat and grabbed her keys.

"Take me around your neighborhood," he said, throwing his hands into his coat pockets. He stepped out onto the driveway.

"There's not much to see," she warned, taking a few extra steps to get to him. "A bunch of houses."

"Do you know any of your neighbors?"

"Most of them." She turned her head to look at him. He was serious about the walk and seemed revived to get outside.

"I don't talk to them much," she admitted. It wasn't the house Sara envisioned her future family to live. It was only a two-bedroom house suited her needs perfectly now, but if Sara wanted children, she preferred a house like the one she grew up in to satisfy the little humans she hoped to welcome into the world one day.

"Did you hear anything about your plane? Is it going to be towed to the airport?"

"I made a call. I'm waiting to see if there's a hanger for rent. I'll need to fix it. My dad will want his plane back."

"I guess if it's his," she agreed. "Will he miss it?"

"I doubt it."

"How about your brother? Does he fly?"

"How do you know about me having a brother?"

"You told me."

"I did?"

She bit her bottom lip. "When you were in the hospital," she said, eyes to the pavement. "You had a concussion," she reminded him, biting her bottom lip. She needed to be more careful. If he found out she spoke to his dad, he might not be forgiving.

"What else did I tell you?"

She sensed the panic growing. "Not much," she soothed. "I wanted you to tell me about Denise. Was she expecting you?" she asked. Wouldn't Colton feel better if he talked about the tragedy? She wanted to understand the weight he'd been carrying around on his shoulders.

He hung his head. The road curved and ended in a cul-de-sac.

"Is it a cut-through between those houses?" he asked.

"Yes. We can take it. It just leads to the next street and back to my house."

"No. I didn't tell her I was coming," Colton continued. "I wasn't sure when I'd make it. So I guess it was a good thing I kept my visit a surprise."

They turned onto the path, through the joining neighborhoods. Sara breathed from the fresh air on her face.

"What's so important about the envelope?" Why didn't he tell her? She had been holding on to the piece and she still didn't know what it was.

"I don't know." He shook his head. "It's from Owen."

"Owen kept it for when he died? How? How did he know he'd die young?"

"He didn't." Colton flashed his weary stare at her, and although it was dark, the street lights caught the fear, the hurt, and the trepidation in his soul. "The job has risks," he whispered.

"Sorry," she said. "It's not my place, I know."

"You don't have to be a reporter when you're not working."

"It comes naturally. Plus, it's a human connection. Tell me about Owen." She tried shifting the mood.

"Great guy." Colton didn't hesitate. "Best friend. Loyal, committed. He didn't deserve to die."

"No, he didn't," she agreed.

They walked to the next street in silence. Colton limped a little more.

"Is this what you do to clear your head?" she asked.

"Yeah, get outside. I sleep better when I do." Colton stopped in front of a large oak tree in front of a two-story house. "I just have to take a minute." He lifted his left foot.

"When we get back, you can ice your foot. You're probably doing too much."

He took a breath and lifted his foot, gritting his teeth. "I'll be okay." He put his hands on his hips and then released his foot to the ground. "You want to know something weird?"

"What's that?"

"We don't know each other, but I feel like we do, sort of." He shook his head into his hand, revealing a boyish grin. He pulled his head up and met her eye.

Something jolted her insides.

"You're getting comfortable here." What else could it be?

"Na, to be honest, I won't be comfortable until I get back on my feet."

"You mean with your friends and family."

"I don't have many of those." His voice dropped.

"You have a family." She didn't want to tell him she knew about his childhood friend Steve, Jenny and knew about his brother, Mom, and Dad. It was too soon to be honest. He would be gone and everything wouldn't matter. "Friends," she pressed, baiting him to tell her more.

His upper body rocked. "I lost touch with many. Found new ones at work but I never kept in touch. After I left." His eyes darkened, and he looked away.

"It happens," she paused. "Time to meet new friends." She gave him a half-smile. For a moment, she thought he was looking at her with desire and maybe even the possibility to have something more with her, but she couldn't have a relationship with Colton. It couldn't happen, and yet, she was standing on the street, in a close distance with a man she hardly knew, enjoying his company and knowing he'd be leaving soon.

"You're in the perfect town to meet people," she said.

"I get the feeling I am."

Chapter Twelve

Colton wasn't used to being welcomed with open arms or fussed over unless he was wearing his uniform. If Sara wanted to learn more about him so she could write about him, she would be wrong. His lips were sealed. There was no way he'd tell her more than she already knew.

Especially how much Owen's death haunted him and the little voice in his head telling him he was a failure for ruining his marriage.

His counselor told him it wasn't his fault and sometimes relationships part because both parties head into different directions without involving each other. But he still felt the blame. He could have done more instead of giving up when Jenny told him it was over.

Sara led Colton inside. "I'm not staying up too much longer," she told him as she hung up her coat. "I have to work tomorrow and have an early start."

"I won't be in your way," Colton said, taking off his shoes. He placed them beside hers and hung up his coat the same as Sara did. By the time he left, he didn't want her to feel like he'd put her out.

"I'm not worried." She grinned and brushed past him to the kitchen. "Do you drink tea? I'm making a cup."

"If it's decaf." He'd started drinking chamomile to get a night of better sleep. It helped him with all the restless nights he'd been having.

Sara was filling the kettle and turned on the burner. She dug through a box of tea, pulling bags out. "I've got mint and sleepy time for decaf."

"Sleepy time," he said — anything to ease his tense muscles and over-active brain.

Sara pulled out two mugs and opened the bags. "Help yourself to the ice for your foot. I'm sure you're going to need it."

Colton was standing in the middle of the room, putting his weight on his right foot because his left was tender and sore to stand on. The walk didn't help his foot, but the fresh air helped his head to relax.

"How will you get your plane to the airport?" she asked, leaning against the counter, she tucked her fingers into the pocket of her jeans. Her hair came to her shoulders, shaping her face. Her brown eyes popped when she spoke and her rosebud lips arched now and again, showing a sliver of white teeth behind them.

"I'll look into it tomorrow."

"Does your commanding officer know where you are?"

"I...I'm on leave." Colton scratched the side of his head. His shoulder began to ache. "I'll deal with it tomorrow."

"You've got a full day ahead of you." She smiled and shut off the whistling kettle. "You can stay here while I'm at work." She poured the hot water into the mugs. "I don't expect you to leave because I need to leave."

"I'm a stranger in your house."

"That's why I let the sheriff know you're staying here, and Brad knows. My brother too." Her eyebrows jumped. She handed him his mug.

"It's good to protect yourself," he said. "I respect that."

"I trust you." She brought her steaming mug to her mouth and put it down. "I'll grab bedding." She left the room to open up a closet. Colton peaked around the corner.

"I can help you."

She took out a folded blanket, sheet, and pillow. "I got it," she said, walking into the living room with full arms.

"I don't mind helping. You're doing this for me." Colton followed her.

"I know." She dropped the bedding on the couch.

"Are you like this with everyone?" He crossed his arms at his chest.

She unfolded the sheet. "What do you mean?"

"Let people stay on your couch."

She bent down to tuck the sheet in and fluffed the pillow. "Not someone I didn't know. Never. If you need another blanket, there's one in the closet. Help yourself."

"Okay, thanks. So, why are you helping me?" He stiffened, anticipating her answer.

She looked away and then back at him, biting down on her bottom lip. "My dad. He would have encouraged me to help you out. I know he would."

So she was helping him not because she felt sorry for him, but because her dad would have been proud of her. A flash of relief came over Colton. Sara was helping him for personal reasons, but he guarded himself not wanting her to find out about him being honorably discharged. It would only give her fuel for a story, but more importantly, he didn't want anyone to know. He had to be careful saying too much. How much did Sara know about his personal life besides the tragedy of Owen?

"They say it's hard when a solider dies young, but it's painful for those who have to live without them," Colton offered understanding, thinking how Denise was surviving without her husband.

"Thanks." She took a step back from the couch. "Make yourself comfortable." She clasped her hands together. "I'm going to go to bed. I have an early morning." She took another step backward. "I should give you the envelope. You know, just so you have it. It's why you're here." Her lips came together and she left the room, returning with what Colton had been missing. She held it out for him and he took it, placing it in his plastic bag with his clean socks and new clothes.

"Can I ask you a question?"

Colton leaned the bag against the wall and stood up.

Sara played with her hands and rocked on her feet. "The accident. With Owen." She pulled a strand away from her face. "Did you have anything to do with his death?"

"You're asking me if I threw him in front of the oncoming vehicle?"

She swallowed, blinking. "I need to know."

"No." His teeth came together, eyebrows knitted. "Didn't you read old news stories?"

"I did." She stood still with only her eyes shifting.

"Well, it's true. I didn't do it. I can't believe people would even think I'd want to hurt somebody on purpose."

"I don't know you," she said softly. "I had to ask."

"Owen was my best friend. For people to think I'd go out of my way to shatter his life makes no sense to me." Colton felt his blood boil. His upper body muscles tensed.

"Thanks for sharing."

He held her gaze. The only way she would find out about him being discharged from the military was if she looked up his record. The pit of his stomach hardened. It was the one thing he wanted to keep to himself. The more she found out about him, it would give her something to write about and keeping his life private was the only way he knew how to heal.

"Feel better now?" he asked, hating himself for sounding bitter.

She nodded. "Goodnight," she said and walked down the hall to her bedroom.

He heard the bathroom door shut. Colton went around the house, double checking the windows and doors to make sure it was locked, then plunked himself down on the couch. He lifted his foot to elevate it and stared at the blank TV. Before turning it on, the bathroom door opened and another door clicked shut.

He heard what sounded like something heavy pushing over carpet. Her bedroom door shook like something was against it. Sara was a smart woman. She was keeping herself safe by barricading herself in her bedroom. The only problem was, Sara still didn't trust him.

Chapter Thirteen

Sara's fingers burned from typing on her computer. Jerry was gone, leaving her to report and edit the newspaper. She had to make the best use of her time, knowing she was responsible for filling space. It would only be for two more papers because Jerry should be back to work before her trip.

If she missed her flight, would Johnathan wait to meet her? It could be another month or so before she got the chance, and then what? He could move on and find someone else? Would her cousin extend his offer? She wouldn't be able to afford a hotel for two weeks. It was a chance of a lifetime and when would she get another opportunity to meet someone outside of Moonlight, and travel to a country and stay for free?

Sara's phone dinged. She scooped it up and read the screen. Johnathan.

She sighed, looked up to the ceiling to stretch her neck. *Not a good time.* She had work to do, and Liam wasn't helping her the way she expected him to. She dropped her phone on her desk and sat up in her chair, focusing on her computer screen. She would message Johnathan later when she didn't have so much floating around in her brain.

Footsteps tapped the linoleum floor. Sara looked to her side, pausing typing. "Liam. I haven't seen you all day." He strode toward the back of the room to his desk. The newsroom was strange without Jerry around. Maybe Liam felt it too, and it was his reason for not being there. "Are you okay?"

His brow wrinkled. "I've got a question for you." He stopped in the middle of the room. "Being a woman and single."

"Don't rub it in." Sara gave him a warm smile. "What's going on?"

"There's this girl, someone I used to know. She's an elementary school teacher." Liam slouched against the printer. "She's coming here to visit." He paused. "And might stay longer if she gets a job."

"Old girlfriend?"

"We never dated." He swayed his head. "She's coming for a visit this weekend. We've been out of touch, but recently connected again." Liam threw the paper he was holding into the recycling bin and shoved his hands into his jean pockets. "Maybe she'll come. I don't know." He flattened his lips. "I can't tell if she's coming here to see me or to see the town because there was a job posting. How do I know?"

Sara leaned back in her chair and rubbed the sides of her eyes for relief. "If she's coming here, I'd say she's interested in you." She rested her hands on her thighs. "Is she coming by herself?"

"She didn't say. I don't think so." He shrugged. "Most girls don't travel alone, do they? I don't travel alone. Especially to a place I've never been to," he said.

Sara swished her lips. "She must be comfortable with you." She wasn't comfortable with meeting Johnathan, but she eased her mind by reminding herself he was a journalist too, and they had been corresponding the past two weeks. What if she didn't like him in person? She had two days to spend with him.

Liam took his hands out of his pockets. "She might hate it here. I don't know." His eyes shifted. "What can I do with her when she's here? Any suggestions?"

"Hot chocolate on the beach, picnic. TJ's will have a band...movie, the fall market. She might like the pig races." Sara gave him a warm smile. What was Johnathan planning for her? Would he take her out to dinner, explore the city? There was so much to do in Seattle. She even searched what places she wanted to see the most.

Maybe he would take her to the space needle, and he would kiss her under the moon. Her lungs expanded.

"Those are good." Liam nodded.

"Oh! And be excited to see her. She'll love it and don't forget to tell her you to have plans with her. You'll want to show her what our town has to offer." Sara clasped her hands in her lap. Her chest lifted. "Give her something to think about...something she'll want to come back for."

Liam turned and looked at her grimly. "Thanks for the advice."

"Hopefully, for you." Sara laughed through her smile. Her stomach rolled with anticipation of her own upcoming adventure. There was so much to see and do with Johnathan; she wondered how he'd present himself. When she got off the plane, would he be holding up a sign with the words, Sweetest Sara on it, so she'd known it was him? Maybe she needed to bring him something from Moonlight Valley to remind him of her when she left.

Sara drove to the outskirt of town to meet Dan Briggs. She had to make a story to fill the pages. It was worth knowing if and when Dan would sell his fruit farm. She contacted the bed and breakfast that was under construction but it wasn't a story.

She drove past Colton's plane still lying in the cornfield and pulled into the long driveway leading to the old farmhouse There was a porch swing on the veranda and a dog's empty dish beside it.

Parking behind a new blue pickup truck, she threw her bag over her shoulder and knocked on the door. Heavy footsteps competed with a dog barking and the door opened. Sara and she stepped back when the dog came toward her. Dan pulled the dog's collar just in time.

"Hello," Dan said. His dog stopped barking and sat beside him.

Sara caught her breath. "Hi."

"She won't bite. Gala's a good girl." He tightened his grip. "Come in."

"Gala. I like it." She smiled at the dog and stepped inside.

"What's going on?" he asked, relaxing his hand on the dog's collar. His jeans were a little loose on him, and it took her a moment to think he had lost a lot of weight. His round face was clean-shaven, and he wore a baseball cap and long-sleeve knit sweater.

"Oh, right. Just wondering. Your farm. Is it for sale?" she asked.

"Not anymore. Why do you ask?"

"I was curious," she admitted. "Of what your plans were, who was going to buy it."

"Come in." Dan turned on his foot. "Gala, go lay down," he demanded, releasing his hand from the collar.

Sara took off her shoes and followed Dan into the kitchen, which was at the back of the house. It had large windows facing a backyard and an orchard. She made eye contact with another man standing in the room. Her heart warmed, knowing he used to know her dad.

"Sara," Dan said. "This is Al. He's from Omak Airport. Came to take a look at the plane on my field. Seeing how he can help."

"Hi, Al," she gushed, walking toward him with arms open.

"Oh, you know each other," Dan said.

"Sara. How are you?" Al embraced her in a warm hug. "Haven't seen you in years."

"It's been a long time," she agreed. "How are you?"

"I'm good. Still running the flight school, although I'm close to retiring. Just need to find a pilot who can take over for me." He chuckled.

"Am I interrupting a visit?" She glanced at Dan and then back to Al.

"No." Al's eyebrows moved. He was wearing a bomber jacket and jeans, looking sporty and youthful. "I heard about the crash and read your story. Thought I might be able to help."

"Can you?" she asked.

Al turned and looked at Dan. "Some of my guys will come and get the plane. We have to arrange a tow."

"Does Colton know about this?" Sara's eyebrows narrowed.

"Not yet. The sheriff was going to pass on the information. We can't have it sit here."

"Who pays for it?"

"The pilot. He'll have to pay." Al raised his hand. "I'll have to track down where he is."

"I know. I can pass on the information." Sara pressed her toes into the hardwood floor. "Where do you think it will be towed?"

"I don't know a day yet, but it will go to Omak Airport." Al zipped up his jacket. "I'll see what I can do." He turned to Dan. "Thanks for being accommodating."

"Anything to help," Dan said, putting a hand on his hip.

"It's appreciated." Al side-stepped and looked at Sara. "I'm going to be at your market this Sunday. We're giving away a free learn to fly package."

"Maybe I'll see you there," Sara said.

Al sauntered to the front door. The dog got off of her mat and waggled her tail, prancing behind the man. "Sara." He stomped his foot in his shoe and looked up from tying his laces. "If I'm not at the tent, I'll be around. Come, say hi." He stood up and stomped his foot. "I don't have a volunteer to work with me, so I'm by myself. I couldn't get a volunteer to build wooden planes with kids."

"No volunteers?" Sara asked. It was one way for Colton to return a favor.

"No," he said with a smile. "I have hundreds of model airplanes I'm going to give to the
kids." Gala licked Al's hand, and he returned the love by petting her. "It was good to meet you too, Gala." The dog's tongue swayed.

"Maybe I can get someone to help you out."

"Who do you have in mind?"

"Colton, the pilot. He'd be perfect. He could sit and talk about planes. I'm sure it's something he might do. I don't know how long he's here for, but it would give him something to do."

"Do you know him well enough to ask?" Dan adjusted his cap.

She felt her cheeks warm. "I don't know, know him, but I've spoken to him, and I think he'd love to be around another pilot and talk about what he knows." She bit her bottom lip. Colton would appreciate the opportunity, wouldn't he?

"Okay. Ask him. I'd like to meet him. I better go. Have a good afternoon." Al bowed and closed the door as he stepped backward outside.

"So, you want to ask me a few questions?" Dan side-stepped. "Come into the kitchen."

Gala returned to her mat and slumped down with a grunt, then closed her eyes.

Sara followed Dan and took out her notepad and pen. "You're not selling now."

Dan's mouth tightened. He took a moment before answering. "It's a tough time to sell." He sat down on a chair, legs spread apart, he clasped his hands between them. "I thought by selling I could find something else to do. Farming is tough." His hands parted. "I'm alone. I've got a big house and acres. Then, I experimented making apple cider and bingo! It turned out. I'm in the process of making my first batch. Do you want to go out back and see?"

"Absolutely!" She jumped to her feet.

Gala got off her mat and wandered over to Sara. She put down her notebook and pet the silky fur. "How long have you had Gala?"

"I got her when she was two years old from Homeward Bound Animal Shelter."

"She's so sweet."

"Yeah, she's a good girl." Dan got up and lifted a lid off a canister. Gala wagged her tail and licked her chops. She sat while Dan lowered the treat for her.

"She's been good for me. They say dogs are the best therapy, and I believe they are right."

SARA FINISHED HER WORK. All she wanted to do was curl up wearing pajamas and watch a movie, but she couldn't because Colton was there and she wasn't that comfortable.

When she left for work in the morning, Colton told her he'd be hanging out at her place figuring out what to do with his plane. Granted, he had a sore foot, there wasn't much for him to do anyway. Walking inside, she dropped her bag to the floor and hung up her coat.

"I hope you're hungry," Colton said coming around the corner. "I ordered pizza."

She froze. "Really?"

"It's on the table." He turned around and hobbled into the kitchen. It was the first time anyone had surprised her with dinner, but then, she had never had a man stay at her house for more than a day.

"There's meat lovers and ham and pineapple. I didn't know what you'd like but I knew you ate meat."

"Yeah, this is great. Thank you." She sat down to a plate and a glass of water with lemon.

"How was work?" he asked.

"Good. Thanks." She took a slice of pizza and put it on her plate. The aroma of cheese made hunger pangs. "What did you do today?"

"I made some phone calls, not a lot." He picked up a piece of pizza. "I called the Traveler's Motel and they have room, so I can head over there after dinner."

"You can stay another night." She took a bite and the cheese was strung to her mouth.

"It's nice of you, but you have your life and I'm interfering. I've already over-stayed. It was supposed to be one night."

"You're not interfering. When are you due back?"

He took a drink of water. "Another week, but I'll be leaving town in another day or two. Just waiting for my foot to heal."

"You can stay another night, but I do have a favor to ask."

"Perfect. What is it?"

"The fall fair is this weekend, and they need someone to help out."

"First of all—" He held up his hand. "I don't dress up in clown costumes or sell fifty-fifty tickets, and I can't work in a concession stand."

She put her fingers over her lips and laughed. "Nothing like that." Colton was serious, but he was charming at the same time.

"What would I be doing?"

She took a breath before talking. "Omak's airport will have a tent set up, and the pilot, Al, needs someone to sit with him."

"That's it?"

She nodded, keeping a straight face. "He needs help building wooden airplanes for kids."

"What does it have to do with you? Do you owe this guy something?"

"It's just a neighborly thing to do. He's a pilot, you're a pilot." She shrugged.

"I get it. What's in it for you?"

"Al's an old friend of my dad's. It would mean a lot if you could help him out."

Colton scratched the side of his head. "Okay."

"Thanks." She sighed. "It would be cool to have an Air Force pilot there. Talk about the industry. Maybe recruit people. You can tell people about it. I can print some brochures to display."

Colton squirmed. "How about I build airplanes?"

"Whatever you want. Sure, if you're good with it." She sat back. "Let me ask you something. For a major who is in the Air Force, you don't talk or refer to it much, how come?"

"I don't like talking about work."

"People are proud of what you do. They'd love to hear about the cool planes you get to fly. I know you can't talk about missions and all of that, but people would be interested in you. You're a hero."

"Nice of you to think so." He paused. "But I'm not a hero." He finished his glass of water. "I prefer not to talk about myself."

"What do you like to talk about?" She watched a faint grin touch his lips.

"Anything but memories." His hands were held tightly together, his back straight as aboard.

"Fair enough. What do you think about watching a movie?"

Chapter Fourteen

Colton hadn't spent time with a woman who wasn't his girlfriend, sharing a blanket, eating popcorn and watching Netflix. It was the perfect night. Until she pushed furniture across her bedroom door for fear of an intruder. Maybe one day Sara would trust him, but for now he could gain her friendship.

Despite the fact he hated to socialize with people he didn't know, Colton needed to act on his promise and hang out under the tent for a couple of hours to support her dad's friend. For a small town, Moonlight Valley was widely spread out and nestled between a lake and mountain terrain, leading to Highway 97. Colton would have walked from Sara's to Discovery Hall, where the market was held in the parking lot, but Sara insisted she drive. It was probably a good thing because it would have taken him over an hour on foot to get there.

Dressed in jeans, he had bought a new pack of underwear and two shirts from Well Clothed, and although he needed a haircut, he'd worry about it later when he left for Omak. A flow of shoppers crowded the path and tents on either side with vendors selling honey, baked goods, quilts, wooden spoons and coasters, and locally roasted coffee. If he hadn't already had two cups this morning with his toast and eggs Sara made for him, he would have had another.

"That's the tent there," Sara said, lifting her chin to the Come Fly With Us banner.

Colton clutched his teeth. "Why am I doing this again?"
"You promised me. We made a deal."

"That's right." His lips parted into a smile.

She giggled. "Come on, you'll like it."

"I've never been around kids."

"Either have I, but I'm sure it'll be fine. Al's a great guy. You don't have to worry."

"I'm not worried," he lied. *I'm nervous.*

She tapped him on the arm with her knitted mitt. "You're a celebrity in town. People will be talking to you."

"Great." He rolled his eyes. "Thanks for reminding me I crashed my plane." Colton would have to try to avoid adult conversation. At least with children, he could talk about airplanes and it would be enough. He had to keep pretending he was a major in the Air Force, and he'd be going back to work. A sliver of guilt stabbed him in the chest.

They walked between people oncoming shoppers and ducked under the white tent.

"Al," Sara called out. The man was sitting on a stool, foot perched on the lower bar, his head shot up from sticking a wing in place on a wooden plane for a little girl standing patiently in front of him.

"Hello," Al said and handed the girl the plane. He stood up from the stool and extended his hand to Colton. "Hi. I'm Al Anderson. I head the learn to fly program at Omak Airport."

"Good to meet you," Colton said, taking back his hand.

"Sorry about your plane. I went to take a look at it to see the damage. You did a number on it." He rubbed his hands together. "But it's fixable."

"I did."

"I told Sara—" Al made eye contact. "I can probably arrange a tow and a hanger for it."

"Yeah? You talked to Sara?" Colton turned to look at her. "You didn't tell me."

She opened her hands. "I wanted Al to tell you."

"That would be great," Colton said. "Thank you. I was calling around today trying to

arrange something. I was going to head into Omak tomorrow and enquire about how to get it home."

"No sweat. I appreciate you coming here to hang out with an old man for a few hours. I had a rush of ten kids lining up for one of these." He held up an individual package airplane. "They go nuts for it. You'd think it was candy."

Colton gave Al a loose smile. Colton knew the feeling because he was that kid who'd take a toy plane over candy.

"Sara, how's it going?" a woman shouted from outside the tent.

Sara turned her back. "Oh, hey." She walked over to a woman.

Al rocked back and forth. "Looks like you're healing well."

"I'll be fine." Colton shrugged it off.

"Speaking like a true military man."

Two children with an adult walked in. "Can I have a plane?" the little boy asked.

"Do you want to build it for him?" Al asked. "Pretty easy. I let them have a choice to build it themselves or have you do it, but if they're small, I do it."

Colton pulled the package until it ripped open.

"Hey, you're the pilot that crashed," the dad said.

Colton didn't need instructions on how to build; he pieced the plane together before he

answered. "That's me." He handed it to the boy.

"One for me, too!" the girl beside him said.

Colton chuckled. "Okay." Within seconds, he handed the little girl her plane.

"When I grow up, I'm going to be a pilot," she said.

"You can do anything you put your mind to," Colton said. He looked up past the girl's brown eyes and caught Sara watching him from outside of the tent. She was smiling. His brain fired off an electric charge. His chest heated, and he looked back at the child.

Within a short time, more kids gravitated into the tent, and people surrounded Colton asking questions about the crash and when he'd go back to work. How bad he was hurt and if he would become a permanent resident of Moonlight Valley. Colton didn't prepare himself for questions, and he didn't feel like answering to anyone.

"Thank you for your service, Major," an older lady said. "I read about you. Amazing you survived the crash. You must be built of steel." The lady chuckled. "This here is my grandson." She tapped her hand on his shoulder.

"Do you want a plane?" Colton asked, holding up a package.

The boy nodded.

"Speak up." His grandmother tapped his arm. "Need to hear your manners."

"Yes, please," the boy said, eyes darting up.

"Sure thing." Colton unwrapped the plastic. It seemed ridiculous that they were all individually wrapped.

"My late husband," the woman said, "he was in the Navy. Spent years deployed. Hard work he was."

"Yes, ma'am." Colton handed the plane to the boy. He searched for Sara but she was talking to a guy around the same age as himself. Her upper body arched, she laughed with him, and it sent Colton's pulse racing.

Once the tent was empty again, Al took out a stack of brochures and placed them on top of the others.

"I'm offering a discount when someone signs up for flight lessons."

"Do you get a lot of people interested?" Colton asked, trying to make small talk. He kept an eye on Sara. He was committed for one more hour. As much as he was enjoying the children, he didn't enjoy the adults who accompanied them, but still, it was mindless work for a trade-off, even though he still felt like he owed Sara more.

"Would you ever be interested in an instructor position?" Al asked.

"Teach flight school?" His body stiffened. He put a hand to his chest. "Sounds great." He struggled with not smiling. "I, um, have to go back to base in two weeks," he lied.

"Oh, right." Al put his hand to his forehead. "I'm sorry. I wasn't thinking. Of course." He brought his hand down. "I could use an experienced pilot." Al held up a brochure. "One of my pilots doesn't want to do it anymore. He has other commitments, and I'm semi-retired."

Colton put the airplane down on the table. Sara focused on talking to the same person. "I appreciate the offer."

"The offer is there," Al said. "Do you mind watching this for me? I'm stepping out for a few minutes."

"Yeah, sure." Colton swung his body side to side. There was nothing really to watch but build airplanes which he needed to do. If this was all he had to do to stay at Sara's house, she was getting ripped off. "Take your time." He had plenty of it.

Sara walked in, plucked her mitts off of her hands, and put them inside her coat pocket. "Do you want to grab a bite to eat afterward?"

"Sure."

"I have to go into work for an hour. I forgot I had a piece of editing left to do." She craned her neck, eyeing the tent ceiling.

"Take your time," he said.

"Are you sure?"

He didn't like seeing the worried look on her face. The lines on her forehead creased. If he wished he could bring her into his arms and tell her it would be okay.

"I'll go now." Her body shifted back and forth. "I'll pick you up. Are you going to be here for a little bit?"

"An hour or so, but don't worry about me. I can find my way back to your house."

She made a face. "I feel bad leaving you here."

"It's good. If I get to your place before you, I'll hang around until you get there." He scratched his head. "I'll be fine."

She fumbled with her purse. "Here."

"What are you doing?"

"Take my house key." She dug and pulled a set of keys from the bottom of her purse.

Colton put his hand out. "No, don't. I don't need it. You need a key."

"Not if you're going to be there first." She circled the key around the ring and handed it to him. "Take it."

"I have your cell phone number," he told her as a way to lessen her stress. "If I need to reach you, I will." He kept his voice light, cupping his hand around her house key.

"I'll pick you up," she said.

"You shouldn't. I can't let you wait outside."

"It's fine."

"I'd feel better if you took the key. At least you won't be stuck outside in the cold."

"It's not cold." She walked away.

"Good luck with what you need to do."

She looked over her shoulder. "Thanks." She bolted out of the tent.

Colton blinked, and she was gone. He touched his chest where he felt an ache. It was stupid to feel anything. He wouldn't allow himself to explore being more than friends with Sara. He had a firm grip on the key. She trusted him, but he couldn't let down his guard.

Chapter Fifteen

S ara walked into The Observer and locked the door behind her. She scurried to her desk to re-read the newspaper one more time before sending it off to the printers. In Liam's and Jerry's absence, she'd get more done without distractions. Well, except for Colton being on her mind. There wasn't much going on at the fall market, but she did manage to snap a few pictures she could use in Sunday's paper.

Sara played around with the layout. The photo of Bronco the pig didn't quite fit with the article about the local butcher purchasing a food truck for the spring shindig. She squeezed her lips together. Her eye caught a gap in one of the sections, enough space to place an ad, so she filled it with a new community announcement, but it didn't fit quite right, and neither did the next two. What else could Sara do with it besides place a photo in it? The paper would be so much better if it had something fun to read. Something entertaining to break up the everyday.

She shuffled through extra photos she kept in a subfolder. She combed her fingers through the length of her hair feeling the pulsing in her temples. Colton was probably on his way to her house, thanks to Al driving him. Her mind went to Colton. His sharp blue eyes pierced her heart, making her feel his pain. She wished he'd be more open with her and tell her personal stories and share his regrets. He might be tough on the outside, but she saw through the wall he built to hide his loneliness. She wanted to know what it was like to be in his arms to show him he wasn't alone. If only he'd let her help him.

What would her dad want her to do?

She closed her eyes, reflecting on the past when she was little, sitting on his lap, eating ice cream too big for her to eat. She heard her dad's laughter, saw her dad's gleaming eyes, and felt his hand around her little body. She was safe in his arms.

Sara blinked to rid the piercing tears but couldn't manage so she grabbed a tissue from the box on her desk and dabbed the corner of her eyes. She had to make her dad proud. She would help Colton get back on his feet. It was the least she could do.

Sara ran the cursor over the space. There should be an advice column; she could use an answer to her relationship problems. What would Kelly and Emily say if she told him she had the pilot staying at her house and she was leaving on her trip to meet a guy she met online? An unsettling feeling erupted in her stomach. She fought to think about Colton. He didn't trust her to talk to her about his past, and it bothered her why he couldn't open up, but then she wasn't a friend.

Thinking about Liam's dilemma instead of her own and since Jerry was gone, he wouldn't see a couple of issues anyway. The town could use a little entertainment. She could create an advice column for fun — just one time to fill space.

She played around with the keys and then the idea popped in her head.

DOES SHE LIKE ME FOR ME, OR MY TOWN?

Sara wrote the headline. What would her code name be? She couldn't use her real name, nobody would take her seriously. She needed something cute, innocent, sweet like her dad called her and Johnathan. Sweet like Peaches. The name pinged in her brain. She straightened her back and began to type.

Dear Peaches: There's a girl I used to know. I like her a lot. We've been out of touch for a few years, and out of the blue, she called me and said she wanted to visit. She's never been to Moonlight Valley and said

it sounded like a beautiful place. How do I know if she's coming to see
me or my town?
-Doubtfully Mine
Dear Doubtfully Mine,
Cheer up! She wants to spend time with you while checking out the
sights. You're the
perfect tour guide. Be grateful for the opportunity and use your time
wisely. You never know, it could be the start of something good!

Sara smiled with accomplishment. The page wasn't blank anymore, and the advice column looked rather...intriguing. Nobody would reply to the column anyway. Who would notice? The column was just a filler. She saved it and sent it off electronically before she had second thoughts.

Sara shut down her computer and grabbed her purse. She smelled the flowers from Johnathan. Tension lingered between her shoulder blades, so she stretched her arms above her head, feeling calmer and then her phone rang. Stopping in the middle of the hallway to answer it and her stomach sank. "Hi, Jerry. How are things?"

"Okay. Did you get the paper out on time? You didn't send it to me."

"I didn't want to bother you." Her arms felt weighted. Head buzzed. She was doing all she could do on deadline.

"I told you to send it to me."

"I can do it," she said, shuffling her feet. "There's nothing new. Usual sports stories, photos from the fall market, and I wrote an article about Dan Brigg's farm, not for sale. He took it off the market. Oh yeah, and there's a permit application for food trucks for the spring shindig."

He grunted. "Okay."

"How are things for you?" she asked, scrunching her nose, waiting for his next question.

"Okay. I'm at the hospital now. I've been here the whole time." He breathed out.

"I'm sorry."

"Well, I should go. Let me know if you need anything."

Sara ended the call and locked up behind her. She got to her car when her phone beeped. Riffling through her purse before turning on her ignition, she read Johnathan's message. Why was she worried about being dumped when they haven't begun their journey together? The unsettling feeling rocked her stomach.

I haven't heard from you in a day. Is everything okay?

She shifted in her seat. *Don't tell me you've changed your mind.* Sara slouched. There was still an opportunity to meet him, and if all went well, then what? Could she move away from Moonlight? Could Johnathan move here? He wouldn't leave his job to work at a small-town newspaper. It would be up to her.

In only three weeks, how could she think of Johnathan being anything more when they hadn't yet met? It seemed unrealistic now, considering her heart wasn't bursting with joy like it had been the first week she spoke to him, when it seemed like a great idea. She had Colton on her mind and wanted to be the one to help him get back what he was missing. He deserved a second chance and she wondered if she could be the one to make him feel whole again. When he looked at her with cautiously, blue eyes beaming, her insides pulled in desperation to feel his skin again hers and to feel secure in his arms.

Hey Johnathan. How are you? I'm over my head at work. Sara paused, pursing her lips. **You've been on my mind, and I need to talk to you.** She cleared her throat. **I'm exhausted. My boss is away and I am doing two jobs right now. I might not be able to leave. I'll keep you posted!**

He responded promptly. **I hope everything is well and you don't have to cancel your trip. Thursday is coming quick.** ☺

She threw her phone into her purse. Her stomach growled signaling she should have had a plan for dinner but couldn't think of what to make. Pulling into her driveway, the lights were on. Sighing, picturing Colton watching a football game, made her think of what she was missing. She wasn't used to sharing her space with anyone, but having Colton around made wanting a companion again almost vital.

She opened the front door and undid her coat. The aroma of cooking garlic filled the air. "Hello," she called, shrugging off her coat and hanging it on the rack.

Colton walked in from the kitchen, wrapping his hand in a dishtowel, meeting her in the middle. "Hi." His shirt formed across his barreled chest and wearing a smile as though happy to see her.

Her insides felt like a handful of jumping grasshoppers. "It smells good," she cooed.

"Hope you're hungry," he said, smiling. "I made lots."

Since when did she come home to a cooked meal prepared by a man? A hot man? A man with a chiseled jawline and abs so cut they indented his shirt?

"I'll be right back," she said, beelining it to the bathroom to wash her hands and to check herself in the mirror. Taking a breath to calm her quickened heartrate, she tossed her hair back off her shoulders in a ponytail and met Colton in the kitchen. She eyed the table which was

complete with cutlery, plates, and a salad bowl in the middle. "So, what did you make?"

"Chicken fettuccine, Colton style." He waved tongs in the air and tossed the noodles around in the pan.

"Colton style?" She giggled.

"I used milk instead of cream, heavy on the garlic, splash of fresh-squeezed lemon and pepper. Butter, of course."

"I smelled it when I came in. What can I do?"

"Nothing. Come sit."

"This is amazing," she said, watching him bring food to the table. An act of kindness. A thoughtful gesture. All because she was letting him stay with her?

Sara put her hand across her stomach. Partly hunger, partly enjoyment of having someone home and willing to make a meal.

"Salad too?" She sat down. "This is nice." Not only was he attractive, he could cook! "I don't remember having the ingredients to make all of this."

"I picked up a few things. Al was kind enough to offer me a ride." Colton carried the two plates over to the table and set one down on her placemat. "He saw me walking on the main drag."

"You shouldn't be attempting to walk that far. Your foot is healing," she reminded him.

"It's fine."

She inhaled the smell of the sauce. "This is real food. Like homemade." The inside of her mouth watered.

He laughed. "You don't cook for yourself?"

"I don't," she said, picking up her fork. "Not like this. You know chicken in a can? I can't be bothered to cook a meal like this for myself." She forked a noodle and used the spoon to twirl it before taking a bite. "A meal is just a necessity, not an enjoyment."

"Shouldn't be."

"No." But she'd instead fill the gap and get on with her work then fuss over what she was eating.

Colton looked up from his bite. "How is it?"

"Amazing." She caught his stare across from her. "So good."

He smiled.

"You're a good cook," she said, appreciating the effort.

"Not really." He ate his salad. "It's easy. How was work? Did you get everything you needed done?"

"I did." She drank some water. "With my editor gone, I'm left with a lot to do. Liam, our sports reporter, does a little, but I can't rely on him to edit, too."

"When is your editor back?"

"I wish I knew."

"He didn't give you a date?"

"No. Jerry's mother is dying," she said between a bite. "He wants to stay with her until her passing. I just wished I had someone else to help. I might take some photos to fill a page." She delayed her laugh. "I'm doing my best."

"And it shows. You're working hard."

She looked up from taking a drink from her lemon water. "Because I'm always working?"

"That, and I've read your stories."

She didn't know why it made her blush. It was her job to write about Moonlight Valley and hadn't been self-conscious before. Having Colton stare at her from across the table made her feel like she was talking to an old friend.

"Moonlight has a lot going on, considering it's a small town," he said.

"Do you like it here?" She was dying to ask what he thought. Coming from a city most would go back to the business and crowded streets. Moonlight Valley had some breathing room and had the view for dreamers and people who appreciated the outdoors.

"I do." He chewed and swallowed, taking a drink of water. "It has more than one needs. Nice people." The smile he possessed while talking made Sara's heart flutter.

"So, you would visit again?"

"I would. It seems like a great place to live."

"It is." Wherever Sara decided to live, it wouldn't be the same, and she had convinced herself otherwise. Moonlight was a great place to live. Then why was she in such a hurry to leave? "Tomorrow is supposed to be my day off, but I might need to write an article to get ahead of my work week. If you need me to drive you somewhere, let me know." She stabbed a piece of lettuce and cucumber with her fork. "Unless you have plans."

"I'm figuring something out. I'll let you know."

"Okay, sure. I don't mind."

"How was the market? Did it go, okay?" She forked a bite.

"It was good."

"That's great. So you might be staying for a bit?" She drank some water.

"One more day." His voice lowered. He moved his fork around on his plate. "Are you okay with me staying another night?"

Her stomach sank. "Of course. Totally fine." It was only supposed to be temporarily. He had a home and a job to go to. It just wasn't in Moonlight Valley.

In her dad's honor, she helped Colton the best she could, and now it was time for him to leave. She knew this day was coming; she just didn't expect to feel empty because of it.

Chapter Sixteen

Colton helped clear the table and put the salad dressing back into the fridge. He stood beside Sara as she ran soapy water to wash dishes. It seemed to be their thing, cleaning up, doing stuff together, and he didn't mind.

Colton actually enjoyed it. It was one of the reasons he liked being married and having a partner. Doing dishes wasn't a task; it was a privilege because standing next to someone he cared about, and talking about nothing was an enjoyment. Colton wouldn't take the little things for granted ever again.

"Thank you for making dinner," Sara said, looking over her shoulder as Colton picked up a clean towel from the drawer.

"Oh, yeah, I hope it was okay."

"I loved it." Her voice rose.

"I don't want to leave and you think I was the worst houseguest." Colton grinned from the side of his mouth and took the plate from her hand and dried it. Leaving Sara would be hard. Goodbyes were never easy, but he had a personal mission to deliver the envelope to Denise and he made a promise to Owen. Colton needed to stay true on his word.

"You've been the best houseguest. You can come back and visit anytime."

"If you're offering," he teased and placed the dry plate in the cupboard.

"I hope you're sleeping okay. The couch is pretty soft."

"It's fine." He didn't want to tell her he had been up a couple of times, tossing and turning, thinking about life and what he left behind. His mini vacation ended and now had to get back to reality. His stomach pinched. He didn't have a home to go to and be reminded of his pass when in a new town he saw a future. He could forget about Jenny and all his mistakes, like not being attentive and being self-absorbed caused many of the problems leading to a failed marriage. He didn't need to let the distance between his dad get to him either. Colton had to learn to accept the way things were. The past few days had given him strength and a new outlook.

"Are you okay?" Sara asked.

"Yeah, fine. Just thinking." He shook his head and dried the knives and forks from the holder.

"You're in deep thought."

"I sometimes am."

"Work on your mind again?"

"A little." He breathed out, keeping his secret of no longer being in the military because he

felt displaced with no purpose. He wanted so badly to be honest with Sara, tell her how much he liked her but once again, but nothing could come of it anyway. It wasn't like he was trying to pursue a relationship; they were newly friends.

"I have an idea," Sara said, rinsing a plate and placing it in the rack. She ran her hands un

der the running water and shut off the tap. Colton handed her the towel to dry her hands.

"I'll go into work for a couple of hours in the morning. Promise me you'll be here around two? I've got an idea."

"You're not sharing?" His lips pulsated, trying not to show his emotion. He couldn't re

member the last time he felt some excitement. "That's not fair," he teased back.

"Just in case it doesn't work out. I don't want you to be disappointed." She brought her hands together.

"I'd never be disappointed. The suspense is killing me." He put the empty rack under the sink where it belonged. He staggered his feet as he stood in front of the counter.

Sara stepped toward him, her mouth open, eyes bright with enthusiasm. "You don't like the suspense?" she asked.

Colton's mouth tugged at the side. "It's not usually me who gets the surprise," he said truthfully. He was a giver, and by the look in Sara's eyes, she too was a pleaser. "I don't need anything." She had already done enough for him.

"It's the least I can do, spend the last few hours showing you around town." Her lips came together. She put her hands on her hips, her light fabric shirt fell into a scoop to reveal the dip in her cleavage. His heart began to pound like it did every time he thought about taking her into his arms and exploring what he had been missing. He didn't deserve a relationship, but damn, did he crave it, and he wanted to know how Sara felt in his arms.

He grabbed the drying towel behind him, balling it in his hands to try and take his mind off of reaching out to her and pulling her into him. He fought the urge to hold her, kiss her.

"What do you need me to do?" Colton asked. His mind was fuzzy. Distracted by her pretty mouth and fitted jeans, he had to get out of the house before he made a mistake. Again.

"Nothing," she answered.

"Do you want to go for a walk?" he blurted out. Maybe the fresh air would change his mind about a woman he couldn't have.

"A walk?" Her eyebrow lifted in amusement. "Your foot's okay?"

"It's better." He tossed the towel on the counter. "Fresh air would be good." The faster he got out of the house, the better it would be for him. He was fighting the urge to tell her something he knew he'd regret. He didn't know how if he tried. Snapping the thought from his mind, he said, "I'll meet you at the front door."

She rubbed her sleeve. "I probably should put something warmer on. It's getting cold."

The nip in the air is what Colton wanted to clear his head. Sara went into her bedroom and came out wearing another layer.

"It's not freezing," he said, zipping up his coat.

She brushed past him to unhook her coat from the rack. Colton sidestepped to get out of her way, and she stumbled backward, he reached out to catch her and she fell into him.

"Sorry," she said scrambling to her feet.

"I got you."

Sara's hand went to Colton's arm, and she held it there for a moment. She had changed into a long, black sleeve shirt, tight against her breasts, and puckered at her sides when she moved her hand down his arm. Colton felt his pulse, and he lowered his hand to help break away from the moment stirring in his gut. It took all his willpower not to pull her into his arms.

"I wouldn't have let you fall," he whispered, staring her down. His hand came to a rest on her hip, and she let her arm fall against his. Her face fell.

His bicep twitched from the pressure of her hand. "That was close," he managed to say through a shallow breath and shaking the idea of kissing Sara out of his mind. Heart thumping and staring back at Sara's gaze, he turned his chin in and eyed her fingers resting on him. A shot of adrenaline came through his veins. Burning and irritating his senses. He put a hand on her hip, testing himself at how far he could go without jeopardizing what they had, but cripes he failed at resistance.

Colton swallowed not wanting to let go. He felt the heat of her skin through the thin fabric. Wide-eyed as though hopeful, Sara's chest expanded, and he lowered his neck to her, gently pushing her against the wall. He brought his lips to hers and she opened without hesitation. Soft, slow, and satisfying, she kissed him back, drawing him in for more.

Sara's hand curved over his shoulder and he shuttered in response.

"I forgot you're ticklish," she said between a kiss. Colton's heart to beat harder and the desire to feel his hands on her body became stronger. Following his instinct and desire for more, he slid his hand under her shirt, resting against her lower back. Kissing her seemed surreal.

All the pent-up frustration, loneliness, and heartbreak had vanished from his mind. All Colton could think about was being with Sara and the growing temptation of her in his arms. He closed his eyes and opened them again to her heavy gaze, kissing him back.

You're not good with relationships. Better stop now before Sara thinks you want her as your girlfriend.

He rubbed his thumb along the channel of her spine and a warm sensation filled his chest. Colton couldn't resist the idea of Sara not being his. He shook off the idea of anything more because he couldn't give her what she deserved, and he didn't want to fail.

His thighs tensed, groin throbbed, he nipped at her lips, while his hand traveled from her head over her breast and rested on her hip.

I shouldn't do this, the voice in his head whispered. She'll regret it tomorrow.

Colton lifted his chin, breaking away from the kiss, she looked at him with a blank expression.

"What's wrong?" She took back her hands. He wanted her to touch him, taste him, love him and feel his need because he had something to offer her. But he didn't. He couldn't give her what she deserved.

Colton took a step back and rubbed his neck, trying to get a kink out that wasn't there.

"You can talk to me." Her voice was delicate and sincere.

And he would talk to her if under different circumstances. He didn't want to show her his heart if there was nothing between them.

"I don't know if I can," he said. He took another step backward and told himself he was doing the right thing because he didn't want to mess up Sara's life. He was saving her from making the wrong decision.

"Okay," she whispered and nodded. Cupping her chin with her index finger, she turned on her foot and headed down the hallway.

"Where are you going?" He scratched his head.

"Giving you space," she called back.

Colton's eyes darted around the living room. He wanted space also, but it was a different kind of space, reasons he didn't want to go back to Bellingham. He enjoyed being by himself and didn't have to get anyone involved with his problems. There were zero risks of disappointing others if he was left alone, and he didn't have to worry about heartache and to crush someone else's dreams.

He raked his hand through his hair, circling the room to shake off the idea of being with Sara if there was a possibility. It didn't matter how good she felt in his arms or how sweet her kisses were, she deserved more than he could give, but damn, it was hard to resist another kiss.

Chapter Seventeen

It was the most uneventful night Sara had in a long time. First, a heated kiss, and then Colton decided to pull away and needed space? She had heard the bathroom door open in the middle of the night, and she laid awake, thinking about what she should have done differently.

It wasn't like her to kiss a guy she hardly knew but knew him better than her date five months ago, and it ended with a horrible kiss. Last night, she got caught up in the moment. Who wouldn't? Colton was hot. She wanted to lay her hands over every part of his body. So, what was the problem?

"Morning," Sara said, walking into the kitchen toward the cupboard. She inhaled the roasted beans of coffee.

"Good morning," Colton said, sounding raspy. With a mug in one hand, he lifted his gaze from his phone in the other.

"Did you sleep okay?" It was the same question she asked him every morning, and she had yet to hear a bad rating.

"Good." He went back to his phone.

Sara poured a cup and opened the fridge, taking out a container of yogurt. "Did you eat? Can I make you a parfait?"

"I didn't eat. Sure, I'd have one." He dropped his phone and stood up. "What can I do?"

"Nothing. It's easy," Sara told him, going into the freezer and pulling out a bag of peaches and blueberries. While waiting for the microwave to defrost the fruit, she pulled a bag of granola from the drawer. Why did being in the same room now with Colton feel awkward?

"I was arranging a tow truck with Al," Colton said, putting his phone down. "It looks like I can have it brought to Omak by the end of the week."

Sara scooped yogurt into two bowls, added the granola, and topped it with the fruit. "Okay." She brought their breakfast to the table.

"Gourmet," Colton said, sliding the bowl toward him.

"Thanks for making coffee," she said, meeting his eyes from across from her. "I forget to remake it the night before."

"What are your plans today?" he asked as he circled his spoon around in the bowl.

"Nothing really," she said. If Colton weren't there, she'd probably go to the gym, check-in with her mom, or visit a friend. Since Colton was there and she was working more than usual, she hadn't made any plans. "How about you?"

He chewed, swallowed, and sat back in his chair. "Figuring out what to do with my plane." He picked up his phone. "Now, I know a tow truck will be calling to confirm; I don't have

anything going on." He crossed his arms across his chest.

Sara avoided looking at him. She had already caught a view of his biceps, and it reminded her of being in his arms.

"Might check out the lake if it's not going to rain," he said.

"It's not supposed to." She looked up from her bowl.

"About last night," Colton said, leaning back in the chair.

"We can forget it." It was hard not to with a kiss so tantalizing; it made her head spin, but she had to if they were going their separate ways.

"I don't want to." His jaw muscle bulged. "I liked it."

"You liked it?" She brought her mug up to her lip, feeling the burn on her sensitive skin.

"I did. I'm sorry." He rubbed his forehead.

"It was nothing, so..." She looked into her coffee mug. "We can forget about it."

"We might have gone too far." He gulped down his coffee. "I don't want to lead you on...I was taking complete advantage of the situation."

"You were taking advantage? I kissed you back. I won't hold it against you." She tried to keep her voice light.

"I don't want you to think I'm taking advantage of the situation. I'm staying here, and you want nothing for it. I'll pay you." He brought his chin up. His mouth softened, his lips came together in a line as though he was thinking.

"You're not taking advantage, you're accepting my offer," she said, sipping her coffee. If Colton only knew how much she wanted him to kiss her and still, it wasn't enough. She wanted more and yet she was caught in-between her desire to go away and meet a guy she might not even like or staying here, helping a man who needed her. "I wanted to help."

"You've done a lot." He breathed through his teeth.

"Are you always hard on yourself?" she asked.

He cleared his throat and picked up his coffee cup. "I want to do things right."

"What are you doing wrong?"

"It's not like that."

"What is it?"

"Just stuff." He shook his head. "I don't want to screw up."

The pit of her stomach hardened. Colton was carrying around a burden. "Want to talk about it?"

"No, it's nothing."

"I promise I won't write about it." Her lips held tightly together.

"You already did." He clutched his jaw, eyebrows creased.

"I'm sorry. Though to defend myself that was all public knowledge. But I should have asked you, I know that now."

"Fine but this is something I'm trying to forget."

"What's something good you want to remember?" she asked, leaning in, hoping to see his eyes bright again.

His mouth pulled to the side. Her toes pushed against the floor, doing half circles, anticipating learning something else about him.

"I used to have a dog, Charles. My ex-wife took him. I guess it made sense. Charles kept her company when I was away." Colton pushed his back against the chair. "I miss the push he used to give me, getting me out of bed in the morning because he wanted to eat," Colton chuckled. "When I was home, we'd go for a jog. Jenny hated running, but Charles loved it."

"Do you miss Jenny?" Sara asked, taking in his wandering eyes and uncomfortable posture. She needed to get him out of the house.

"No. I did at the beginning." He rubbed his jaw. "Not anymore."

Sara sucked on her lips, dying to know what happened to them. Why did they break up, but too many questions for Colton would push him away.

"She's with an old friend of mine. Can you believe it?" Colton shook his head. "She leaves me for my friend."

"That sucks," Sara admitted. "It must have been painful to see." She took her questions in stride, taking whatever Colton wanted to give her.

"Yeah, it was." Colton got up and headed to the sink with his bowl and empty coffee mug.

Sara followed him and put her dishes in the sink. "I can do these later." Her grin deepened. "I want to take you somewhere."

He shot a concerned gaze her way.

"It's all good. I'm going to get ready." Sara left the kitchen to have a shower. She couldn't sit at home all day when it was her chance to get out and spend time with Colton, allowing him to learn about Moonlight Valley. She wanted him to know he was safe in

Moonlight Valley. It was an excellent place to relax. If Colton needed to heal, he didn't have to go far.

Forty-five minutes later, they were both showered and dressed for the day. Colton waiting at the entrance holding his bag of belongings.

"You don't need to bring anything," she said, slipping on her boots.

"Where are we going?" His eyebrow crinkled.

"You'll see. It's something I've meant to check out on my own, but I think you might like it." She smiled, locking the door behind her.

"That doesn't help me." He rested his hands in his hip, then turned around and walked to her car.

Taking Colton to Homeward Bound Animal Shelter could go either way, but it was the only thing that came to mind when she thought of what to do for the day. It was about to rain, so she didn't want to go for a walk, and there wasn't a good movie playing at the cinema. She tried to stay out of restaurants and Betty's Bakery because everything filled up around lunchtime when people came out of the church.

"This is where you wanted to take me?" He stared at the building before undoing his seatbelt. "Are you getting a dog?"

She snatched her purse from behind the seat. "I haven't been here in years."

"Why don't you have a pet?" He got out of the car.

"I hate to think about losing them." She slammed the door and headed to the two front steps and tugged on the knob, stepping into the building smelling like wet fur and kibble.

Sara unzipped her hoodie halfway and met the owner's stare coming from down the hall. "Hi Josie," Sara said.

"Hi. Have you come to do a story on my shelter? I might be closing."

"Closing? Oh, no, that's too bad."

"Not enough funding."

"I'll have to come by another time and talk to you about it. I brought my friend, Colton," Sara said, touching Colton's arm. "We were just stopping by to take a look at your dogs if you have any."

"Honey, I've got a dozen dogs." She wiped her hands on her jeans. "All my dogs are outback. I'll show you."

"I have to leave here in around ten minutes," Josie said over her shoulder. "I have lunch plans. I don't usually close, but I have a family member visiting, and she's going home today."

"If it's a bad time," Colton said. "We can come back."

"If it means taking a dog off my hands, it's a good time." She rubbed her hands together.

"Have you finally decided to adopt?"

"Maybe," Sara said and smiled when she heard the barking of dogs and one whining.

"They know someone's here." Josie raised her eyebrows. "I'll let you look, but it doesn't give you a lot of time."

"It's okay," Sara said. "I want to show Colton. We'll be quick."

"Adoption isn't a quick process anyway," Josie said. "If you like one, then you'll have to come back later." She opened the door to the covered outdoor shelter.

There were rows of kennels. The dogs were barking, and some were whining about being let out. Sara wiped the top of her nose. "Poor thing," Sara said, puckering her lips at them.

"They don't come inside?" Colton wanted to know.

"They stay here during the night, it's warm enough, and I let them out in the morning."

Sara's heart dropped when he saw dogs squishing their noses to the grated metal door.

Colton went over to the black dog pushing on the door. "How's it going?" He put his hand up for the dog to smell it through the metal bars. The dog tried biting the cage and Colton pulled back his hand. "Maybe he's not as friendly."

"I'll leave you two for a moment. Let me know if you want any out of their cage."

"How about this one," Sara pointed to the yellow lab, laying its head between its paws.

Josie turned around. "That's Bella. She's friendly. Loves people. Got her in the other day." Josie pulled out her keys, looking through them to find the right one to open. "Here it is." She opened the lock and the dog ran at Sara almost knocking her off balance. Sara laughed and bent her knees to ruffle her hands through the dog's fur. "Awe, you're adorable," she told Bella. "Where's your toy?"

The dog went into her kennel and brought back a rubber ball.

"That's your special toy?" Sara giggled some more. Her heart doubled in size. She threw the ball into the kennel, and the dog came back with it drooling in her mouth.

Colton crouched beside Bella and petted her. "She's pretty."

"Looks like Bella has a new home," Josie said. "I hate to cut it short, but I have to go."

Sara got to her feet. Bella was wagging her tail, and the other dogs were barking.

"You can come back later if you want," Josie said.

Sara didn't think she was ready to bring a dog home, but having Colton by her side and getting some love from a dog gave her hope that one day she'd be completed.

COLTON WASN'T SURE why Sara brought him to the animal shelter when all he kept thinking about was Charles.

"Do you need to stop anywhere?" she asked, pulling out of the parking lot.

"Do you mind if we stop by to see my plane?"

"Yeah, sure. It's just up the road here," Sara said.

He looked out the window taking in the curved highway.

"This is where I saw you." Sara pointed to the spot up ahead. "When I noticed something was wrong."

Colton nodded, envisioning Sara's astonishment when she came across him descending. His stomach did a little flip, taking himself back to the moment when fear of the unknown started getting to him.

Sara parked along the road and got out. "There's a bit of steep slope," she said, leading the way.

"Shouldn't we tell the farmer we're in the field?"

"Dan won't mind," she said, struggling through the dirt toward the upside-down plane. It was on an angle, the wing to the earth with the remittance of fuel marking the airplane.

Colton slowed his steps as he came up to the Cesena. He walked around it, noting the

visible damage and the damage he couldn't see. Colton squatted under the propeller, looking for cracks and any parts missing. Stepping to the side, he touched the body of the plane and viewing the cracked window. Once he got it to a hanger, he'd be able to assess the damage more thoroughly.

"It's amazing you're alive," she said.

"It could have been worse." Colton held her stare. A cool breeze whipped around his neck as though a wakeup call to stop thinking about the softness of her eyes and the gentle tone of her voice. A sweet concoction he needed but couldn't have. Sara deserved someone stable and mentally stronger.

Colton brought his hand back to his hip and refocused his attention on the plane. A dark cloud moved over them. He looked up at the grey sky, but it felt like a sunny day when Sara was there with him.

"You're here," she said, giving him an encouraging smile. "Now I'm looking at this, I definitely couldn't fly in one of these."

"Not even with me?" He flashed her a smile and in return, she giggled.

"No offense, but I wouldn't go with anyone," she said wide-eyed. "You're an experienced pilot and look at what happened." Her face was all serious. "I mean, anything can happen. It's out of your control."

"Some things are." He touched her arm and her mouth closed, eyes darting to his. "An experienced pilot knows what to do in bad situations."

"There's a chance, though." She took a deep breath. "A chance you may not get out of and how scary is that?"

Rain pegged their heads and tapped on the metal like a xylophone.

"Most of the time, you do," he said gently. He could see fear of flying building in Sara's mind. "We can get out of here." He nudged her. "Before it pours."

She looked up to the sky.

"It's starting to." Colton grabbed Sara's hand and pulled her along, ducking under the raised wing. Falling into his arms, Colton did what came naturally: he wrapped his arm around her waist and tucked her into him as though he needed to protect her from harm.

"You know it could rain for the rest of the day and night?" She batted her eyes at him.

He loosened his grip not wanting to let go. "I guess we'll have to make a run back to your
car."

"I'm not sure running is a good thing for you right now."

"Then I'll get soaked."

"I wouldn't leave you." Her head tilted, lips parted.

Her words penetrated his mind. The flame in his chest burned. He wouldn't leave her either given the chance. The hardest thing was, he couldn't promise her anything more than a kiss. If she was looking for a relationship, she had the wrong guy.

"Tell me when you're ready," he said, staring into her eyes. "And we'll make a run for it."

The rain came down a little harder, hitting the plane with a rap-tap-tap.

"Not yet." She stared him down. "I'm not ready to get soaked." Her body shook as though cold.

He pressed his hands into her waist. "How long can you wait it out for?"

"As long as we need to." She raised her chin and slightly tilted her head.

Colton grinned. "I know what we can do to pass the time."

"Ya?" Her playful response sparked an electrical current running fierce through his veins. Sara's leg brushed up against his, she slapped her hand on his chest, the other on the base of his neck.

She looked at him with hopeful eyes. Pressing his fingers into her hips, he didn't give himself an option to opt out. He liked how Sara made him feel wanted and normal. Would she when the truth came out? Without contemplating, Colton brought her in and there was no turning back. He held the back of her head and brought his lips to hers, making the kiss last as long as he could without coming up for air.

Chapter Eighteen

The next morning, Sara flew through the kitchen, just missing Colton, standing in a white T-shirt against the counter, eating a bowl of cereal.

"I'm running late," she announced, grabbing a spoon, and shaking the granola out of the box.

Colton took out a mug and poured a cup of coffee, handing it to her with sensitive eyes.

"Thank you." She paused, taking her coffee from him. "Did you sleep well?" She set the mug down and took the milk out of the fridge.

"It was okay," he said, shoving a bite into his mouth.

Thank goodness, he was wearing a shirt; although he was distracting, it kept her mind from wandering off track. She had already showered and dressed in her usual work attire and flat ironed her hair. She might have added a little extra makeup and this time swapped a pair of studs for small hoops.

"I'm going to find a place to stay," he announced, taking another bite.

She took a seat at the table. "Oh yeah?" She shouldn't be disappointed. She knew the time was coming. His two-night stay had turned into four. She pushed her spoon into the bowl.

"It's time."

"I can help you find a place." She took a bite of her cereal, crunching and swallowing.

"I got it." Colton turned on his foot, putting his bowl in the sink and took a swig of coffee.

"Does that mean you're staying in Moonlight longer?"

"A few days longer," he said.

Would she see him again? It was hard to hide her disappointment. "Then what?"

"I leave," he said straight-faced. "Back to work."

Sara finished her breakfast not wanting to think she'd never see him again, but they both had their plans and it wasn't her right to make things difficult when she knew he had a job to go to and she was taking a trip.

"I'll be at work if you need anything." Sara dumped her bowl in the sink. She gave Colton one last look before leaving the house. There was a heaviness in her stomach as she drove away, leaving Colton to breakfast dishes he said he didn't mind doing. She couldn't get the image of the kiss out of her mind. Why wasn't she enough for a guy to take a chance on her? Would she ever settle down with someone? Sure, Colton was physically active, but mentally she wished she could crack him. It wouldn't do her any good though, Colton was on a different page than her and was probably not ready or willing to give her a chance.

In a few days, she got to know him, and she liked having him there, but their time had come to an end. She shouldn't be sad about it, but she would miss Colton. In just a short time she learned what it would be like to have someone in her life who cared.

Her stomach turned as she pulled in front of The Observer. She had been fighting her inner emotions about finding adventure, but it turns out the past week was more than she bargained.

"Oh! Sara!" Deloris jumped up from her desk. "You didn't mention we had an advice column."

"Oh. It's just a one-time thing."

"One time? We've got at least a dozen emails."

Sara's heart sank. "A dozen?" She held her breath.

"Who's Peaches? Do I know her?"

"Oh. Yeah, no." Sara's teeth went together. "She's a—" Sara swallowed. "Someone."

Deloris clutched her beaded blue necklace, holding a questionable gaze.

"No one you know."

"Who do I send these emails to? There's no contact info."

"Right. Sorry." Sara gritted her teeth. "It was only meant to be a...one time thing." She slid her hot hands together. "Send them to me."

"Ha." Deloris' eyebrows peaked. "By the looks of the emails, it won't be a one-time thing. People love this stuff."

Sara pulled on her strands. "Did you read them?"

"Two or three of them. Maybe four."

"Any good ones?"

"There's a lot of people in need of advice," Deloris said. "Next time tell me when something new happens around here. I had no idea how to respond. I emailed one guy back, telling him we don't have an advice column." Deloris' plump cheeks flushed. "I felt like a fool."

"I was filling space and didn't think anyone would read it," she soothed. "I couldn't have a blank space."

"You can use a picture."

"That's what I usually do, but I didn't have one and it was late."

"When Georgia finds out—"

"How will she know? She doesn't pay attention to the details." Sara's heartbeat faster. She could get fired for overstepping her bosses.

"You didn't ask?" Deloris' eyes sprung open. She gathered her beaded necklace in her palm.

Sara shook her head, biting her bottom lip. "I might have messed up," she whispered.

"Does Jerry know?"

"I'm not speaking to him unless a bomb goes off."

"Oh, it could go off when he finds out his paper has an advice column. You know him. Wants everything to look like it did thirty years ago."

Sara chuckled nervously because Deloris was only a few years younger than Jerry.

"It's small," she wavered. "Unnoticeable. Jerry's preoccupied with his mom. The paper is the last thing on his mind. He won't care about a concerned resident needing advice. I was helping."

The phone rang. Sara flinched.

Deloris looked up at her with a sharp eye. "You know how Jerry feels about change."

"Yes. Jerry wouldn't hire a temp and expects me to do everything."

Sara went straight to her desk and plunked herself down, relieving her locking knees. She turned on her computer and went to work. Colton flashed in her mind. If she stayed in

Moonlight, would he come to visit her? She stopped herself from thinking about Johnathan. Her online dating didn't excite her the way Colton did. Coming home to him gave her all the feels she had been wanting.

She wrapped her cardigan around her for comfort not warmth and edited Liam's story. Once saved, she scrolled through the mock-up for Thursday's paper and returned to editing and checked her work emails. There was a whole list of them forward from Deloris. By the time she scrolled through them, it was almost lunchtime. Where had the morning gone?

Sara chewed on her lip. It was ridiculous to think she could make a relationship work with a guy she hadn't even met. Was Johnathan the cure to her adventure because everything was fitting so perfectly? Until she met Colton, who challenged her heart and made her think about what mattered in her life. Was she throwing everything away for a chance to be with someone she truly cared about?

Maybe Colton wasn't ready for a relationship, but having his friendship was essential to her. He told her he didn't have anything to offer her. What did she need besides love? Sara opened the emails for the advice column. Her stomach sank. Okay, so people responded to Peaches. She could answer one more for and then end it. There was no use in creating a new email address. This column wouldn't last. Besides, she had enough to do. She read through some of the questions and concerns people had.

Help! My wife took my cat, and they're not coming back!

She giggled and opened the next one. *Can I date two guys at once?*

Sara laughed and scrolled to the next subject line. *I married the wrong man.*

"Can you imagine?" she whispered, leaning forward in her chair. Sara clicked on the email and read.

Dear Peaches,

I fell in love twenty-eight years ago with a married man. I married his friend, and since my husband has passed away, I began seeing my first love again. We have been seeing each other, but fearing ridicule and abandonment by our friends. Do we keep this a secret or tell our children? We don't want to lose the ones we love over it.

Sincerely,

Seeking courage

Sara breathed out, staring at the question. Poor lady. She's been in love with a man for so long, and finally, she can have him? Sara stared at the words, conjuring up her response. People shouldn't be upset by it. They love each other.

Sara created a folder for the column and pasted the question on a blank page and started to write.

Dear Seeking Courage,

You must be scared and worried you'll lose your children when they find out you've been in love with someone else. It's a lot to process, but it's also been a long time, and your children are adults now. They should understand you wouldn't do anything to hurt them. You deserve to be happy and to be loved. Tell them gently. Prepare them by telling them you are dating so they know you're not planning on being alone. Once they know you are open to having a relationship, they'll know you are ready to start again; then you can tell them who you love without
disrespecting their father.

Best of luck!

Peaches

Sara flexed her hands, and her stomach dipped with nervousness. She saved the document and shut off her computer.

"Hey, Sara," Liam marched over. "Since when do we print an advice column?"

"Since Sunday."

He slumped to his desk. "Is it weird, or what that the question asked was similar to mine?"

"I never thought about it." She wheeled her chair around to her computer to get back at it and to end the conversation.

"Good advice, though." He stopped and touched the top of his floppy black hair. "Are you okay?"

She spun her chair halfway to meet him. "I'm spending way too much time here. I need a day off too." Her chest knotted and she rubbed her hand over the spot. "I've been writing and editing, doing layout..."

Liam's lanky frame loosened. "You should have asked for help." He put a hand on his hip. "I can do page layout."

"But, can you do the layout for the sports section and page two?"

"Yeah, sure." He shrugged.

"Thanks. I would appreciate it." Sara swung back and forth in her chair. "How did it go with the teacher?"

"Good."

"Just good?"

"Great. She likes it here." He smiled. "She doesn't know if she got the job yet."

"Good luck to her." Sara grabbed her purse. "I gotta go." She stood up and pushed her chair in. "See you tomorrow."

Sara drove home and pulled into her driveway, turned off the ignition and hopped out, sprinting to the door. She pushed on the knob, but it was locked, and the lights were off. Did Colton go back to bed? She fumbled with her keys and stuck the right key into the lock and opened the door. "Colton? Are you home?" She slipped off her flats and raced around the house, opening her bedroom door. He wasn't there. She went back into the kitchen and flicked on the light. He wasn't home, but he left a note.

SARA,

There are a few things I need to do to set my mind straight. Please forgive me for not saying goodbye. Thank you for everything you've done. You're amazing. I'll see you soon.

Colton

Sara's stomach flip-flopped. Did he leave for good? Her eyes teared. But as she stood dumbfounded, she noticed his bag of clothes sat beside the couch. Why would he leave his belongings?

Bringing her hand to her forehead, she fought the urge to drive to find him. It would take him hours to walk to Omak. He could have texted her or called her. Maybe Colton didn't feel the same way about her as she did about him. She wiped the tears away. Maybe if she didn't work until the late afternoon, she could have helped him.

Her phone rang, and she stumbled for her purse to answer it.

"Hey, Sara. Did you forget?" Emily's voice caught her off guard.

"Forget about what?"

"Oh, you did. I told Kelly you'd forget." She took a breath. "We're at TJ's Tavern."

"Ah!" Sara smacked her forehead. "I forgot. Sorry."

"I got off work early, so no rush just wanted to remind you. We'll be here when you get here."

Sara hung up and cleaned herself up before heading out. At least hanging out with her

besties would take her mind off of Colton, work and Johnathan.

Sara's phone beeped when she parked her car and fumbled for her purse to read the text. She sighed when she saw it was her brother contacting her. Where was Colton? She couldn't call him or send a message because he made it clear he needed space.

Have you spoken to mom lately? She's acting strange.

Hi Evan! Strange? How?

She's all jumpy. I asked her how she is, and she said okay.
She doesn't look fine. She's wearing makeup. Think she's
dating someone?

I doubt it. Mom says she doesn't want to.

She told me the same thing, but I'm starting to wonder.

If she were sick, she'd tell us, wouldn't she?

Sara replied as she got out of her car. **I'd hope so. Don't worry. I'll call her later and see how she is.**

Let me know.

Oh, yeah. Sorry to hear about you and Jessica. I had no idea things weren't going well.

It's been rocky for a while. It's better this way.

Sara put her phone away and pulled on the pub's door. Her friends were sitting in their usual booth. "Hey," Sara said, shrugging off her coat and hanging it on the hook beside the booth.

"Hey, yourself," Kelly said. "Haven't seen you in so long."

Sara plunked herself down, sliding in beside Emily.

"You look a little...pale," Emily said. "Feeling okay?"

"I'm good. Sorry, I don't know why I forgot about tonight." Sara shook her head.

"I haven't spoken to you either," Emily said. "Since you took pictures of Mason at his dad's hockey game."

"It's been a while. Not intentionally."

"Everything okay?" Emily lowered her head.

"I've never been this busy. Honestly." Sara laid back into the booth to take a load off.

"Because Jerry is away?" Kelly asked.

"Yeah. Liam's got his head in the clouds. I'm writing, editing and—" she took a breath when she saw the waitress's shadow.

"Something to drink?" the waitress asked.

"House red would be great, thank you."

The waitress sauntered away. Sara put her elbows on the table. "I may have to cancel my trip."

"Nooo," Emily screeched. "Why? Cause you don't have anyone to cover for you?"

"Jerry doesn't want anyone taking my place and he might not be back in time."

"What if he's a day late and Liam works by himself?" Emily smiled through clutched teeth.

"It's a no-go." Sara shook her head.

"That sucks," Kelly said. "He can't do that. Can he?"

Sara squirmed. She hated lying to her best friends. It was hard enough lying to her mom about meeting Johnathan.

Kelly swirled her wine glass. "Since when did The Observer have an advice column?"

"Since Sunday." Sara tapped her hand on the table. Her muscles tensed. "We have already received around fifteen emails." She puffed out her chest.

"Who's this Peaches? Is she like a therapist?" Emily asked.

"She's not." To lie or not to lie? The advice column will only happen one more time or two more times if Jerry comes back by the weekend.

"Do you know her?" Kelly pressed.

"I do."

"Who is she?"

Sara fluttered her eyelashes. "Me."

"You?" Emily and Kelly yelled out in unison.

"You have to promise not to tell anyone, okay? Please!" Sara begged. "I don't want anyone to know."

"You're giving advice?" Kelly asked. "Since when?"

"I know," Sara sighed, feeling her cheeks warm. "I know. I was filling space. I've been writing and editing; I panicked when I couldn't fill the room I had, so I entertained myself. I didn't think it would result in anything." She slumped into the seat.

"So, Jerry doesn't know about it?" Emily asked.

Sara folded in her lips and held them tight. The waitress set down her glass of wine in front of her. Sara sat up and scooped the glass, taking a gulp.

"So, what are you going to do when Jerry finds out?" Emily asked.

She opened her palms. "I needed to fill space. I didn't think the column would cause so much attention. I hope he doesn't care." She knew he would, but to what degree, she didn't know, and it worried her. "How's business?" She directed her question to Emily.

"The winery is finally running smoothly. I don't want to jinx it. Mason will be here next month for two days," she said giddily.

"He's coming all this way for two days?" Sara shrieked.

Emily's cheeks brightened. "I miss him."

"And he misses you." Sara batted her eyes what she would give to have a guy love her the way Mason loved Emily.

"We've set a wedding date. Tentatively," Emily said, her shoulders moving up and down.

"Really?" Sara smiled. "When?"

"Probably July. After playoffs. So don't plan any vacation next July."

"Exciting!" Sara brought her glass to her lips. Her muscles relaxed, and she eased her back into the booth. "Thanks for the heads up."

"And Kelly said she'd help plan it, right, Kel?"

"My first wedding," she said coolly.

"You'll do great," Sara said. "If you need an assistant..."

"Plan on it," Emily said, eyeing them both. "Cause you both will be bridesmaids." Emily's eyes lit up as she took a drink. "Good thing you're going away now. I won't have to worry about coordinating dates."

"Oh, by the way," Sara said to Kelly. "Brad was asking about you. He says hi."

Kelly nodded, lips pursed. "What's the scoop on you two?" Emily asked. "Are you two back together?"

"We're talking, but nothing more."

"You've got to be kidding. How is that possible?"

"It is," Kelly reassured, taking hold of her glass.

"What's it going to take to put the past behind and get on with the future?" Sara asked.

"It's probably not going to happen," she said matter-of-factly.

"What? How?"

"I gave him a chance, and the ball is in his court now. It's up to him." Kelly shrugged.

"So what? You're waiting to see what he does?"

"I'm not waiting, but I'm not looking either. With my job and launching my business, I don't have the energy to be looking for someone." Kelly took a sip from her iced drink. "Did Brad help you out the other day?"

"Oh, you mean talk to Colton?" Sara asked.

"Who's Colton?" Emily shook her head, darting eyes from Kelly to Sara.

"The pilot." Sara felt her cheeks warm. "I took care of him. Brad was busy."

"So, he's not some crazy guy?" Kelly said, running her hand along with the table.

"Not at all." Sara took a sip. "He's adorable." She bit her lip, knowing she probably said the wrong thing because, without a beat, Kelly was quick to call her on it.

"You're seeing him now?"

"No," Sara said, wishing for a different answer.

"How are you helping him?"

"Oh, well, you know, lending him my couch for a few nights."

"And you never told us? What?" Kelly's eyes bugged out. "Tell me more. So this pilot is staying with you?"

"I know it sounds ridiculous and probably not the best decision I've made." She closed her eyes briefly and inhaled. She couldn't mention Johnathan at all. "I'm helping a civilian."

"Yeah, you are!" Kelly blurted out.

"How old is this pilot?" Emily asked.

"Our age," Sara answered.

"Good looking?"

"He's adorable, remember?" Kelly said, arching an eyebrow at Emily.

"Yeah, he is." Sara's heart began to beat a little faster.

"Single?"

"Yes, but don't get any ideas. He's not interested in me."

"Are you kidding?" Emily pushed her head back.

"He's not staying here permanently. He's from Bellingham, and besides, I'm leaving for a trip. I don't want to get involved with anyone right now."

"If you go," Kelly said.

"I don't believe you," Emily shot back, narrowing her eyes. "This Colton guy is bunking at your house for free?"

Sara's squeezed the stem of her glass between her fingers. "I don't want anything. I just want to help. My dad would be proud."

Kelly lowered her eyes. "Your dad would have had Colton at his house. Not yours."

Emily leaned into the table. "Are you guys like...together?"

"No. No." Sara shook her head. But the kiss? What did it mean? "We're not—" Her tongue tied.

"Where is he now?" Kelly's one eyebrow lifted.

Sara's stomach tightened. "I don't know." She wished she did. "He left his belongings with a note and told me he had to clear his head, and he'd see me soon."

"He obviously likes you," Emily stated.

"Oh, ya," Kelly added. "Clear his head? You are his unexpected. You've given him something to think about."

Sara laughed. "I doubt it."

"When did he leave?" Kelly asked.

"What is this?" Sara said laughing. "I saw him this morning. We had coffee and I was running late to work. I haven't seen him since."

Both women sucked in a breath.

"This morning?" Kelly said, grinning and staring all serious. "Good for you."

"Good for me? No. If you knew what I was up against, you'd have a different view."

"Would I?" Kelly asked. "Try me." She pushed herself back against the booth.

"Another time." Sara looked away and then back at Kelly. "Why are you looking at me like that? Nothing is going on."

"Okay." Kelly gave a stern look.

"You don't believe me."

"I have to believe you."

"Maybe when I get back...from my trip, things will be different." Would they? Sara questioned herself.

"You're leaving on a two-week trip, and when you get back, he'll be gone," Kelly said.

"Then, it's not meant to be." Sara's stomach clenched.

"You can't roll the dice." Kelly flicked her hand. "You could miss your chance."

"What chance?"

"An opportunity to be with someone." Kelly pulled on her dyed red strands. "You complain there's nobody here for you and a guy falls from the sky—good looking you say, and you're not even interested? I don't get it. Something else is going on."

Sara breathed out.

"No pressure," Kelly said, smoothing her lips. "Is he your secret admirer?"

"How did you know about that?" Sara had forgotten Johnathan had stopped sending her gifts. Was he feeling the distance too and losing interest like she was?

"Doesn't matter," Kelly said. "Spill it." She waved her on. "I want to know who it is."

"I haven't had anything delivered in over a week," Sara said. "It stopped."

"Weird," Kelly said, pruning her face.

"No card?" Emily asked.

"No. He's over me." Sara laughed and pulled up her shoulders.

"Now, we know why you seemed preoccupied." Kelly brought her glass to her mouth.

"Why?"

"Look what's going on in your life? Even I can't keep up."

Chapter Nineteen

Colton hated crowds and being around lots of people tested his anxiety and the only way to conquer his fear of the unexpected was to get out of the house. He never used to be so cautious. There was a time when he used to party and challenge a drinking game. Now he was happy being by himself.

His counselor told him to take baby steps. Get out of the house every day, even if it was for a walk. Say hello to a passing stranger. Anything to break the mold, so he spent most of his day hanging out at Homeward Bound Animal Shelter while Sara was at work. Josie was kind enough to trust him to take dogs for a walk. It was what Colton needed. There was no threat of

conversation when he was with animals. He didn't worry about how he was perceived or worry who liked him. A dog loved attention, so it was a win-win.

Colton walked inside, holding a dog by the leash on either side of him.

"You've been out all day," Josie said.

"Sorry."

"I appreciate your time, but I can't pay you."

"I'm not looking for a paycheck."

She shoved her hands into her jean pockets. "If you need a job, Tucks Automotive and Car Detailing is looking for someone. You might even want to try the community center. They're looking for fitness people." She stopped sweeping the floor and eyed him sternly.

"I'm not qualified," Colton said.

She swept the dirt into a pile and scooped it up with a hand broom. She emptied the pan into the garbage pail and left the brush beside it.

"I'm going to go."

Josie reached out and took the leashes. "Come back anytime."

Colton walked out the door. He needed to think about his options for staying in Moonlight Valley without getting Sara involved. It was an excellent place to be and close enough to Omak airport. Tomorrow he would make his way there and deliver the envelope.

Colton fought the urge to find a place to shoot some pool. He had time to kill before going back to Sara's house and collect his things. He hobbled into town, focusing on where he was going, and the only place he remembered was TJ's Tavern. Colton couldn't go wrong with a Monday evening. He wouldn't have to worry about being social and wouldn't have to fight a crowd. He may even eat there.

Colton entered the dim-lit pub. Country music played over the speaker. He looked straight ahead to the back of the room where the pool tables would be, and sure enough, there were two, side by side, with a couple of guys using them.

He turned on his foot and headed to the bar, trying to hide his limp. At least he'd get himself a drink while he waited for a turn.

Colton sat down on the barstool, put his hands down on the counter.

"What can I get you?" the bartender asked. "I've got draft beer on special tonight."

"A soda water with lemon or lime would be great," Colton answered.

"You visiting?" The bartender flicked a couple of wedges into his iced cup and filled it with a press of a button.

Colton nodded.

"You look familiar." He set down the cup, and Colton scooped it up and took a long drink.

"I get it a lot." He placed his cup down and spun around on his stool, watching the game finish up.

"Hey, Colton," a voice said.

Was he hearing things now?

"Colton." Click-clack of boots were pacing toward him. He heard his name again, this time, closer. He picked up his cup and looked over his shoulder.

"Sara," he said. His heart quickened. He put down his cup and stood up, wiping his hand on his new pair of jeans.

"If you told me you were coming here tonight, we could have come together." Her smile faded and she touched his arm. "Are you okay?"

"Fine. Yeah." He took a sip of his drink and she took her hand back. Why did he have to come across edgy?

"Do you want to join us? I'm here with some friends."

"I don't want to intrude." He didn't feel like being social.

"Come on. You're not. I want to introduce to you." She grabbed his hand and he snatched his glass from behind him, taking extra steps to keep up with her. She led him to a booth and dropped her hand from his. He squeezed her hand. "Colton, this is Kelly and Emily," she said pointing. "This is Colton." She rocked on her heels and smiled as though giddy.

"Sara's told us a little bit about you," Kelly said.

"She has?" Colton cleared his throat.

"So, you're a pilot. You're with the Air Force," Kelly said.

He swallowed. "I took a short flight to Omak but landed here instead." He kept a straight face.

"Looks like you landed the best person," Kelly said. "But let me put it out there. You screw her around, and you screw with us."

"Yes." Colton nodded. "She's safe."

"Figured so. Military man." Kelly lifted her glass, smiling and took a drink.

"Okay, that was awkward," Sara said, grabbing for her drink.

"Is this what you ladies do on a Monday night? Hang out here?" He took a drink to wet his throat.

"Sometimes," Emily said. "It was the only day we could all meet up."

"We're saying goodbye before she leaves on her trip."

"What trip?" His stomach fell. He forgot about her trip, and she hadn't mentioned it since he was in the hospital.

"The one I told you about. I'm headed to Australia to stay with my cousin for two weeks. It was supposed to be Thursday."

"Of this week?" Colton tipped his half-empty glass back and forth. Had he been drinking alcohol he'd have asked for another right about now, but he wasn't planning on it. He wanted to get mentally strong again and not depend on anything to soothe his mind. It was easy to self-medicate or rely on prescription drugs to ease the pain, but Colton was determined to fight through it.

"Yeah."

"Are you packed?" He hadn't seen a suitcase and she hadn't escaped to her bedroom in the middle of a movie. He was getting to know Sara just by hanging out with her.

"Not yet."

"Why don't you sit down?" Sara asked him, taking a seat beside Emily.

Colton took a step back. "I shouldn't stay."

Sara reached for him and tapped his arm. "You're not intruding," she reassured. He could sit for a minute or two and then he could go play a game of pool as planned.

"You're not interfering," Kelly said. "Not at all. We're here cause it gets us out of the house. Change of scenery."

Colton sat down beside Kelly, across from Sara. "I guess there's not much happening on a Monday night."

"Unless you belong to the chess club over at Discovery Hall or are part of the knitting club at the Baptist church," Emily said.

The women gushed in laughter.

"Where do we belong?" Kelly asked, raising a shoulder.

"We'll have to make our club," Sara said, taking a sip of her wine. She caught Colton looking at her and surprisingly didn't shy away. She held his stare, warming his chest. His fingers slipped down his glass.

"And what would it be?" Kelly's red lips as she took a sip from her glass.

"Women who travel," Sara said. "We can plan our next vacation."

"Colton can fly us," Emily added.

Colton tapped his foot, his elbows wide, he lifted his glass to his mouth.

"He doesn't fly commercial," Sara said. "But it depends where we're going. His plane, the broken one, I would never in my life get into it. First of all, if it were a car, it would have been a total write-off."

Colton crunched on an ice cube, enjoying Sara's reasoning.

"It only has two seats," Sara went on. "Which I can only imagine would feel claustrophobic."

Colton swallowed and chuckled, sliding his back up the booth.

"Am I right?" Sara asked him playfully. She tilted her head to get his attention. "He won't even admit it," she teased and he held her gaze.

"I'll get it fixed," he said with a loose grin.

"Fix it. It needs a lot of fixing, and I'm not brave enough to get into a tin can and risk my life."

"I had a safe landing," he said coolly.

"You had a concussion and a sprained foot."

"It's healed."

"Getting there," she argued. "You're lucky to be alive."

"Okay, you two," Kelly interrupted, leaning over the table with her hand spread out to get their attention.

Sara smiled and blinked at her friend. "It's amazing he's here. Seriously." She glanced at him and then Kelly. An electric current radiated over his skin. If he could take Sara into his arms again he might not let go. Her touch, her kiss...he craved more of her. If only things were different. With him.

"Tell me the truth," Kelly lowered her head, eyes darted at Colton. "Are you afraid to fly now? I would be. I'd take it as a warning." Her eyes flashed.

"Na." His lips parted. "Planes are still safer than driving."

"He's flown bomber planes and jets," Sara boosted. "This was nothing for him."

"Yeah, well." He shrugged it off. He took his glass and drank the rest of it. The iced cubes clanged as he tried to slide one into his mouth.

Sara twisted her body. "What made you stop here?"

"I was going to play some pool. Do you play?" Colton scratched the side of his head.

"I don't, but I can learn." Her eyebrows peaked.

"Okay. Let's go." Colton stepped out of the booth. "Maybe those guys are almost done."

"I'll be back," Sara told her friends as she walked away.

"The tables are being occupied. I guess we can wait," Colton said.

"Hey," Sara said to the two guys playing. "Are you guys playing another round after this one?"

"We were going to do one more. You want to play teams?" the one guy asked.

"Ah, I don't think—"

"Sure," Colton called out. "We'll play teams." Nothing like getting out of his comfort zone.

"Can't play for money," the one guy with a shaggy beard said. "I just spent my last dollar."

"Just want to play a game, no bets." Colton threw his hand down.

"Alright. Cool." The guy took a shot and cleaned up the table.

Colton grabbed a pool stick from the wall and handed it to Sara, then took one for himself.

When the guy racked the balls, he threw the triangle underneath and asked, "solids or stripes?"

"Solids," Colton said and looked at Sara.

"Doesn't matter," she said and shrugged.

"You start," the bearded guy said.

Colton eyed Sara. "You break. Have you done this before?"

"I have." She smiled and broke the triangle, dunking a solid.

"Hey, way to go," Colton said. "You didn't tell me you're a pro."

"I'm not." She laughed.

He watched the game unfold and thought of strategies to win, but it wasn't about the game. He could care less if he won, it was spending time with Sara which had him thinking of what he was missing. He couldn't have her, but damn, did he want her. Naked. In his arms. He wanted the chance to kiss her again and feel her body against his, but was afraid if he did, she might not be so giving. They were both going their own ways. She had a trip planned and he had to pretend he was going back to work. A relationship wouldn't work.

"You're up." The guy flicked his chin at Colton.

Colton blinked, snapping out of his thought and positioned his cue stick. He took a shot. It wasn't good enough to win because the other guy took a shot and cleaned up the table.

"Good game," Colton said.

"Yeah, thanks," the guys said and walked away.

Sara pressed her heels down; her stick clutched under her arm; she had one hand on the table. "You didn't tell me you were good."

"I'm not." Colton's forehead tensed. "I play for fun."

"Yeah, me too."

"Hey Sara," Kelly said with Emily meeting Sara in the middle.

"We're going." Kelly handed Sara her purse. "Work tomorrow," she said with an eye roll.

"Yeah, me too," Sara said. "Talk to you later."

"We'll see you before you leave," Emily said and threw her arms around Sara for a hug.

"Nice to meet you, Colton." Kelly waved and leaned into Sara, "I popped something into your purse. Just in case." She leaned back and winked.

Her friends walked away, and Sara turned to Colton. "I should probably think about going home," Sara said with a pouty bottom lip. "I don't want to think about work. I have to get there a bit earlier tomorrow." She pursed her lips. "I don't want to."

"We can go," he said. Either one of them moved. The light in Sara's eyes zapped him with temptation. "It's getting late anyway," he whispered. He reached for her cue stick, so he could hang it up for her. Colton touched her hand, his heart thundered. He might regret it tomorrow but tasting Sara again would be worth the self-punishment. He'd hate himself for even trying when he knew he couldn't make anything out of his attraction for her.

Colton closed the gap between them and lowered his lips to hers. She kissed him back, and if it weren't for being in a public place, he would have taken her into his arms and see where it would lead, but he was self-conscious and worried about causing attention, even though there were only a handful of people there minding their own business.

"Need to go home," she said, breaking away. She turned on her foot and looked over her shoulder. "Are you coming?"

Colton hung up the cues and followed her. For once, he didn't want to be alone.

Chapter Twenty

Colton got out of Sara's car and followed her into her house, locking the door behind him.

He wrestled with his hands. Why was he so afraid of losing what he didn't have?

"What's wrong?" she asked, searching for his eyes.

How could he tell her she should stay away from him because she was better off without him?

"I am." He was positive he was, but it didn't make trying to move on any more
comfortable.

"Then kiss me."

He must have stared at her for a moment too long, because she didn't wait for him to make the first move. Her lips found his, taking his breath away, he kissed her back. The long sweep of her tongue caused some sort of explosion within him. He kissed her harder, pulling her into him, she threw her arms over his shoulders, loving how her hands found a place on him like he was keeping her safe.

Sara took a couple of steps backward, breaking away, but still holding on. He touched her cheek, and she stopped moving, her eyes searched his. Colton slid his hand over her ear to the back of her head; his fingers threaded her strands.

Moving toward the wall, Colton pinned her with his leg between hers. He kissed her with hunger, pushing his hand against her hip, he slid his hand under her shirt to feel warm, silky skin. She shuttered, tilting her head back, he drew his tongue down her neck and toward her earlobe. Her hands on his shoulders, fingertips pressing into his muscle, a moan escaped from her, escalating his desire. Holding back would be torture, but he needed to know how far Sara wanted to go.

"Tell me to stop," he whispered, praying she wouldn't. "Say it and I will." He breathed on her neck, but couldn't break away, she tasted so good, and his mind was blanking out except for the passion he was feeling. The need she was creating. A want he desperately craved for so long, but with Sara it all felt right. A part of him wanted her to change her mind so he didn't have to revisit these built-up feelings he had for her.

"Don't stop," she said, kissing him back. Her hands sliding over his shoulders, bringing her closer.

Every muscle in his body seized with an affirmation. He wanted this. He wanted Sara. Kissing her long and hard, triggered his body into feeling a deeper need. His jeans tighter, he gave her a gentle squeeze against his thigh. Colton's hand climbed under her shirt, his other on her hip to anchor him. Her arms fell in, hands to his chest, her lips on his. Heart racing, he wanted to take it slow, but Sara was moving just as fast as his mind could take him. Her hands ran over every cut of his abs, moving slowing upward to his pecs. His insides vibrated with excitement, but he proceeded with caution. He had to take it slow, but he wasn't sure he could.

Colton slipped his hands under her shirt, feeling up to cup her breast, lifting her shirt so he could taste her delicate skin. He trailed kisses around her bra and she closed her eyes, kissing him harder. Her hand played with his T-shirt, bunching it up to his chest, tugging to lift it off him. The turn-on too great to think twice about regret, Colton tore off his shirt and tossed it behind him, covering his hands on her back, her leg rubbed against his. Friction inside his jeans grew with an intense pulse. She kissed him, her tongue touching the corner of his mouth, and he lunged into a deeper kiss — hands in her hair, his palm against her hot cheek. His body stiffened, and he shuffled his socked feet on the carpet.

Parting his lips from hers, he trailed kisses along her jaw, to her earlobe and down to her neck. She let out a soft moan, sending his heart galloping. He wanted to satisfy her and make her his for one night because it was all he could commit to. He pulled at her shirt and lifted it up her to her shoulders. Sara took hold of the shirt and threw if over her head. Her hands against his neck, her fingers sliced through his hair, making the tiny hairs on his neck stand on end, he traced his tongue over her lips.

"Tell me you want this," he said. "If I'm going to stop—" He caught a breath. "Now would be the time."

"I want you." she said, breaking away, their noses touching." I want this."

He exhaled, breathing into her neck.

Her body slid against the wall, pulling them apart. With a daring look, she whispered, "Bedroom."

Each step down the hall was clumsy as they kissed and touched each other like they hadn't done something crazy as this before. When they got to her bedroom, Colton slowed down, kissing her as he unbuttoned her jeans, not missing a beat. Every kiss, he used his other hand to slide them off until they were stuck on her thighs. She broke away and fell back onto the bed. Colton pulled them over her heels, leaving them on the floor.

They locked eyes and Colton's chest filled realizing he were about to make love to a woman he had feelings for. She gave a wavering smile and lay down beside her. How could a connection with someone new be this strong? His hand rested on her high cut panties, his finger pushed through the band, rolling it over, and he leaned in to kiss her soft flesh. She moaned and played with his hair as he gently slipped off her panties and crawled beside her to feel the warmth of her skin. With her hands on his chest, he looped his arm around her to bring her closer. She swept a strand away from his forehead and looked into her dreamy-state eyes. There were no words. Her actions said it all. She liked him and although he wanted to push her away because she deserved better, he selfishly held onto the time he had with Sara. There would be

nobody like her who made him feel worthy and accepting.

Colton pushed himself up against her body, kissing her, he swiped his thumb against her cheek, admiring her beauty and passion for wanting this as much as him. Her hands slid over his arms, and she tucked them into the back of his unbuttoned jeans, sliding them off with one push at a time until he was able to wiggle them to the floor. Sara was proving she was just as eager as him, putting his mind at ease and letting him know it was okay.

Colton smoothed his hot hand over her body, kissing her shoulder blade and down to the fullness of her breast. His erection pulsing, he slid her bra strap over her shoulder and kissed her while unhooking the clasp.

"I have a condom," she said, wiggling away from him. She jumped out of bed, grabbed the throw blanket from the armchair, and wrapped it around her as she ran down the hall.

He held his breath, not wanting to lose the momentum. Like superwoman, holding her cape, she dashed toward him and slapped a condom package on his chest. He sighed with relief. He didn't have one and didn't carry one because he wasn't expecting an affair.

Colton took off his boxers. Sara watching him which sent a flurry to his gut, he rolled the condom on himself and moved up on the bed, clamping his hands around her waist to lift her on top of him. At the same time, she unraveled the blanket, revealing her perky breasts and narrow waist. He deepened the kiss as he squared her body with his.

The heat between them ignited, and the fire started.

He wasn't testing himself anymore; he was beginning to know his boundaries for getting through life while torturing himself in the process.

Chapter Twenty-One

Sara scrambled out of bed to shut off her alarm clock. Plopping her head back down on her pillow to let her heart return to a normal rhythm.

"Good morning," Colton said, his lip curling, he rolled his head toward her, with unruly hair and eyes half open.

"Morning. Sorry," she said with a pout. "I didn't mean to wake you. I have to get ready for work. Feel free to sleep." She moved to the edge of the bed, and Colton put his hand on her arm.

She looked over her shoulder.

"I'll make you breakfast while you shower," he said, dropping his hand.

"Really?" Her heart swelled. "I was just going to have a piece of toast."

"I got this. You do what you have to do." Colton flipped the blanket up, got out of bed wearing his boxers, and slipped on his jeans. Sara rubbed her lips together as she watched Colton bare-chested walk out of her bedroom, making her hungry for more than just breakfast. If she didn't have to be at work, she could think of other things she'd rather be doing, and staying in bed for a couple more hours in Colton's arms was one of them.

Sara wrapped herself in a robe and made her way to the bathroom. How could she be in love with a man she had known for less than a week and also have the idea of dating a man she met online? Although Johnathan was a second thought now, she needed to sort herself out.

Sara showered and dressed. She headed into the kitchen, and Colton handed her a cup of coffee.

"Oh, nice. Thank you," Sara cooed. Since when did she wake up to breakfast made and coffee poured for her?

Colton, wearing his T-shirt from last night, flipped eggs in a pan.

"Can I help you with something?" She stood in the kitchen, watching him comfortably moving around. He opened a cupboard and took out two plates. "I'm good. How do you like your eggs?"

"Doesn't matter." She shook her head, lips pursed. "However you are making them."

He had his back to her. His T-shirt stretched across his shoulders, and his jeans hugged his butt. She licked her lips. "What are you doing today?" They hadn't talked about the next couple of days. Would he be looking for his own place? Colton was hard to read, and he wasn't one for sharing voluntary information. She wanted him to tell her on his terms, but she wasn't sure how much longer she could go without knowing his plans.

"I've got a few things to do," he said, buttering the toast. He plated the food and spun around, offering breakfast.

She eyed it and smiled. "Thank you." She carried her plate in one hand and coffee in the other toward the table.

"How about for you?" he asked and scooped his eggs onto a plate.

"I have stories to write." She brought her cup to her mouth. "Do you think you'll, um, stay in Moonlight?" She wrinkled her nose. She was never afraid to ask questions, so why was it hard for her to ask him his plans?

"Soon." He glanced at her and took his snatched the toast from the toaster. "You haven't mentioned when you're leaving on your trip. It's coming up, isn't it?"

Her shoulders caved. "I'm supposed to be leaving Thursday if Jerry came back in time. My boss." She cut into her egg and took a bite.

"You're going to Australia for two weeks, is that it?" Colton brought his plate to the table, sat down, and forked a bite. "You don't seem excited about it."

"That's right." She took a bite of her toast. "There's a lot going on and I might not be able to go, so..."

"What's in Australia? Why do you want to go there?" he asked between bites.

"My cousin lives there." She washed down her bite with a sip of coffee. "I'm staying with him."

"Your cousin?"

She nodded and scooped another bite.

"It's not an ex-boyfriend?"

Would it matter if it was? She grinned, making eye contact with him. "Nope. I've been saving all year for this trip. It's a place I've wanted to visit and he invited me." She flattened her lips. "My cousin is a geoscientist and teaches at the university. It seemed like the perfect opportunity to go, so I booked my flight." She watched him slow down his bite, nodding, thinking. "You're going to be going back to Texas."

"Yeah. I'll be leaving soon too." He brought up his head to meet her eyes.

What would it take to crack him? What was he afraid of by not telling her his plan? He had to have a plan. Avoiding making eye contact, she scraped her fork against her plate to scoop up the last bite of egg. "What are you doing today?"

"I'm going to figure out what needs repairing on my plane."

Sara looked over at the clock on the stove. "Oh, no! I didn't notice the time." She jumped up. "I'm sorry. I have to go. Thank you for breakfast. We'll chat later."

Colton jumped up, meeting her in the middle. He held out his hand to touch her arm. "I'll see you later? Maybe tonight?"

"Yeah, sure." She ran out of the kitchen and gathered her bag and coat, struggling to put it on. Colton pulled out her coat sleeve to help her and she pushed her arm through and at the same time, slipped her feet into her thick heels and stomped her feet in her shoe as she flipped her hair out of her coat. Grabbing her bag with her wallet and notebook inside, she jangled her keys from her pocket. "Thanks."

As she turned around, the sparkle in his eyes sent an avalanche to her stomach. Colton was here because he had something to accomplish. It wasn't about her. What they shared last night didn't matter. It was only an affair and wouldn't amount to anything more because she wasn't what he wanted, and she had a trip pending and he had his life to go back to.

SARA GOT TO WORK ON time and clicked off her document she was working on and opened her emails.

Liam came by her desk, cupping his hand through his flopping, dark hair. "I'm doing the page layout. Where do you want the advice column?"

She tore her eyes away from the screen and put her teeth together. "Page four?"

"Put it anywhere on the page?" Liam held his hand behind his bent neck.

"Wherever you think," she said. It would be the last one to print before Jerry came back anyway.

"Do you have one ready to go? Deloris said there's like twenty emails. We don't even get a lot of response from Letters to the Editor." Liam shuffled his feet toward her desk. "When I was at the rink on Sunday, someone came up to me and asked if I knew who Peaches was." He stared. "So, who is Peaches?"

"Oh, someone I know who gives good advice." Her stomach flip-flopped.

Liam flexed his shoulders. "I haven't seen this much interest in our paper since Thomas Wallace ran for mayor."

She held her stomach. What if people didn't like what Peaches had to say? Would Jerry fire her for overstepping her boundaries?

Her cell phone rang, and she leaned over to grab it, and Liam turned on his foot and sauntered back to his desk. Sara brought her phone to her ear. "Hey, Kel."

"Sara. I got a favor to ask you. I know you're getting ready to go on your trip, but are you busy after work?"

"Not too busy." She didn't know if she was going and she hadn't packed. She was losing Colton for good. "What's up?"

"Can I ask you to take a couple of photos of me? Maybe two? Three max? My website's ready to go, but I need a photo of myself, and I only have goofy ones, nothing serious. Ugh. I'm cringing thinking about it."

"Sure. I can do it. I'll be home by five."

"Is the pilot going to be there?"

"His name is Colton." She laughed. "And I don't know."

"What do you mean? Didn't he stay the night?" She sounded disappointed.

"I mean he is. Yes, I'm sure he will be."

"You slept with him, and now you're having second thoughts."

"Kel," Sara snapped. "I'd love to chat, but I'm at work."

"Talk about an instant husband," Kelly mocked.

"It's not like that."

"I can't wait to hear all about it," she sang and hung up.

Sara butted her lips. She liked coming home to a man, but she wanted whoever she was with to feel the same way she did.

Chapter Twenty-Two

Colton took the mountain bike from Sara's shed. It was the only thing he could think of using to get twenty miles to Omak without asking anyone for a ride. Ignoring the ache in his left foot, Colton peddled harder so he could get into the next town before noon. Grey clouds moved

overhead, and he maxed out on the speed his legs would take him down the highway.

He saw the Omak Airport sign first, but it was Denise's house he was looking for. He needed to get it over with because the anticipation had been built up for months. He rehearsed how he would tell her why and explain why he had the envelope. He would apologize for taking so long to get it to her, but he had to see her in person. Give her his condolences and plead his innocence.

Colton's thighs burned, reminding him he needed to push himself to full capacity if he wanted to be healthy. Being physically and mentally fit wasn't an option when he was in the Air Force, he wouldn't allow himself to be anything else. After Owen's death was around the same time, his divorce papers went through, his life fell apart, and he didn't know how to fix it without asking anyone for help. Not like anyone could fix it for him, but he'd lost his friends, his wife, his dog, and himself, and he may even lose Sara.

Colton kept his eyes on the road. He past the welcome sign and entered green sporting fields and a Dunk & Donuts. He slowed down. Leg muscles twinged, but he arrived. Pulling into the parking lot of a gas station to check Google Maps, he'd be at his destination in twenty-five minutes.

Colton took out a protein bar he bought earlier, took a big bite, and opened bottled water he had placed in the holder. He drank and ate while vehicles passed him, and airbrakes from semi-trucks thundered. Colton took a long drink and put the lid back on his bottle, placing it into the holder. He had to keep going.

With wobbly legs and an achy foot, he peddled and listened to Google Maps give him directions, taking him into town and through a residential neighborhood. He slowed down, reading the address numbers. The houses lined both sides with few cars parking on the street. He was taking a chance if Denise was home. He didn't know if she worked but followed his heart and his mind to a bungalow similar to Sara's. Colton checked the address on his screen and looked at the house. His eyes fell from the house to his phone, making sure there wasn't a mistake because he didn't have another address.

Reviewing the house address one last time, he got off his bike and walked it up the driveway and lay it against the beam, which held up the front awning. His stomach squeezed. He flexed his hands and put his hand inside his coat pocket, pinching the envelope. He took a breath, releasing his hand to his sides and knocked. He stepped back on his trembling legs, and his chest flared from expanded lungs. Would she recognize him? Would she know who he was?

He tapped on the door and took a step back and waited. There was a child's high-pitched voice on the verge of crying coming from inside. He knocked again.

"Mommy, door," the toddler said, just as the door opened, and the boy peeked his head around his mom's leg.

"Hello," Denise said, tilting her head. Her eyebrows narrowed and then relaxed. "Colton?" She froze. "Colton?" She covered her mouth. "You're here? What's going on? Come in!" She extended her arm and touched his hand.

Colton smiled and bowed and stepped inside.

"I can't believe it." She shook her head and threw her arms out, embracing him in a long hug. Colton clamped his eyes shut, not wanting to cry too, but tears began to form, and he fought to make them fall.

Denise brought her hands back. "You look great. How are you?" She searched for his eyes.

"Good." Colton rocked on his feet.

"What are you doing here? I mean, here? Sorry." She swiped her hair out of her face. "It's good to see you."

"I should have called."

"Mommy." The toddler tugged on her jogging pants. "Mommy."

"Your timing is perfect," she said and bent down to scoop up her son. She brought him to her hip. "It's Uncle Colton," she said, smiling at her son and patting his belly.

Colton's stomach squeezed like ringing out a wet cloth. He wasn't an uncle, but he accepted the reference.

"Owen would tell Riley you're an uncle." She smiled at her son. "Do you want something cold to drink? I have apple juice, water? You look hot. Tell me you didn't ride from Bellingham." Her eyes brightened. "You didn't, did you?"

"No. No, Moonlight Valley." Colton rubbed the sweat from his forehead. "A water would be great, thank you."

"So, what brings you to Omak?" She put her son down, and he wiggled to his scattered toys on the living room carpet. "I wasn't expecting company." She looked around and patted her shirt. "It's a mess in here."

Colton lay out his hand, shaking his head. He didn't even notice. "I should have called, but I didn't know when I'd be able to visit." He spoke slowly and glanced at the little boy with bright eyes like his dad.

Denise disappeared into the kitchen. "It's a hard day today."

"Of course," Colton said, following her. "Anniversary." He couldn't even say a full sentence. The word caught in his throat. "I'm sorry." He touched his mouth.

"Yeah," she sighed and handed him a tall glass of ice water.

He guzzled it down and put the empty glass on the counter. "I guess I was thirsty."

She took the glass. "I'll get you another."

"Thanks. How have you been?" Colton asked.

"I'm okay. I take it day by day."

Colton's heart crushed for a young family torn apart. "The reason I came to see you is...I have something to give you." He pulled out the envelope from the inside of his coat.

She walked at a turtle's pace, holding the refill, and eyeing the envelope. "What is it?" There was a flicker in her eyes.

"I don't know," he whispered. "It's from Owen."

"From Owen?" Her mouth dropped, and she brought down the glass. She hadn't notice it was slipping through her hand.

Colton leaped forward and took the glass from her before it fell. "Yeah. We had this, um, this deal." His stomach turned. It was a thoughtful conversation when he had it with Owen, but now, talking to his wife made him feel displaced. Colton flexed his jaw. "He and I...we sealed an envelope with..." He paused. "I don't know what it is. I'm guessing a letter. He gave me this to give to you in case anything happened to him." The words stuck in his throat, and Colton paused again, pulling in whatever strength he could to tell her what he knew. "I promised Owen I'd give it to you if anything happened." His voice faded. "He told me when your anniversary was, and I haven't forgotten." The side of his mouth twitched. "I thought it was important for you to have it today."

She stared at the envelope for a long moment and cried.

"I wanted to give it to you sooner," Colton said, planting his feet. Agony twisted his heart seeing Denise emotional. "I'm sorry. I wasn't ready then." His mouth dried, and he picked up his glass and gulped water.

"You lost a friend too," she said through tears.

Colton nodded, but she lost her life partner. "I didn't want to mail it. I wanted to give it to you in person." Colton tapped his lips. "I made a promise. We had this thing, this pact, if one of us didn't make it, we'd give a letter— I don't know what it says." Colton swallowed. He lifted his shoulders and pointed his hand at the envelope. "It's something from Owen. It's all I know." He could guess it was poems, but he'd let Denise find out for herself. "I told him I'd hold onto the letter until we retired, then he'd take it back." He squinted to hold back the tears filling. "I needed to fulfill my promise."

Denise blinked, tears streaming. She put her fingers to her lips and closed her eyes, staring at her name on the envelope.

"I'm sorry for Owen's death," Colton whispered and swallowed, trying to lose the lump in his throat. His eyes swept the floor. He knew it would be hard, but he wasn't expecting to feel sick and irritated by Owen's death. "I tried to save him."

"You don't need to apologize. You didn't do anything wrong," she whispered and wiped the back of her hand across her wet cheek.

"It's just...I...there was a report..." He couldn't even say it without feeling a pang in his chest. "I would have given Owen my life."

"I know you would have." Denise glanced at her son, who was stacking giant building blocks. "It was an accident." Her face pruned, and she touched his arm. "A horrible accident."

"It shouldn't have happened. We didn't see it coming." Colton visualized it like it was yesterday. He squeezed his eyes shut and then opened them desperately wanting to forget the feeling of helplessness and despair every time Owen entered his mind. It brought him back to the horrible place. "Anyway." Colton looked down regaining his thoughts and composure.

"It's okay." She rubbed his arm. "I never blamed you for his death. Nobody did." Her soft and courteous voice soothed him. "It was a bad situation."

"I blamed myself. I should have reacted quicker, but I swear, I did what I could. I should have been stronger. Owen saved my life."

"You can't blame yourself." Her eyebrows came together. She took a step toward him. "How are you doing?"

"I'm trying to get my life back," he admitted. "You know, I was honorably discharged? My anxiety got the better of me." He bowed his head. He hadn't disclosed it to anyone outside his family.

"Oh, Colton, that's okay." She nodded in sympathy.

"Everything happened all at once," Colton continued, feeling relieved. "Jenny left me and..."

She furrowed her brows. "I know, I'm sorry."

"Then, Owen died, and I couldn't think straight." He rubbed his forehead.

"Did you get some help?" her voice gentle, soothing his mind.

"I did. Yeah. I'm a work in progress." There was a pause, and he chuckled with embarrassment. "It must be hard for you." He couldn't imagine how Denise was coping.

She wiped the tip of her nose and her eye. "I'm thankful I have our son. I have a piece of Owen with me every day." She clutched the envelope and forced a smile. "Do you have something of Owen to remember him by?"

Colton darted his tongue in his cheek and said, "Memories. Good memories." He breathed. "Owen made me laugh. He was my therapy when things went sideways. Never met another guy like him." He looked to the ceiling to hold back tears.

There was a moment of silence.

"I'll be right back." Denise spun on her foot and headed down the hall. A door creaked and a minute later, she came back into the kitchen, holding a small, metal airplane. "I want you to have this."

Colton cradled it in his palm. "Don't give me anything. It belongs to your son."

"He has a match." She smiled proudly; her body jittered. Flaring her hands out, she put them on her hips.

"Why do you have two?"

"They were on sale." She snorted a laugh, and Colton chuckled.

They cried and laughed some more. Denise was talking at the kitchen table with a box of tissues between them. Colton told her about the past week, and Denise shared with him how she was surviving on her own.

"It's good to see you," he told her as he got up to leave.

"If you ever come this way again, stop by."

"I will."

"Promise?"

"I promise." They embraced in a hug. "I keep my promises."

She hugged him tighter.

Colton would be in touch. There was a little boy he wanted to watch grow up and tell him about his amazing dad, who loved him. He wondered if the boy would have Owen's humor or the love of planes like he did. Colton's chest lifted. A weight he no longer bared and tasted the freedom of a past he thought would challenge him forever, and finally, he could let go.

It was time to let go.

It was time to live again.

Chapter Twenty-Three

Sara played around with the layout of the newspaper. Her phone rang and she pushed away from her desk and scooped up the receiver.

"My mother passed," Jerry said in a shallow voice. "Thought I'd let you know."

"Oh, I'm so sorry." She crossed her legs, elbow bracing her hand as she listened to the soft voice of a usually boisterous man. "Are you on your way back?" Sara's stomach tightened. She needed to know if she was leaving or not because she still had to pack. Her adventure was

waiting, and she was supposed to meet Johnathan. Maybe she would feel different when she arrived in Seattle. She let her body fall into her chair. What was she thinking? She wasn't

interested in Johnathan, not even a smidge, and although Colton had a piece of her heart, it wasn't enough to make a relationship out of it.

Her fingers pressed her forehead. Worried about what Colton was doing, she fought to think about him and let him interfere with her work.

"She did," Jerry said. "I sang to her, and she went to sleep." He sniffled and coughed. Sara extended the phone from her ear and brought it back to a muffled sound followed by another sniffle. "Sorry." He let out a breath. "She was a wonderful woman. Full of energy. Seeing her fight until she was at peace. It was, well, hard."

"Of course."

"How is it going? Is the editor from the Omak editing?"

"I've been doing most everything."

"Liam's not covering the news?"

"He's writing sports and has written opinion pieces while you're gone."

"He could have written one news story."

"We have it covered." Sara looked over her shoulder to see Liam at his desk.

"I trust it's going well. I'm not missing too much, am I?"

Sara flexed her hand, her ear burning against the phone. "Not much. No bombs are going off," she said lightly.

"Good. Good. You're doing a fine job. I haven't had a phone call. I assume it's running smoothly."

"It is."

"I've been giving some thought to your suggestion about freshening up the paper."

"Oh?"

"Make it...lively. I'm considering it. Maybe it needs different fonts, bigger pictures. Can you come up with something, and I'll run it by Georgia? Can't do anything without her approval, or I'll get my ass chewed out."

Sara swallowed. Her arms tingled. "She hardly pays attention to us."

"She does. You know she's like a cat? Waits for the opportunity and then pounces."

Sara sucked in a breath. "Good to know."

"Stick to what we've been doing. Can't go wrong with it. Come up with some ideas. Ask Liam, too. I won't be back until next week. I have a funeral to plan."

"Next week," her voice faded. Sara sank in her chair. It was the answer she'd been waiting to hear. She hung up the phone. If Jerry wasn't coming back until next week, she could run one more advice column or do what she used to do and add a photo. "Liam?" She called over her shoulder. "Do you have a photo I can use for a filler?"

"Probably. I took lots from the minor hockey game I was at. There's one of a couple
getting engaged."

"In the stands?" She swung her chair around.

"Yeah. You should have seen it. Quite funny how it worked out. I found out the mom's kid was playing, and the guy planned it. The lights flickered after the second period, and the
announcement came on to look at their section. Just then, an announcement came on telling
people to look at their section. The guy got down on his knee and proposed. The crowd cheered, and then the kid, I don't know how he did it without skates, but he jumped into the stands, and the three of them hugged."

"How sweet." Sara puffed out her lips.

"It was. People were crying and yelling from across the arena, congratulations."

"We'll put that one in for sure." Sara tucked herself into her desk and adjusted to fit a story
into the grid and added a photo.

"Did you get it?" Liam asked. "I sent it."

Sara clicked on her email. "Got it. Thanks. Send me the caption." She saved it and dragged it onto the page. She had spent more time doing layout than getting out and finding stories.

"What happened to your friend who came to visit? Is she still here?"

"No. She went home." He played with the top of his hair. "She might get the job at the school. She's coming back for a second interview."

"That's good news. So, you two are dating? How are you managing if she's not here?"

"It's only for a week. We talk every day, but so far it's working. She'll be back in a few days. I couldn't do the long-distance thing. It's impossible to get to know someone without being with them." He leaned back in his chair, hands behind his head. "It helped we knew each other already." He laid back and rocked in his seat. "Whatever happened to your secret admirer? You haven't had a delivery in a while."

"Over a week." Sara grinned. "But I'm okay with it. It is hard to know someone if you're not seeing them in person."

"So, you've never met the guy?"

"No. It was probably a good thing. I'm not moving away from Moonlight."

"I feel the same. I don't feel the need to leave here."

"Dan Briggs said the same thing. He isn't selling his farm now. He wants to get into the apple cider business. He's happy being here and living with his dog."

"Can't blame him." Liam bounced back and forth in his chair, staring at his computer.

"Speaking of dogs, the animal shelter needs funding, or it'll have to shut down. Did you hear, I was going to check it out for a story, but I have an interview with the men's baseball league. They're talking about expansion."

"I can probably check it out for you."

"If you want, go for it. You don't have any pets, do you?"

"I don't, no. I've thought about it lots of times." Maybe now was a better time.

"When you get there, don't get sucked in by the sad puppy faces. Don't look them in the eyes, or you're doomed."

"Thanks. I'll keep it in mind."

Sara drove to the Homeward Bound Animal Shelter, which was on a big piece of property, and got out of the car. A shepherd and a Ridgeback ran to the fence, barking.

"Hello," she called out and went to the door, wiping her feet on the mat and walked in.

RESCUING HIS HEART   207

Josie met her carrying a floppy ear dog. She was wearing her usual, three-quarter inch sleeve, button-down shirt, and jeans with a rip in them. "Have you come to take this little guy off my hands?"

"Aw." Sara's heart grew five times bigger. *Don't look at his eyes.* "He's so cute, but no. I haven't. Not yet," she admitted.

Josie placed the puppy down, and it sniffed Sara's leg.

"I've come to ask you about you closing your business. Can you tell me a little more?"

"If it'll help me save these animals, sure." Josie shooed the dog away from Sara's leg. "Come here." She scooped it up. "Follow me. I'll put this guy back into his crate."

Sara swung her purse around her while she walked and dug for her notebook. "Are you planning a fundraiser to help with the funding?"

"No, I don't know what to do." She shook her head. "I'm dipping into my savings just to feed them."

"Do you have any sponsors?"

"No. Whenever I ask, people say they'll contribute, but they don't."

"How many animals do you have?"

They walked outside to the covered area.

"Let's see, I've got the puppy," she said, pointing to the crate. "Five adult dogs outside, two females and the other is in her crate. I've got a couple of rabbits, a guinea pig, a budgie." She rubbed the middle of her forehead. "Cats. Got eight of them."

"Have you thought about doing an adoption day? An open house?"

"I don't have the money for it."

"It shouldn't cost you anything. You could get the vet involved. We live in Moonlight.

People will help if you ask them."

Josie scratched her arm. "It's just me here. I had help, but I can't afford to pay a salary."

Sara jotted down her notes. The woman gave so much to save animals, and nobody was protecting her.

"I'll tell you what." Sara flicked her pen. "If you set up an adoption day, let me know, and I can run a story about it. It will get the word out and hopefully create buzz."

"You know people will leave animals at my front door? I hate it." She pouted slightly. "I feel sorry for these pets no longer getting the love they deserve. Just yesterday, I had a budgie in a cage at my door. Can you believe it? A budgie." She cackled. "It's cold for a bird living inside. There needs to be awareness. People can't just drop their pet off and expect them to be safe."

"Does it happen often?" Sara was scribbling down her notes.

"No, but if people knew the next time it happens, I might not be able to give their pet home, maybe they'll think twice about doing it." She tightened her jaw.

Sara lowered her notepad. "Can I see some of the animals?"

"Sure." The lady wandered past Sara. "Down the hall is where the cats are." She opened a door to a room with stacked cages. Meow's and a high-pitch squeaky meow came from one of them. Sara got out her camera, quickly focusing on the black and white cat with its nose up to the cage door. The litter smell got stronger, and Sara sped up the pictures and stepped out of the room where she heard chirping.

Down the hall, toward the backdoor, there was another room. "This is the other room where I let the small dogs play."

Sara stepped inside. Fluffy faces were staring back at her. A miniature poodle was on all fours, watching her come closer. "Can I get a picture of you holding some of the dogs?"

"Oh, I don't know. I don't look the best." She brushed off her legs and pulled her strands across her neck.

"You can cuddle the dogs," Sara instructed. "People will be more focused on the dogs than you." Josie grabbed hold of the beagle before it ran at Sara. A shaggy white-haired dog wagged its tail, and two more mixed breed dogs ran circles around the room.

"Come on, you guys," Josie shouted.

Sara walked in a circle, trying to take a few shots. The dogs bumped into her legs, one jumped up and left an imprint of its wet nose on her jeans.

"Come here," she yelled, scooping one up and getting another to sit. She reached into her pocket and took out a milk bone. "Sit," she told the one, and it did, panting for a treat. The other dogs yelped and barked for attention. "I don't know if I can hold them. They're all excited." She sat on the floor and curled one under her arm. One dog put a paw on her lap and licked her cheek. Sara snapped pictures and was pleased she got a good one. She reviewed her shots on the screen of her camera. "Here, look at this one." She held it up for Josie to see. "I love this one." Sara smiled.

"They take turns in this room. The bigger dogs are outside. They needed to run, so I let them out. Want to come to have a look?" She looked at her feet. The two mixed breed dogs had calmed down. "I'll let them play," she said and shut the door behind Sara. "Out here, I have two dogs." The Shepherd barked madly when they went outside and met them at the gate. "You have a lot to say today, Barney," Josie told him, and he stopped, licked his chops, and sat. "Are you done out here? Wanna come inside? Okay. In a minute." Josie walked to the next gate and opened it. "These two are friendly. This here is Stanley."

Sara bent down to pet the Australian Shepherd. "You're sweet." The dog licked her hand.

"And you remember Bella."

Sara put out her hand, and the dog licked it like a lollipop. "How old is Bella? She looks young."

"The vet figures she's around three years old." Josie waved her hand.

"Aw, beautiful!"

"The yellow Labrador Retriever ran away, and her owner didn't want her anymore."

"Why? She's a good dog."

"The owner got her from a family member, and then she was passed to the next person who said she didn't have the patience for a dog." Josie shrugged. "Oh, look, she's bringing you her ball."

Bella came running back with a florescent pink ball and dropped it at Sara's feet. Sara picked up the slobbered ball and threw it as far as she could. Bella charged for it and brought it back. Bella made Sara play over and over. As soon as Sara raised her hand, Bella was already running for it.

"She has energy," Sara said. "She's like a puppy."

"Smart too."

"It's so sad why nobody wanted her." Sara frowned. Bella would make a good companion. Bella came back with her tail wagging and dropped the ball at her feet. "This is their home. What would happen to them if you closed?" Sara asked.

"I don't know," Josie said, eyes glossing, she put her hand under her bottom lip and staring at the dogs in the yard. "I don't know what else to do."

Sara picked up the ball again and threw it.

"You've got a best friend now."

She shouldn't have looked Bella in the eyes.

Chapter Twenty-Four

Colton rode toward the TAKE A FLIGHT flying school banner, got off the bike, and placed it against the portable. He sauntered inside, unaware if he had the right place, he looked side to side.

"Hi there. How can I help you?" A woman attaching papers with a clip looked up from her desk.

"I'm—" Colton pulled at his earlobe. "Looking for Al Anderson."

"He's in hanger number two." She stretched her arm and pointed behind her. "Straight out and to your right. If he's not there, come back, and I'll page him."

"He's okay with me stopping by?"

"You're here, aren't you? Go ahead. We're not formal here." She grinned.

Colton walked out, and when he saw a plane bumping along the runway preparing for

takeoff, Colton had to stop to watch it. Fascinated by the ability and power a double engine had, it didn't change his mind about flying. The plane slowed to a stop and waited for the okay to go. He anticipation the takeoff, as though he were the pilot, feeling the revving in his legs and the extra beats in his chest. The plane jerked, and Colton leaned over in reaction then straightened up, giving the pilot his mental courage. It started to move again, gaining speed, the flight took off, and Colton made a fist as though to congratulate his efforts and turned on his foot, heading in the other direction.

As he headed to hanger two, there was clanging and voices. He rolled his shoulders and clutched his hands, blowing out a sequence of short breaths to gain control. He walked into the open hanger, looking around at the organized workplace and the six-seater plane.

A grey-haired man ducked under the wing. "Hey, Colton. How are you, doin'?" He came toward him with his hand extended, and Colton met him in the middle.

"Good, thanks." Colton nodded, shaking his hand. He lifted his chin to the plane. "Is this one here rebuilt?"

"Na, just needed some maintenance." Colton cupped his hands and rubbed them together.

"Do you want to take a look?" Al asked.

"Yeah, sure." Colton eagerly treaded to the plane, put his hand out to feel the cold metal against his skin. A rush of excitement hit his nerves. "This yours?"

"Yeah." Al smiled.

"Nice."

"Don't use it as much. I used to charter short flights. I mostly instruct." He spoke through a grin.

Colton bobbed his head, looking around.

"When are you headed back home?" Al asked.

Colton shuffled his right foot. "I decided to stay. I'm not going back." His chest muscles contracted, his feet planted firmly. He should tell the truth, but he hadn't told Sara, and he felt maybe he should. The only way he could start over was to start living somewhere new, and Moonlight Valley seemed like the place to settle.

Colton bowed his head and brought it up to meet Al's shining eyes and weathered skin. "I was honorably discharged."

Al gave him a long, understanding gaze. "I'm sure it's a good decision." The warmth in his eyes gave Colton hope.

"It was." Colton swallowed. Being honest about it meant being honest with himself. "I haven't told many people."

"Nothing to be ashamed of, son. It's an honor you served our country. Thank you for that."

Colton tried clearing the tightness in his throat with a subtle cough.

"Do you need a job? I could use someone like you."

His pulse quickened. "Yes, sir. I'd appreciate it."

"Why don't you come by Saturday. I can show you around and introduce you to the gang. You'll get along great with them. Do you like pizza?"

"Love pizza."

"Do you want to stay for a bit? Just ordered in. The guys are working in hanger one." He pointed to the building next door. "Should be coming out once the food arrives. They can smell food from the runway." Al laughed, and Colton chuckled.

"Thanks. Maybe next time. I've gotta get back."

"You've got my number."

"I do. Thanks."

"Call me anytime. You know, Sara? She's a good person. She knows lots of people. Don't be afraid to ask her for recommendations; she can probably help you out."

Colton grinned. His chest heated. "She's helped me a lot so far."

"It's her nature to help. Her dad, he was a good friend of mine." Al clutched his teeth, his lips stretched. "It was a real loss when he died. It crushed the family."

"I bet."

"It's a shame when you lose a good person."

"I know all about it." Colton gave a slow smile. His chest lifted and an overall lightness filled his body. Owen wouldn't be forgotten but remembered with honor and love.

It was the first time since the accident; his mind wasn't circling the repercussions of the accident. He had Sara to think about and wanted to get the chance to have her in his life.

Chapter Twenty-Five

Sara rushed home to open her photography studio before Kelly got there to make sure her shed didn't feel like an ice bucket, she flipped the heater on and set the volume a little higher on the radio to drown out the buzzing of the blowing heat.

The door flew open. "Hey!" Kelly said, stepping inside.

Sara hung her coat and rubbed her hands together.

"Sorry to put this on you. Is it a bad time?" Kelly asked.

"It's good," Sara sighed. "We'll probably go white background?"

"Doesn't matter to me." She took off her coat and placed it with Sara's. "You're the
expert."

"Are you sure it's okay? I feel bad, but you're going to be leaving in two days, and if you
go for two weeks." Her mouth came together.

"It's all good." Sara stepped over to her camera on the tripod, checking her settings.

"Tell me," Kelly said playfully. "Did you sleep with the pilot?"

Sara couldn't hide her grin. Her lips tensed as they moved to the side and looked up from the camera. "I did."

"I knew it!" Kelly's eyes widened. "I saw him kiss you at the pool table, and I just knew something would happen."

"I thought you left."

"I came back to use the bathroom. So, was it good?"

"It was good." Sara gave a little smile. She squeezed her hands together. "Like it shouldn't feel so right, you know?"

"Then what is it?" Kelly waggled her eyebrows. "You're unsure about something."

"I haven't heard from him since this morning. I know it sounds weird, but since he's been here, I know what he's doing and where he's going. He's usually here, waiting for me to get home."

"For saying you've known this guy for what, a week? You're talking like you're dating this guy."

"I feel like I do know him and it's been a week and a half." She hadn't thought there was a connection until their first kiss. Now Sara worried if she went on her trip, would she lose out on an opportunity with Colton?

"You did help him recover," Kelly said.

"He doesn't need me anymore, I guess."

"You don't know. Maybe he feels better and wants to see what's in Moonlight."

"Maybe." Sara looked into the viewfinder to make lighting adjustments. She thought she liked living on her own until Colton proved to be the perfect house guest, the instant boyfriend, and yet, a relationship didn't seem feasible.

Sara pulled herself back from the camera. "It's one thing to lead a girl on, and it's another to disappear without saying what she did wrong."

"I don't think you did anything wrong unless you told him you wanted to marry him."

Sara gushed. "I didn't say that." She laughed.

"Then, you're good."

"Do you want to stand on the spot." Sara pointed to a black circle on the floor of the backdrop. "I need to check the lighting."

"This is fine," Kelly said.

Sara took a few test shots. "I've never been with someone who was into me physically," Sara said, clicking and then popped her head up. "Does that make sense? You know, connected. So sure of where this was going. He even kissed me goodnight before we went to sleep."

"I get it." Kelly sighed. "I felt that way with Brad."

"What do I do?" She lifted her shoulders.

"I don't know. What would Peaches do?"

"She'd say if it were meant to be, he would come back. Don't wait around for him."

"She doesn't believe in going after what you want?"

"Sure, but you can't make someone be with you if they don't want to." Sara felt a dagger to her heart. Was it how it was? Colton had troubles of opening up and talking about his past. He didn't want anything more than what he gave. At least it's how she perceived him even though she didn't want to believe it. They'd never have a relationship if he couldn't be honest with her.

"Ready?" Sara asked, changing the subject. "You look great, by the way."

"I feel like I'm going for a job interview." Kelly patted her navy suit blazer.

She looked through her viewfinder and snapped pictures. "Hold that pose. Good smile."

Kelly broke into a laugh. "I'm trying to be serious." She folded in her lips. "I guess you have to wait and see if he shows up later. Do you have a cell phone?"

"I do. I don't want to annoy. I don't want Colton to think I'm that girl." Sara twitched.

"We're doing headshots, too, right? Cause I was thinking of doing both. If you don't need them right away, at least you'll have them."

"Sure. Thanks. What do you mean by that, girl? You're caring, and nosey is part of your job, he's staying with you. You should have a clue where he is." She turned up her hand.

"You think I'm nosey?"

"Not as much as you used to be."

"Okay," Kelly laughed.

"Can you face the window and turn your body slightly this way?" She waved her fingers.

"That's it. Right there. Stop. Pull your shoulders back. I know it's awkward." Sara snapped a couple of shots. "And turn a little more to your left." She clicked again. "This is good!" She held up her hand as she zoomed in. "You know, I didn't think I'd feel different after sex, but I do...a little." How could she not? Colton made her feel appreciated and loved if she dared to think it.

"Oh, it's different. Why wouldn't it be?" Kelly fluffed her long, dark hair over her shoulders. "It meant something, or you wouldn't have done it. You're not one to jump into bed with anybody."

"You're right about that." Sara looked up from her camera. "It meant something."

"This guy is into you. He was practically drooling over you at TJ's."

"No, he wasn't." Sara snapped her tongue on the roof of her mouth, eyes to the ceiling. She didn't want to believe it because if he did, why did he leave without a word?

"He was. Please tell me you used the gift I gave you."

"I did. I don't know how you knew I needed it."

"Always be prepared," Kelly laughed.

"I don't keep a box of condoms in my night table drawer."

"You should."

"It's not going to happen again. He left, and it's probably for a good reason. He got what he wanted, and now he's gone."

"How did you know he left?"

"I have a feeling."

"Relax. He probably went out for the day. He'll be home for dinner, and you'll wish you had a box by your bed."

"It was a one-time thing." Sara set down the camera on the tripod.

Where would Colton walk? He didn't know anyone in Moonlight, at least she didn't know if he did unless he went to Dan's house to see about moving his plane. She hadn't thought of it, and she felt silly for not coming to mind. "You're probably right. He's probably fine."

"What does he do when he's here, and you're at work?"

"He cooks and cleans, goes out. Okay, hold steady." She clicked her camera. "And one more." She slid the toggle to view the shot. "I didn't realize how lonely I got living alone."

"That's why Britt's living with me. There's someone to come home to, and the house doesn't feel so empty."

"And it's working out okay?"

"She has the upstairs, and I have the downstairs. I'm turning one of the rooms into my workspace. We have our quarters, but we end up having dinner together most nights."

"I didn't tell you, Evan and Jessica broke up."

"No way."

"Evan said they went their separate ways. Okay, let's do some headshots." Sara went over to grab a chair and brought it to the circle.

"We should hook him up with Britt. Didn't they used to date in high school?" Kelly sat down, and Sara took a step back to see if she was angled perfectly.

"It didn't last," Sara said.

"Why?"

"I don't think either one of them were really into dating, were they?" Sara backed up. "It was more about hanging out with friends, and Evan was more interested in playing sports than having a girlfriend." Sara got behind her camera. "I think we've got them. Do you want me to do anymore?"

Kelly jumped up. "That's good. You took more than I need."

"I'll edit these and send them to you right away."

"Thanks. I appreciate you doing this for me," Kelly said. "Let me know how much I owe you."

Kelly left, and Sara tidied up before stepping outside. Walking the short path from the

studio to her backdoor, she turned her head to the small shed used to store a lawnmower and her dad's bike. The latch hung, leaving a gap. Did she forget to lock it? She trusted her neighbors but out of habit she locked the shed and she wished she did because her eyes widened in disbelief taking count of the empty space. The bike was gone. Her mind raced. Who would take an old bike? *Colton.* Her body ran cold. How did he know it was there? If he did, why didn't he ask?

Her mind whirling with questions and concerns of where he was, Sara plunked herself down on her computer and downloaded the pictures of Kelly. She tried not to let her mind wander too far but she feared she may already have.

Clicking on a picture to edit, she stopped to check her phone. No message. She checked email, and there was a message from Johnathan. She hadn't even thought of him. Her body sunk into the chair, losing her energy and excitement for a man she didn't know. Out of fairness for Johnathan, she knew she needed to call it off and not follow through with her commitments. She shouldn't be falling for Colton either, but she feared it was too late. How could she worry about Colton's safety when she didn't really know him? The continuous gnawing wouldn't allow her to relax, so she closed off her computer and decided to take a drive towards Dan's house thinking that Colton might be checking on his place. Her phone rang and before she had a chance to pull over, it went to voice mail. Easing her grip from the wheel, she turned onto the shoulder to listen to her message.

Hey Sara, it's Johnathan.

His voice was direct and fluent, like he was covering a story.

I'm making dinner plans for Thursday night. Sushi or Thai? We never discussed what restaurants you liked. I love Sushi, hope you do too. Call me or text me. I have to make reservations.'

There were lots of things they didn't know about each other, and food was one of them. What about concerts verses theatre? Bars verses clubs? She sucked on her lip. Maybe she was being over the top. Surely couples didn't need those things to make it work, but Sara wanted as much energy and compatibility if she were making a significant effort to start something new.

And just one thing, I have some information about Major Colton Brooks.

Chapter Twenty-Six

Colton peddled the airport, down Highway 97, wanting to get back to Moonlight Valley before dark. He felt an ache gather in his calves, but didn't want to stop.

The grey clouds brought its promise of rain. Colton gripped the handlebars and coasted down the main road, breathing heavily, and pushing himself to get to Sara's house to tell her he wanted to start a relationship with her, even though in the back of his mind, the idea threatened him.

The rain pelted harder, blinding Colton's vision and he wiped a flattened strand off his forehead, focusing on Sara's face and kissing her pretty mouth. He turned down the quiet road, eyeing Sara's house in the distance. Slowing down when he got to her driveway, legs shaking from exhaustion, he got off the bike and walked it to the back of the house where he found it — working on getting his balance on his wobbly legs and making it to the front door. He raked his hand through his wet hair. Coat soaked, his cargo pants splatted with dark spots from riding through puddles and the splash from oncoming vehicles, his sneakers squeaked with every step.

Putting his hand up to the door, it flung open before he had a chance to knock.

"Where have you been?" Sara's eyebrows knitted together; she breathed a heavy sigh.

"I left you a note," he said. Women liked notes, didn't they? He stepped inside and closed the door behind him, Sara backing up and crossing her arms to her chest, staring him down.

"A note? How about a phone call? I had no idea if I should go out and look for you."

"Sorry. I had things to do." He threw his hands into his wet pockets of his coat.

She unhooked her arms and threw her shoulders back. "It would have been nice if you called. Where did you go? You took my dad's bike."

"Yeah, I needed transportation. I went to Omak. I thought you wouldn't mind."

"You biked there?" Her forehead wrinkled.

Colton pushed his head back from her response. "It wasn't bad." Compared to being mentally challenging. He did what he came to do. Sure, he could arrange to go back to Bellingham and live with his parents for a few weeks until he found a job and a place of his own, but that's not what he wanted. Wherever he was going to live, he needed his own roof over his head and income. It came down to where he'd rather live, and Moonlight Valley had been everything he wanted in a town.

"I tried calling you." She threw up her hand in protest. Her lips butted, and her shoulders came up. "You didn't answer. You could have been dead on the side of the road. How was I supposed to know where to find you?"

"I'm sorry."

"I know you didn't want to talk to me, but you could have texted me to tell me you were okay."

"I guess I should have, but I told you I was gone for the day. I delivered the envelope."

"Okay. I could have driven you. Why didn't you ask for a ride?" Her fingers clutched onto her sleeves.

"You've done enough for me already. Besides, you were at work. I'm not going to bother you for something I could do on my own. I'm capable of doing things on my own."

"Yeah." Her eyebrows narrowed.

How could she be so upset when he didn't concern her?

"Had I drove, you could have been there and back in just a few hours," she said. "You've been gone the whole day." She straightened her back, cheeks flushed. Why was she so angry?

"I didn't know there was a curfew," he snapped. He put a hand to his forehead, wishing he had of taking a breath before answering.

"It would have been nice if you at least told me where you were. You could have gotten hurt. You don't have anyone here. What happened if you got hit by a car? You weren't wearing a helmet." She pointed to his head while she spoke. "The highway isn't safe. And you didn't have a flashlight?" She flung her hand out and then crossed them at her chest. "Even worse!"

"I appreciate what you've done for me, but I'm capable of handling myself. I don't need a sitter, and I sure the hell don't need someone telling me what to do." He clutched his jaw. His words were meant to be driven with power, authority, and with conclusion, but it did none of those things. He didn't need Sara. He wanted her, but maybe he was moving too fast. He swore he didn't want to be involved with anyone, and now he was reminded of his insecurity.

"I'm trying to help you."

"I don't need you interfering and coaching me, okay?" He survived his past. He had a second chance to do something else with his life. He wasn't looking for recognition or love; God knew he was a failure at it. Keeping a low-profile would suit him just fine in Moonlight Valley, but maybe Omak was a better choice. He wasn't sure. What he was sure of, he couldn't ask Sara for anything more, and couldn't offer his heart because there was a chance hers or his would break.

"You're not fair to me!"

"You're not responsible for me," he shot back.

Her eyes shot open. "I'm trying to help you. I deserved to know what you're doing, so I know you're safe. It's respectful. Of all people, you should know the meaning of it." Her eyebrows came together and then fell. "Major."

Colton closed his mouth and stared at her.

"When were you planning on telling me you were honorably discharged?"

"Did Al tell you?" Did he call Sara after their conversation?

"No," she snapped. "You lied to me. You told me you were going back to work. Back to base." Her eyebrow arched. "You were never going back."

Colton's stomach turned and ground his teeth, looking away in shame.

"I could have written about you about your past," she said calmly. Her eyes strained and he fought to look away. "I showed you respect, and you didn't have the decency to tell me the truth."

Colton walked past her, snatching his bag of possessions.

"Where are you going?" Her voice hitched. "You're soaked. You should get dry. Have a shower."

"I stayed too long," he muttered. That was his first mistake. The second was getting

involved with a woman he couldn't have.

Droplets from his hair ran down his face when he stood up, clutching his bag. "I should have never come here." Colton needed space. He needed to figure out his next step because he didn't want someone telling him what he should do when he didn't know himself.

Sara took a step toward him, crossing her arms. "Are you scared because I care about you?" Her bottom lip quivered.

"Do you care?"

"I do." Her body stiffened. "Yes. Of course I do."

"Then why haven't you told me details about your trip? Going to Seattle for two days? Who are you meeting there?"

"Because I—I don't know if I'm going." She raised her hand and took a deep breath. A dead giveaway that there was more to the story. More than what she wanted him to know.

"You're planning on it." Her friends even knew.

"I was."

"You're not now?"

"I don't think so." She nervously pulled at her hair. "I can't."

"Why not?"

"Because I don't know if I have time off." She brought her fist to her mouth, eyes to the floor. "My circumstances have changed."

"But you're supposed to be leaving tomorrow?"

She nodded slightly, her eyes on his.

"Who were you going to meet?" He shifted his jaw, feeling the burn in his chest.

"Someone I met. Another reporter."

"A guy?"

She nodded, holding his stare.

"You're dating this guy while sleeping with me?"

"I'm not dating him. I'm not seeing anyone. It's not like that."

"No?"

"I wasn't expecting—" she opened up her arms. "This."

"You were still planning on going?"

She bowed her head and folded in her lips. "I don't know."

"Let me say this." Colton's stomach hardened. He refused to think of the outcome it would bring. He wasn't doing either one of them any favors by sugar-coating how he felt. "If it weren't for my title when you first met me, you wouldn't have had anything to do with me." He took his hand out of his pocket. "You helped me because you wanted to make your dad proud, respect the military." Colton's mouth twitched. "He's not alive and yet you're looking for acceptance from a man who's not here."

Sara's face fell. Her lids closed and she rubbed her hand over her chest. "My dad." Her bottom lip quivered. "Taught me to respect, and I honor the men and women who fight for our country. There's nothing wrong with wanting to make him proud. He reminds me of what I can do to help those who need it. So, if you're going to tell me who I should and shouldn't care about, then that's your problem."

Colton took a step outside, clutching his possessions. He should have known Sara was only thinking of her needs. It was better to leave and say nothing than to face the battle neither one of them would win. Colton lowered his head and walked down the steps in the pouring rain. He didn't know where he was going, but he couldn't stay there.

Chapter Twenty-Seven

The next day, Sara met Kelly at Betty's Bakery for a cup of coffee in the middle of her workday, but an hour didn't seem like enough time to ease her mind. The day had been full of sitting in front of her computer, thinking about everything other than work.

"It's like he's disappeared," Sara was explaining Colton's exit the night before. "Not like I've gone looking for him. He doesn't want my help anyway, and we're not a couple, so it's weird."

"You told me about Peaches advice. If it was meant to be, he'd come back and don't wait around for him."

Sara grunted, clutching her coffee cup. "And didn't I say you can't make someone be with you if they don't want to?"

"Okay, well, not talking to him isn't helping the situation. You care. You told him you care. It's all you can do." Kelly put down a manicured hand. "You're all Colton has while he's here."

"But he wants his space, and I'm giving it to him, but I just want to know if he's okay."

"When he's ready—" Kelly gave a gentle smile. "You'll see him."

"Will I?"

"Sure." Kelly shifted her lips to one side.

"And if it's not?"

"Move on." Kelly shrugged. "You need to live your life too."

Sara picked up her coffee cup. "I don't know why I thought it would work." She sat angled on the chair and crossed her leg over the other.

"It's not over. Colton has to figure out what he wants too, and maybe he feels like he owes you. Guys are proud. Maybe he feels like you've helped him enough, and he wants to do things on his own."

"You should be the one writing an advice column." Sara drank her coffee.

"It's easier when it's not your life's problem."

"So, how long should I wait?" Sara pursed her lips.

"There's no expiry."

"Like you and Brad."

"Yeah, well, all you can do is carry on with your life." Kelly folded her arms on the table. "Thanks for my photos. I've already uploaded one of them to my website." She took out her phone and tapped on it. "Here it is." She flipped her phone to show the homepage.

"That's great. Looks good."

"Do you think you'll be ready to launch in a few weeks?"

"I think so. I'm working on the details." Kelly took back her phone and stuck it in her
purse.

"I can't believe you're doing it." Sara squealed. "You're following your dream."

"I didn't think our town needed an event planning business," she said with a flick of her wrist. "But I think there's a need for it."

"I think so too. I'm proud of you. I hope it's successful."

"Thanks. I'm going to work part-time at the bank. At least for now, until I can get my business off the ground. I don't know how business will be."

"Have you seen Brad around?"

Kelly buttoned her lips. "No." She shook her head. "It's better this way."

"Is it?" Sara's top lip arched. If there was one couple who seemed like the perfect fit, it was Kelly and Brad. "It's hard to believe."

"He doesn't want to get married. He's caught up in his work, taking extra courses. He's gone away a couple of times to learn about fighting forest fires. I haven't paid attention to it. We ran into each other at TJ's but haven't spoken since."

"He's not seeing anyone?"

"Not that I know of." Kelly's lips squeezed together; her eyes darted to the table. "Men are difficult. They say women are hard to read, ha!" Her eyes flashed. "They either can't make up their minds, or they don't like change."

Sara's phone buzzed, and she jumped to retrieve it out of her purse. Heart racing, she anticipated hearing Colton's voice. She picked up her phone, she read the screen. "Ah. It's work." She brought her phone to her ear. "Hello."

"Sara," Deloris said. "Jerry is here."

"Where?" Sara's heart raced.

"At the office. When are you coming back?" Deloris asked in a rush.

"Is he asking for me?"

"He asked where you were. I said you were on assignment."

Sara picked up her coffee. "Okay, tell him I'm finishing up and will be around later. I have one more stop to make before coming back in." She hung up her phone.

"That sounded urgent," Kelly said with a half eye roll.

"Jerry's back. Finally. He's wondering where I am. Jeez, like I've been sitting around at work. It's the first break I've had in a week."

"I have to get back to work, too," Kelly said, finishing the last drop of her coffee. She stood up and put on her coat, wrapping a scarf around her neck.

"I have to stop by my mom's before I go back into the office. I picked her up some face cream she uses."

"Your mom is capable of looking after herself."

"I know, but I was at the store..."

"I think you like looking after her." Kelly lowered her chin as she secured her scarf. "How are you going to meet someone if your focus is caring for your mom? She's not ill, is she?"

"Well, no." Sara grabbed her purse and swung it over her shoulder. They walked to the doors. "How is she going to meet someone if you're constantly doing things for her?"

"She doesn't want to date."

Kelly laughed. "Of course, she does! Why would she want to be alone? She's a beautiful lady who deserves a companion."

"She doesn't want to replace Dad."

"It's not about replacing. It's about living. How is your mom going to live when you and Evan have relationships?"

"She's fine." Her mom seemed happy, like she found a new lease on life. "She says she hasn't been happier."

Kelly narrowed her gaze as she stopped beside her car. "She has a man."

"She doesn't," Sara said. "She's excited about the new programs she's coordinating. A slight job change at the retirement home, and she says it brings her joy to see smiles on their faces."

"I'm just saying, you don't need to do everything for her. It's taking away your social ambitions. You're talking about traveling and exploring new places, but what I think you need is a change of scenery because you're focused on taking care of your mom's needs."

She turned her head away. "She says she's happy when I come to visit."

"She should be. You're her daughter."

Sara bounced.

"Try giving each other some breathing room. Maybe your mom will share more about her personal life with you." Kelly got out her keys.

"I know everything there is to know about my mom, and dating isn't something she's interested in."

Kelly narrowed a sympathetic gaze. "Really? You don't live with her. How do you know?"

"I—I don't. I'm not stopping her from finding someone." It wasn't a conversation she's had with her mom because dating hadn't been a topic. Anytime Sara brought up a man, her mom got all flustered and changed the subject.

"Maybe she needs your consent."

Sara swallowed the lump in her throat. After her dad died, her mom said he was the only man she ever wanted. What if she changed her mind?

"I think your mom deserves to find love just like you deserve to find someone."

"I'm not stopping her." Sara put her hand to the base of her neck.

Kelly opened her car door. "Give her Peaches' advice." Kelly winked and got inside.

Chapter Twenty-Eight

Colton left his room at the Traveler's Motel and walked to the opposite side of town to Homeward Bound Animal Shelter. He had to do something with his day, and staying in watching TV wasn't an option. He needed to move. It was the only way to figure out what his next step would be.

Dressed in a clean pair of jeans and his dried sneakers, Colton spotted the open sign in the window. He rubbed his jaw and headed to the front door. Once inside, his nose twitched from the scent of sweaty dog and urine. He looked around.

"Hi there," Josie bellowed.

Colton didn't see her. He craned his neck, looking for a camera, and then took a step to see if someone was down the hall.

"I'll be right there," she yelled.

Colton circled the room and Josie came through the door. Her black hair was pulled back into a ponytail under a ball cap. "I was cleaning up last night's mess." She took off her gloves and threw them into an empty pail by the desk. She wore jeans and a baggy shirt. "Have you come to walk a dog?"

"If you're okay with it." He wiped his hand on the sleeve of his coat. "I want to walk down to the lake."

"I can't pay you." Her eyes strained. "It's a volunteer basis."

"I know. I'm not looking to get paid. I miss walking my dog." *And I need something to take my mind off of Sara.*

Josie nodded. "I'll probably have to close this place, you know. I don't have enough money to run it. It's just me." She sighed and shook her head. "You can take Tera. She has energy to burn."

"Sure. Any dog as long as it likes long walks." He threw his hands on his hips.

"Let me get a leash. As long as you tell me when I'd expect you back."

"Two hours. I'll be back by lunchtime."

She turned and snatched a leash that was hanging on a hook behind the desk. "Come with me."

Colton followed Josie down the hall. The scent of disinfectant got stronger as they headed to the back door to the undercover area. Dogs barked, and one howled. Josie stuck a key in one of the pens and grabbed the collar of a black and grey, medium size dog.

"This here is Tera." She gripped the dog's collar. The dog barked and wiggled, trying to break free. "You can see she needs some exercise." Josie attached the leash and handed it over.

"Hi there, Tera." Colton grabbed the leash and put his hand down for the dog to sniff and gave her a pet on her head.

"I think she likes you," Josie said, wiping her hands on her shirt.

"Ready, Tera, for some exercise?" He roughed up the dog's fur, ending with a pat on her head.

"Do you have a job?" Josie asked. "A place to stay?"

"I have a temporary place, and I got a job at Omak airport as an airplane mechanic."

"That's fantastic. Well, if you're looking to rent a place, long-term, Cottage Hills winery has some one-bedroom cabins."

"They do? Where's that?"

"They're nice for one person. Better than a motel." She put her hand on her hip. "It might be all you need. Just go back into town and take the first right and it's up on the hill."

"I'll have to check it out later." Colton turned on his foot. Funny how an animal could help one's mental state. It was time to find a place to rent until he could get his life back in order. Maybe even get a dog. It seemed like the perfect solution. Right now, he needed to walk.

SARA SAT IN THE PARKING lot of Betty's Bakery to make a dreaded phone call. She hated to let anyone down, and she especially felt obligated to meet Johnathan when her heart wasn't into it. Sara made a mistake not being upfront with Colton, but Sara didn't expect to fall in love.

Grabbing her phone from her purse, her hand trembled as she brought it to her ear.

"Johnathan here," he answered.

"Hi. Johnathan," she said in a rush, squeezing her eyes shut to ease the painful conversation.

"Sara?"

"It's me." She opened her eyes.

"Are you okay?"

"I'm fine," she said with a slow breath. "Thanks for sending me the information about Colton Brooks." She licked her lips. Her throat was dry. "I have some news. Not so good news." She paused. The line was quiet. "About Thursday. It's not going to happen." She clutched her fist. "I'm working. My editor is away, and I have no one to cover for me."

"It's his problem. He knew you were going away."

"But his mom died. I don't know when he's back, and I have to handle things here."

"There's no one to cover? Not a junior person?"

"We're a small town," she reminded him. "There's three of us putting out the paper twice a week." It might sound like a chore for some, but looking out at Betty's Bakery, Sara liked the feel of knowing people and sharing events that matter to the people she lived with.

"You gotta work in a city." He exhaled a breath.

"No, I like it here. I enjoy the town I live in."

"You wanted a change," he protested.

"I thought I did." She pressed her shoulders into her seat. "Moonlight is my home, and I can't leave. I don't know what I was thinking." She hadn't met Colton then. He reminded her of what was important.

"I'm sorry. I..." Sara brought herself up to the wheel and blinked. It was getting dark, and little traffic was on the road. The small town was where she belonged. She had a life here. "I have to go." She had to stay strong.

"What about us?"

"It was great getting to know you. I hope you find someone." She hung up, relieved, knowing he wasn't the one for her.

SARA PARKED ON THE street down from The Observer and reached for her ringing cell phone in her purse. She took off her seatbelt. "Hello." She stared out the front window, watching cars pass and hoping she'd see Colton.

"Sara," Deloris huffed. "Are you coming into the office? Jerry's here!"

"I thought he wasn't back until tomorrow, but okay. I just parked."

"He's not in a good mood."

"Thanks for the warning." What could she expect from a guy who lost his mom and had to get back to work? She gave him the benefit of the doubt.

"And Georgia is here too." Sara's hands began to tremble.

"Maybe I'm going to be fired, and then I'll be able to take my trip."

"Sara. You won't get fired. We need you."

Sara hung up and snatched her purse from the passenger seat. She might as well prepare herself. Maybe she could travel and write a blog about her adventures.

Her feet hit the pavement with determination. Strutting up to the front door, she put on a brave face, ready to take the next step, whatever it was.

She gave Deloris a faint smile as she walked past the front desk and down the hall to the open office space. The shuffling paper through the photocopier, the ringing telephone and Jerry's voice echoed in Sara's ears. Feeling flushed, she hung her coat up on the back of her chair. Her heart hammered. Why did she think she was going to be in trouble? If it weren't for her, the newspaper wouldn't survive.

Liam swiveled his chair around to face her. His eyes widened, and his mouth stretched across in a terrifying manner.

"What?" she asked him, wide-eyed.

Liam flicked his chin toward Jerry's office. The light was on, and the door closed.

"What's going on?" she whispered. Her knees locked, body stiff. "Is everything okay?"

Liam held up his hands. "I don't know. Georgia came in unexpectedly, and she went right into Jerry's office."

"Am I...in trouble?" She took a shallow breath.

"I don't know what's going on."

"What's Georgia doing here?"

"No idea." He shook his head.

"Huh." She bit her bottom lip, avoiding the door.

Taking a seat at her desk, Sara checked messages and answering what she could, she noted potential stories and then went into her folder and opened up where she left off on the animal shelter story. Knowing there were animals without any homes made her think about what she could do to help.

The town needed Josie and the service she provided. Sara typed faster, her fingers and brain worked at top speed. Maybe it was to avoid what was about to happen next. She could feel it. Georgia would be coming out of Jerry's office at full swing, ready to pounce and demand changes to be made. Sara would be the first to go. Her skin prickled.

Georgia's high heels tapped against the floor, and Sara tried to be natural, pasting on a smile and looking over her shoulder in a friendly manner.

"Sara," Georgia said. Her black hair cut to her shoulders came around as she lowered her head to meet Sara's eyes.

"Hi. Georgia. How are you?" Sara looked up and threw her hands in her lap. "I haven't seen you in a while." Sara tried to hold her lips in a constant smile, preventing them from trembling.

"Good. Thanks. Yes, well, I should be stopping in more, but you all seem to have

everything under control." She jerked her head, hands to her side with her shoulders back in perfect posture. Her burgundy lipstick popped with her dark, full lashes.

"Do you have a minute?" Georgia asked. "Can we talk in Jerry's office?"

"Um, yeah, sure." Sara pulled herself off the chair, legs shaky.

She followed Georgia into the open office and met Jerry's perplexed face.

"Hi. How are you?" His glasses couldn't hide the bags under his eyes, and there were new wrinkles around his mouth. Maybe he was really stressed. She put her hand to her stomach.

"I'm okay," he said. "Have a seat."

She's getting fired. It would explain why Georgia was here. Sara wiped the sweat from her hands on the thigh of her pants.

"How did everything go?" Sara asked softly. If she kept talking, the firing part wouldn't be so harsh. "You're back a little earlier."

Because she was getting fired.

"Turns out my mother didn't want a funeral. We had a family gathering instead."

"Nice," Sara whispered. "That seems...thoughtful." She cringed. Maybe she chose the wrong word.

"It was. Nice." He moved his hands across his desk. "While I was away, some things didn't go as planned."

Sara held her breath.

"You did a good job, taking over for me. I appreciated you stepping up. It's not easy. I told Georgia how well you did, considering."

"I noticed you started an advice column," Jerry said bluntly, his eyes darted above his glasses. "I didn't approve of it, and neither did Georgia."

Her face heated. "Sorry. I needed space to fill, and it seemed like a good idea."

"A photo would have worked. Who's idea?"

"Mine."

"Where did you find Peaches, and who's paying her?" Georgia asked.

Sara clutched her teeth. "Peaches, um, is me."

"You're. Giving, advice?" Jerry moved his glasses up his nose. "You're not qualified. We could get sued."

"It's practical advice," Sara said. "People know they're asking a friend, not a professional." Wasn't everyone in Moonlight a friend? "I think that's why I've received over twenty-five questions so far."

"And people know it's you?"

Sara shook her head. "Not many, a few people do." Sara pressed her shoes into the carpet. "I did write a disclosure."

"You should have asked for permission," Jerry grunted.

She puffed out her chest. If she was going to get fired, she was ready.

"I kind of like the idea," Georgia said, leaning sideways, elbow on the armrest, she placed her hand under her chin.

"You do?"

"It changes the format, but it makes it for an interesting read. I just don't know how long you can keep it going before people get tired of reading people's problems."

"It's never a problem in Moonlight," Sara explained. "People want to help or listen... it's better than reading about the fall market every week." Sara crossed her leg over the other and squeezed her hands together.

Jerry pushed up his glasses. "Georgia and I feel your commitment with the paper is key...while I was away, I had my issues to take care of, including my health."

"Oh, no. Is everything okay?"

"I'm taking early retirement."

Her stomach twisted. She'd never go on her trip. Whoever was stepping in to replace Jerry won't want her to leave.

"I'm stepping down as editor."

"What? Who's going to take your place?" A newbie? Someone from another town? She

uncrossed her legs. Her knees weakened.

"If you're interested," Georgia said. "It would be my pleasure if you took over for Jerry."

"It's not right away," Jerry interrupted. "I'll be working less and less, ease you into it. Not like you need to be." He gave a lofty smile. "Are you interested?"

"Oh. I'm, I'm not sure." Sara put her hands on her thighs. "It's a great opportunity and thanks for thinking of me—"

"You don't have to decide right now," Georgia said. "But it's something we're looking at for the end of the year. Higher salary, three weeks' vacation and you can pick your days off."

"Okay. Sure. I'll think about it," Sara said. Was it what she wanted? It was a hefty workload, and she still enjoyed reporting. "While you were away, two reporters weren't enough. It was hard to get everything done. And I worked day and night. Liam did what he could do. It would have been helpful having at least a part-time person in to read copy or do page layout. Anything to cut down on time used on production days."

Georgia and Jerry's heads bobbed.

"I'm sure we can figure something out," she said, eyeing Jerry then doing a head turn to look at Sara. "Thanks for bringing it to my attention."

Sara walked out of the office with her head held high, returning to her desk.

Liam spun around in his chair. "How did it go?"

At the same moment, Georgia walked out of Jerry's office and went down the hall toward Deloris. Liam went back to his work, and Sara opened the story she was writing about the need for funding for the animal shelter. She placed a photo of Josie on the floor, laughing, with dogs hoping in and out of her lap. Sara smiled at the one of a dog licking Josie's cheek.

Her phone rang, and Sara broke away from the computer and took her phone out of her purse.

"Hi, Mom."

"Sara. Are you planning on coming over this afternoon?"

"I was."

"Can you make it a bit later? I have company and, um, well, it would be better for me if you came later."

"No problem, Mom. I'll see you then."

It wasn't like she had to rush home to see Colton. Those days were over.

Chapter Twenty-Nine

Colton dropped off Tera and said goodbye to Josie then headed into town to find Cottage Hills. He didn't know where he was going, but he'd figure it out. At least it was worth enquiring about a place of his own instead of staying at a motel.

He followed a sign which led him up a hill and down a road. He didn't know the winery existed, and he was in awe when he reached the top. The view of the lake was incredible. It took his breath away just as it had when he flew over.

He walked up the road, which split. On one side, there was a two-story house and, on the other, the winery. In the distance, there were four cabins and rows of grapevines. He breathed in the clean air, feeding his soul with peace and freedom.

Colton walked through the parking lot and into the building. The open sign was on, but inside there was a woman behind the counter, shuffling bottles around.

"Hi there," she said, smiling. "Would you like a wine tasting?"

"I've come to enquire about the cabins."

"You'll need to talk to Emily. She's the girl you need. I'll grab her for you." The woman flashed through the backdoor. A moment later, a woman with blond hair pulled back in a

ponytail came out. He recognized her from TJ's Tavern when he ran into Sara.

"Hi. Oh, Colton," she said, walking around the counter to greet. "How are you?"

He gave her a half-grin. "I'm good. I didn't know you worked here."

She stood in front of him, her petite body swaying, hands open. "It's my family's winery." Her eyes were bright and cheery. "What can I do for you?"

"I was told that you rent out some cabins."

"Yeah. I do." She nodded. "Usually in the summer and fall."

"Are there any vacant now?"

"Yes. Are you looking to rent one? For how long?"

"Maybe two months, three, I don't know." He was taking it day by day.

"Do you want to have a look? Let me get my keys." She went around the counter, into the back room and came out wearing a coat and jangled a set of keys. "We'll go out this way." She led him outside, through the parking lot and around past the house.

"So, you're planning on staying here in Moonlight." Her ponytail whipped around. "That's good."

"For a little while. I don't know. I got a job at Omak airport."

"Moonlight's a great place for a fresh start. I mean if that's what you're thinking."

The first cabin was beside a row of grapevines.

"This one's my favorite. It has the best view." She stepped up on the porch. "You can bring a chair out here...well, it might be too cold now, but it's nice to look out at the lake."

Colton put his hands on the wooden railing and stared straight across at the mountain/lake view.

"I'll show you inside." Emily opened the door and flicked on the light. "Burr. It's colder in here."

"There's heat?" Colton rolled up his shoulders from the chill.

"Yes, there's heat. Full appliances, bathroom, and bedding. Go ahead and check it out."

Colton took off his shoes. If he was going to live there for a few months, he wanted to keep it clean. The living room had a couch and TV. The kitchen was small, but he didn't need much. The bathroom had a tub and shower; the bedroom had a window facing the front of the cabin.

"I'll take it."

Emily laughed. "I didn't tell you how much."

"How much?" he asked.

She eyed him skeptically, and it made Colton flinch from knowing what she was thinking.

"I'll give you a deal. If you stay for a minimum of two months, I'll charge you six hundred a month instead of eight."

"Okay. When can I move in?"

"Right now, if you want it," she laughed. "You're staying with Sara, right?"

How much did Emily know about him?

"Not anymore. I've got a room at a motel." He cupped his fist in his hand. "I wanted to give her some space. She's done enough for me."

"Sara doesn't mind. She likes helping."

"Is she still going on her trip?" He crossed his arms at his chest.

"No. She couldn't go." Emily's eyes swept over him. "You really haven't spoken to her."

"I'm giving her space," he said, scratching the back of his head. "Thanks for showing me the cabin. This is great. I'll come by tomorrow with cash."

He had a permanent place for as long as he needed — a perfect place to start over.

COLTON'S PHONE RANG, and he snatched the TV remote and turned down the volume. His dad's number was on the screen, and he contemplated answering it. He didn't feel like talking to anybody. If there was one person he owed his attention to, it was Sara, and he didn't have the energy for her either. He rubbed his forehead, massaging it as he brought the phone to his ear.

"Hello."

"Colton," his dad said.

Colton's head shot up, and he stared at the blank TV screen. He tried to make his voice uplifting, so there would be fewer questions.

"Where are you staying?"

"At a motel."

"Is it the Traveler's Motel?"

He jumped off the bed, standing stiff, clutching his phone. "How did you know?"

"I've been looking for you. What's your room number? I have something for you."

"Room? What? Are you here?" Bubbling laughter made its way to the top of his throat.

"I'm outside," his dad said laughing.

Colton bolted to the door with his heart racing and his phone to his ear, scanning the parking lot. He did a double take at his dad wearing his typical long, black coat, the one he wore when he was going to court. The only thing that was missing was his briefcase.

"Is Mom okay?" Colton's chest tightened.

"She's well." He stepped toward Colton. His black, patten shoes sunk into a puddle and he lifted his foot, eyeing the mess on his shoe. Colton's chest tightened. His body stiffened. The feeling of shame and disappointment washed over him like he was six years old again and running through the house with his muddy boots on.

He had to tell his dad he wasn't coming home. Colton had started a new life. Thanks to Sara who helped free him from his past and showing him what he was capable of. His dad stood on the sidewalk in front of Colton's room. "Are you ready to come home?" He shoved his hands into his coat pockets.

"I'm staying here."

His dad rocked side to side. "It's a beautiful place. I drove to the lake."

"I like it here." Colton's muscles began to ease. "I have everything I need."

"So, you're not coming back?" It was more of a statement than a question, and Colton didn't feel like replying. He stared at his dad, finding the courage to stand his ground.

"I told your mom I'd bring you home."

Colton's body ached with growing tension. Since when did he need to explain to his dad what he was doing with his life?

"We miss you." His dad stood still. "We worry about you."

"You don't have to worry about me, Dad."

A dog barked in the distance. Colton craned his neck around his dad to see where the sound was. The last couple of days brought a flash of fall weather. He brought his shoulders back and eyed his dad.

"I'm proud of you."

Colton's limbs lightened.

Another bark.

"I failed," Colton said. "Too many times."

"No, you didn't. You handled the situation better than I would." Roger's face pinched. His cheeks reddened. "You're human. You had some unfortunate things happen, but that's not going to stop you from trying again."

Colton's toes curled. He clasped his hands.

"I understand why you felt the way you did, and I'm sorry." Roger flexed his gloved hands. "If living here makes you happy, then I respect you for doing so."

Colton's chest lifted. "Mom still hasn't gotten over Jenny."

Roger snapped his wrist. "Don't worry about it. It'll take her time, but she will."

Colton breathed easier. "How did you get here?"

"I drove."

"You drove?" It wasn't like his dad to drive if he could fly, not because he was luxury, but because time was always an issue. There was never enough of it. He lived work. The five-hour drive here probably added extra stress to his already stressful job. Add another five home, and it would take up his day.

"It wasn't too bad. I had a company." He turned around to see his BMW in the final parking spot. His dad walked to his car. Colton stiffened. If he took another step, he would have wet sock feet.

His dad walked to his car and opened the backseat door. A black, shaggy dog jumped out with his tail wagging and tongue hung out, running across the parking lot.

"Charles," Colton yelled and ran toward him. His feet soppy wet, but Colton didn't care. He bent down, holding himself steady and the dog ran into his arms, licking him, his body jiggling with excitement. "How are you doing, buddy? Huh?" Colton asked and petted him. Charles licked him again, and Colton laughed, unable to get enough of his dog's love.

"Jenny says you can take him."

"She doesn't want him?" Colton slowed down his petting and looked up with curiosity.

Roger's eyes grim. "She says he's better off with you. She wants to get on with her life, and says Charles misses you. He belongs to you."

"She realized that now?"

"I guess she needed time." Roger opened his palm and stuck his hand into his coat pocket. "Have you had enough time to figure out what you want? I miss having my son around."

Colton licked his lip and got to his feet. He didn't know he was missed. "You have two sons." His brother was always the good one, the one who would be missed if he moved away or took a long vacation. Colton didn't think he was needed.

"Yes, and I didn't plan to only have one around." Roger brought his lips together and eyed Colton. "Can I expect you to come home?"

"I like it here." He looked down at the pavement. "I think there's something here for me. I have a second chance."

"You're smart. You'll do what is best for you."

Colton's heart expanded.

"I support your decision. Whatever it may be."

"What changed?" Colton needed to know. His dad wasn't the affectionate type.

Straight-forward and curt, it wasn't easy for Colton to express his emotions, but he was learning and Sara pushed him to come out of his shell, even if it felt awkward at first, he knew he was on the right track.

"I realized the good work you've done. You're alive," he said simply. "The only thing I've lost is the time we haven't spent together when you were home. I'm sorry about that."

Colton rubbed the back of his neck. He wanted a better relationship with his family and with Sara. It would take time, just how it took time for him to be receptive to his dad's love.

The dog pushed himself to the side of Colton's leg, lifting his head for another pet.

"Looks like it's you and me," he said to Charles. He looked up at his dad. "Do you want to get something to eat? I know a place we can bring Charles along."

"I'd like that." Roger smiled. "I could use a meal." Colton knew from that moment on

everything was going to be okay.

Chapter Thirty

It felt good leaving work and not having to worry about her job and Jerry's, although she didn't mind being editor if she had an extra body working to elevate the stress of getting so much done at once.

She pulled up to her childhood home and parked in the driveway behind her mom's compact car. Sara tossed her purse over her shoulder and stepped up to the front door, turning the knob, it didn't budge. Was the door locked? She tried again just to make sure. Her mom's car was in the driveway, and her mom told her to come over. Sara knocked and waited.

"Coming!" her mom yelled.

The door swung open to her mom, wearing makeup and hair styled welcomed her with a warm hug.

"Hi, honey. Come in."

Sara stepped inside. "The door was locked."

"Oh, I must have done that when I got home. I wasn't thinking." She laughed. "I made coffee."

"I'll have a cup."

"What's the story today?" Her mom poured two cups of coffee. Sara plunked herself down on her usual chair and took the cup, warming her hands with it.

"The animal shelter might close its doors due to a lack of funding and too many animals."

"That's sad."

"It is. There's so many. I don't know how Josie does it. Feeding and caring for all of them. She even has a turtle."

Her mom grinned, holding her cup in her hands, she stood in the middle of the kitchen. "I have something to talk to you about. Something that's been on my mind for a while." Her mom put down her cup on the counter and gave a weary look.

"What's going on?"

"You and Evan are older now. Adults..." She paused, glanced at the window, and then back at Sara. "That's not how I wanted to start." She sighed, her eyes swept the floor. "I am seeing someone."

"You're dating? Like actually dating? Really? Who? Anyone, I know?"

"Yes." She bobbed her head. "It's about time I did things for me."

"I thought you were happy."

"I am. I was. It's just now I'm happier." She flashed a faltered grin.

"Okay. I get it. So who is it?" Sara pushed.

Her nostrils contracted.

"Al."

"Al?" Sara let the name roll off her tongue. "I only know Al Anderson and he—"

Her mom's eyes lifted. "Yes."

"What?" Sara tapped her lips together.

"How did it happen? Never mind. I don't want to know. Seriously?"

"I knew you wouldn't agree, and I'm sorry you don't, but I'm a grown woman capable of being happy with a man who loves me."

"He loves you?" Her eyes bugged out even more.

"He does."

"Can you be happy for me?"

"I am happy for you, Mom. I am really. I'm just shocked. That's all." Sara gave advice, and she couldn't back out of what she wrote even if she wasn't going to tell her mom who Peaches was. Not yet, anyway.

"It's your life, Mom. You deserve to share your life with someone." Sara got out of her seat, meeting her mom in the middle, they embraced. Her mom stroked her hair, bringing her back to when she was a little girl. Her mom's hand, comforting and reassuring when she was feeling sad or unsure. Sara had one parent and didn't want to lose their connection. It made her think about what she was missing. Her house didn't feel the same without Colton, but he needed time to settle and figure out what he wanted. She didn't want to push him into something he wasn't feeling.

If love wasn't in her cards right now, she had to accept it and move on, but right now, the only way she knew how to fill the empty space was to provide an unprivileged dog a home.

Chapter Thirty-One

Colton's lungs filled with fresh air as he headed out on a walk to the beach with Charles. Cold, crisp, fall was settling in. He didn't mind the change in season; he was grateful to be alive and embracing life once again. Owen was gone and would never see or experience life, but Colton had the chance, and he was going to do what he could to live with courage and embrace what he had.

Grateful to be starting over, in a new town. He didn't realize how much he needed his own space, until he had a place he could call home. Even if it's for the short term. Holding one hand on the leash, Colton set out on his walk. Emily insisted he could borrow her fiancé's new pickup truck, but he felt weird about using something that didn't belong to him without knowing the person. He hadn't even met the hockey player who people called, generous. For now, Colton walked everywhere. The town had all his essentials, food and clothing were in the same place, making it easy to access. Once he was on the main road, he was practically at his destination.

Charles pranced beside Colton as they walked down the windy, gravel driveway. "I'm glad you're here," Colton said to Charles. "I never thought I'd see you again, buddy." As if Charles knew what Colton said, he looked up at him, tongue hanging, his eyes gleaming. "You're a good boy. I missed you." The dog brushed up against Colton's leg, and Colton laughed.

Colton passed an orchid. He kept on the same path, following the lake on the other side. In the distance, a family was hanging out by a log. The shriek of a child, followed by an adult's voice, Colton slowed down his pace. He didn't know how long he'd stay in

Moonlight Valley for, but it seemed like the right place to start life over.

Colton bent down, looping his fingers through Charles' collar. "If I let you off-leash, don't go running off on me." He unhooked the leash and the dog sprinted in circles with his tongue hanging out, waiting for Colton to throw the ball.

Colton continued playing fetch as he walked around the lake. Spotting someone in the distance with a dog. Colton continued to play, but this time, Charles didn't bring the ball back. He caught up to the other dog with its owner, sitting on a log facing the water.

"Charles!" Colton yelled. He didn't come. "Charles! Come on! Ugh. Damn dog." He was supposed to be a good listener. "Come on!"

Colton huffed and walked briskly, calling Charles as he walked toward him. Whistling didn't help either. Why was his dog so interested? He was sniffing a yellow lab, and the woman was bent over petting Charles.

"Figures." Colton exalted a breath. The closer he came, he realized the woman was enjoying his dog's company, and her dog was bumping against her wanting to be pet. She was giggling and talking to the dogs. Colton got closer calling his dog. The woman looked up. Her blond hair tucked under a knitted hat, she smiled and waved a gloved hand.

"Sara," Colton said. His heart leaped and for a moment he didn't stood there, as though in a trance. He snapped out of it and jogged toward her. "I didn't see you there."

"Hi." She pulled her dog into her leg. The dog sat and wagged its body to her petting.

"You got a dog?" He cocked his head and grinned. Colton took Charles by the collar.

"Two days ago. We're still getting acquainted. Her name is Bella."

"Bella." Colton nodded. "I remember. She's the one you liked at Homeward Bound."

"I did. Yeah." Sara blinked. "Bella needed a home, and the house was too empty." She gave a wavering smile. "I felt a little lonely." She shrugged.

He felt lonely without Sara so it made two of them.

"This. This is Charles. He's my dog. My dad drove him here."

"So you're staying," she said, squinting, meeting his eyes. "Have a seat." She wiggled over on the log and Colton sat beside her. "I don't know for how long." He might as well be honest. He wasn't going to make plans when he didn't know his future."

"Oh. How did it go with Al?"

"Good. I start this week as an airplane mechanic. I might even be an instructor."

"That's great. Really." Sara pet her dog. "I'm happy for you." She looked at him and his pulse raced. "Things are working out. How do you like staying at Cottage Hills?"

"How did you know?" He paused. "Oh, right. Emily." He shook his head and grinned. "It's good. It's all I need. It's perfect. Emily's been great. She told me I could stay for as long as I want. I'm paying her rent."

He brought down his chin to look at her, feeling as though he needed to prove to her that he was doing better than when they first met. He was getting his life together. "What happened about your trip? You didn't go."

"It's the wrong time." She smiled at Bella and pet behind her ear. "My editor didn't get back in time, and we had to straighten some things out... I got a promotion. I'll be the editor in the new year."

"That's great. Congratulations. You deserve it. Are you happy about it?"

"I think so as long as I can hire another reporter. I'll take over in the new year. I'll go on a trip when things have settled." Her lips came together. "Maybe. I'll see."

Bella was sitting, licking her chops, and wagging her tail. "I think Bella wants me to move. Mind if we walk?" she asked.

Colton jumped to his feet, and Charles followed.

"I've been walking more."

"You have Bella now."

"Even before her, I was walking around my neighborhood after dinner."

"I was doing it too."

"You were?"

He felt her disappointment because he would have instead walked with Sara than himself. His chest ached to hold Sara in his arms. He made love to this woman, and he still cared about her. How could he get her back even if he wasn't fully ready to commit? Or was he? "You walk more when you have a dog," he agreed.

"Thanks to you," she said. "Walking has been a great stress release for me. I've done yoga in the past and hit up a good workout at the gym, but going for a walk seems to help clear my head. It has its advantages."

"I agree."

They walked along the beach on a pebbled path.

"Is this the ice cream shop?" Colton asked. "The one you used to go with your family to?"

"That's it." Sara smiled, her shoulders caved and she tucked her hands into her coat pockets. "We'd sit right here on one of these logs, or at a picnic table." She pointed to the side of the boarded-up shack with a poster hanging on the front, closed until May. She put her hand back into her pocket.

Colton stopped to take in her memory. "We'll have to get ice cream when they open."

"I'd like that," she said and smiled.

"Two scoops." Colton felt a pull in his chest.

"Waffle cone," she added.

Colton chuckled. "It's the only way." He stepped toward her. "You were right." The words came out without him thinking, and he stopped himself from what he wanted to say next, but it was too late. He had to clear the air between them. Not that there was tension or anger, there was a gap between them though that Colton didn't like, and he needed to close whatever it was preventing him from moving forward and accept life as how he wanted it. Time would help heal, but it was Sara who pushed him to be better and to recognize a friendship he was desperate to have. Colton didn't want to lose her again. He needed Sara in his life.

"Right about what?" She cocked her head, eyelashes fluttered.

"I needed to figure out my life before anything else. And I have. Landing in Moonlight was what I needed. Meeting you was what I needed more." He shuffled his foot on the pebbled sand.

"I was scared." He bowed his head. "More of a fear," he corrected. "Fearing what was next. I didn't want to believe there was anything good going to happen." His chest ached. "I didn't deserve it. I couldn't make anyone happy until I found you. I might not deserve a second chance, but it's all I have. I'm happier now than I've ever been, but I'm not as happy without you." He touched her arm. His hand fell to her side. "I'm sorry."

"I am too." Her lips came together.

"What can I do to make things work?"

"You mean between us?"

His stomach clenched, fearing they weren't on the same page.

She folded her hand over his. "I think this is a good start."

His muscles eased up, and he pulled her into him, putting his arms around her. "Since I met you, I've learned to accept change and to accept myself. Had I not come to Moonlight, I don't know where I would have been or what I would have been doing with my life. I was lost. You came into my life at the perfect time, and I'm in the perfect place." His eyes skimmed the mountain terrain.

"I was a little lost too," she said. "You gave me a purpose. It was like my dad was watching over me."

"He was a smart man. I wish I could have met him."

"You would have liked him." She smiled thoughtfully.

"I'm sure I would have."

Her gaze met his.

"We can take it slow," he said. "Whatever we have. Whatever this is. I want to be with you. I'm in no rush to go anywhere."

"Are you staying? Because there's only one thing," she said, staring at him with glowing eyes. "Moonlight Valley is my home. It will always be. I'm up for an adventure, and I can't wait to travel one day, but I'm home. Here is the only place I want to be."

"I'd be anywhere as long as I'm with you." He lowered his head to hers and kissed her gently on her warm, smooth lips. They would make their own adventure. Charles barked, and Colton broke away. "And the dogs." He laughed.

"And the dogs," she agreed, scrunching her nose, and laughed into his chest. He wrapped his arms around her, holding her tight. His chin rested on the top of her head as though they didn't miss any time apart. He had a second chance at love and grateful to be in a town where people accepted mistakes and honored friendships.

His heart was full and the love he felt for Sara ran deeper than the lake and higher than any plane he flew. Loving her was the answer and Moonlight Valley was the perfect place to be for a second chance at life and love and everything else in between.

Epilogue

Three months later...

Discovery Hall held the first-ever Homeward Bound Animal Shelter fundraiser. There were round tables set up with gift baskets, a silent auction, and tea, coffee, and muffins provided by Betty's Bakery. Colton didn't care what he was doing on a Saturday afternoon as long as he got to spend it with Sara.

Living in Moonlight Valley was proving to be the right choice. Colton was still renting a cabin from Emily, but he knew it was a matter of time before he and Sara got a place of their own. With Sara soon-to-be taking the job as editor at The Observer and he was enjoying being an airplane mechanic at Omak airport, they made the best of their free time together.

"Oh! There's Kel," Sara said. "I'll be right back." She jumped to talk to her friend, and Colton reached for his beeping phone out of his back pocket. The thought of Al needing him for an emergency repair crossed his mind. Colton was attentive to his new boss and was grateful for the job opportunity and the free rent for storing his dad's plane until the springtime when it would be fixed and ready to fly again.

Colton tapped on the email message. He flexed his shoulders back when he saw the name Combs as the sender.

Dear Colton:

It's taken me some time to email you, but it's a new year, and I wanted to send you a note to let you know if you're ever in Omak, please stop by and visit us. I want Riley to know who his dad's friend was. I want to reassure you, in case you have any doubts, Owen and you were at the wrong place at the wrong time, and I don't blame you for what happened. I'm sorry for your loss, and what you have to live with, but know, you're not alone.

The envelope you gave me had all sorts of heartfelt notes,

including one, I want to share with you. Owen wrote, "There were days I felt I couldn't survive because I was homesick and I just wanted to be home and reading Riley a story. Colton helped me get through the hard days and celebrated the triumphs. Please tell him he was the best friend any guy could ask for."

Colton paused to take a breath.

Owen was lucky to have you work alongside him, and I couldn't ask for a more dedicated friend he called brother. Thank you for not giving up on him or yourself in the darkest days. In the

envelope, there were poems he wrote to me. I will always

treasure them and thank you for sending them to me. I read them every night. It's given me comfort and hope to move on. They are a savor for me. Although Owen has left us with broken hearts, he did leave our son and me the foundation of love, and hope. I wish the same for you.

Love,

Denise

Colton closed his phone and tucked it into his back pocket. He wished Denise well and hoped she'd find someone to fill the empty gap that Owen left. He would be pleased to know Denise was getting her life back, and it slowly for Colton too. He'd try to know Riley and to live every day with integrity and find adventure with Sara. He looked up and caught Sara walking back to him with a faint smile and extended her hand to his. "Everything okay?"

His heart leaped. "Better than okay." He squeezed her hand to reassure her if she had any doubt from the tone of his voice. Colton was still working on expressing himself and grateful for Sara's patience and understanding. Sara let out a small giggle. She stopped abruptly in her tracks when Josie sprang in front of them with arms wide open. Kelly took a couple of steps towards them.

"I can't thank you enough for putting this all together," Josie said, looking at Sara and then at Kelly. She wore her hair down and had on a sweater dress and tall boots, a change from ripped jeans and an old plaid button-down shirt. "I'll be able to keep the shelter open, at least a bit longer." Her eyes glossed. "I can't imagine closing it."

"Either can we," Sara said, glancing at Colton.

"And we've sold out of the calendars." Josie's eyes lit up. "Thank you." Her lips flattened into a grin. "Nobody can resist animal pictures, and you did such a good job on them."

"I'm glad it worked out," Sara said. "We picked a good day to photograph before the weather turned."

"It was a great idea." Josie smiled. "I don't know how you got the dogs and cats to pose for you."

"Offering a treat doesn't hurt." Sara winked and laughed.

"She has the magic touch," Colton said, putting his arm around her waist.

"We're grateful Charles and Bella have a place to stay while we're away."

"They'll be taken good care of," Josie said.

"It's only for a week," Colton said. "We're saving Australia for when we have more time to plan."

"This was a last-minute getaway," Sara added. "Before my job title changes."

"After the wedding, I hope," Kelly said. "I'll need a sidekick because this isn't just any wedding."

"As long as you promise I can make a two-page spread of the event."

"That's up to Emily," Kelly said.

"You know the town will want to read about it. It is public interest."

"You're speaking like an editor." Kelly laughed. "But it's going to be pretty hard to shoot and perform your bridesmaid duties."

"I've got my sidekick." Sara nudged Colton. "He's a photographer." She beamed.

"Not as good as you." Colton unhooked his hand from hers and placed it on her hip, pulling her into him.

"Well, I have to draw another name for the gift basket," Josie said, stepping out of their circle.

"And I'm meeting Emily to go over some details of the venue," Kelly said.

Colton caught sight of Brad wandering in, dressed in a firefighter uniform, the one Brad wore when he was doing community service. Sara spotted Brad as well, which made Kelly look over her shoulder. She hid her smile with a purse of her lips and looked away.

Brad's boots knocked against the hardwood floor. Kelly's back straightened as Brad joined the group.

"Who's in charge of this event?" he asked, stepping beside Kelly.

"Is there a problem?" She looked over her shoulder.

"Only one." He paused. "You don't have a permit."

"A permit? Are you kidding?" She glared.

"I'm kidding." He laughed. "It's all good." He looked around. "Do you want to grab a drink or something?"

Kelly hesitated. "I'm busy today."

"Even later?"

"Yup." She rose an eyebrow to him. "Don't try sucking up. It's not going to work."

"Wasn't trying to. Just thought you could use a break."

"We have to go," Sara said, stepping back from the circle. "We have to let the dogs out. Talk to you later." She took Colton's hand and pulled him along. When they got outside, the snow had stopped falling. "I didn't want to be in the middle of their dispute."

"What's their dispute? I thought they were friends?"

"They're trying to be, but I don't think Kelly can forgive Brad for not wanting to commit."

"Do you mean marriage?" They walked through the snowy parking lot.

"Yeah, he's not the marrying type. Well, it's what he told Kelly, and that's why they broke up."

Colton unlocked his new truck, walking Sara to the passenger side. "So, how do you feel about marriage?" He wasn't ready to settle down again just yet, but it was something he wanted when the time was right.

"I like the idea." Her warm smile heated his insides. The love he had for her was nothing like he experienced before.

"But I'm in no rush." Colton wrapped his arms around her, squaring his body with hers.

"I'm happy doing what we're doing, but maybe one day." Her eyes sparkled.

"One day," he agreed.

They were building a life together at the right pace, and in the perfect town to settle down. Colton brought his nose to hers. The cold air patted his face with fine prickles. "I love you," he said, holding her tighter. "You're the best thing that's happened to me."

"I love you too." She brought her smiling lips to his and kissed him, warming his insides. Colton wasn't taking his second chance at living for granted. He was taking it in stride, one day at a time with the woman who saved his heart.

Don't miss out!

Visit the website below and you can sign up to receive emails whenever Charlene Groome publishes a new book. There's no charge and no obligation.

https://books2read.com/r/B-A-ZUIF-NWWOC

Connecting independent readers to independent writers.

Also by Charlene Groome

A Moonlight Valley series
Rescuing His Heart

Moonlight Valley
Playing For Love

Standalone
Making Perfect Scents

Watch for more at www.charlenegroome.com.

About the Author

Charlene Groome is the contemporary romance author of the Warriors' Hockey series. She writes about sexy heroes who play overtime with the women they love.

With a background in journalism and radio broadcasting, Charlene is penning stories about friendship, love, and family.

A fitness enthusiast, she loves romcoms, and all things girly, and has a soft spot for home decor. She lives on the West Coast of British Columbia with her husband and three children. When she's not writing, she enjoys hanging out at the lake with her family.

Read more at www.charlenegroome.com.

Milton Keynes UK
Ingram Content Group UK Ltd.
UKHW020728081123
432193UK00018B/682